"She's your dog so you get to pay the bills."

"Oh, no, you don't," Mark replied. "I do not have room in my life for a dog. She's probably not housebroken, she's probably sick and I'm away a lot of the time."

As though she understood that her fate was being discussed, the puppy wriggled over and laid her head on Mark's hand with a sigh. Her little rear wagged as she looked at him hopefully.

"See that?" Sarah said. "She *is* your dog. Besides, someone has to pay for all the treatment we've given her. Isn't that what you always say, Mr. Scott?"

"Whoa."

"No whoa. *You* found her, *you* helped me work on her, *you* saw what we did. It all costs money. The clinic has to make money. That's also what you always say. Well, Mark, you've just spent about two hundred bucks, and by the time I get through loading you with all the things you need for her, you'll have spent a bunch more."

She rubbed the pup's ears. "Sweet baby, Mommy *loves* a paying client."

Dear Reader,

Those of us who love romance tend to love all God's creatures. Personally, I draw the line at poisonous snakes, but I'm sure there are those of you out there with a soft spot in your hearts for copperheads. Our pets give us so much more than we could ever give them, and when they're sick or hurt it's up to us to help them.

Our veterinarians and their staffs are truly special. Who else would work through the night in a freezing barn to save somebody else's calf?

Medical doctors need to know about one species—human beings. But a vet has to know that aspirin will kill a cat, that chocolate will poison a dog and that pythons sometimes can't tell the difference between eggs and tennis balls. And then there are the owners—much more trouble than the animals, to hear my vet friends talk.

In *The Money Man*, Sarah Marsdon has completely uprooted her life to take over as large-animal vet for a new clinic, only to find that the equipment she needs—and was promised—hasn't even been ordered, thanks to Mark Scott, her personal roadblock. He's not going to spend another dime. After all, a bankrupt clinic can't help even one animal.

Until the clinic is out of the woods financially, Sarah must make do with what she has. But she isn't willing to offer less than the very best to her charges. She's certain Mark could find the money if he really wanted to.

They're both too bullheaded to give an inch, even though the romantic sparks fly between them from the minute they meet. Can they find some way to compromise before their conflict destroys their love? Or will everyone lose—the animals, as well as Mark and Sarah?

Carolyn McSparren

P.S. I love to hear from readers. You can reach me by email at cmcsparren@aol.com.

The Money Man
Carolyn McSparren

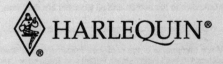

TORONTO • NEW YORK • LONDON
AMSTERDAM • PARIS • SYDNEY • HAMBURG
STOCKHOLM • ATHENS • TOKYO • MILAN • MADRID
PRAGUE • WARSAW • BUDAPEST • AUCKLAND

ISBN 0-373-70996-X

THE MONEY MAN

Copyright © 2001 by Carolyn McSparren.

Visit us at www.eHarlequin.com

Printed in U.S.A.

ACKNOWLEDGMENT

To all the veterinarians I know, their families
and their staffs. These wonderful people answered
thousand of questions, let me watch procedures,
recounted funny and heart-rending tales and taught me
about the inner workings of a veterinary clinic.

DEDICATION

For Dr. Melissa Poole of Mississippi State University,
Camille and Dr. Mark Akin of the Akin Equine Clinic;
everyone at the Bowling Animal Clinic; Elizabeth Lee,
a great veterinary technician from Albuquerque,
and Sam Garner and Bobby Billingsley,
who convinced me all cows are crazy!

CHAPTER ONE

DR. SARAH MARSDON shoved open the double glass doors and walked into the reception room of Creature Comfort Veterinary Clinic.

She breathed in the faint odor of damp fur, disinfectant and enzyme cleaner used to remove doggie scents from floors.

From the area to her left came the occasional barking and yipping and the persistent baritone yowl of a Siamese cat. In the week since she'd left her job in St. Paul, she'd missed the sound of a waiting room filled with animals.

She'd paid a high personal and professional price to get here, but this job at Creature Comfort was a dream come true. At last she was going to be treating large animals—horses, cows, goats, sheep, even pigs.

"Why do you want to be a large-animal vet?" Steve, her previous boss, had asked. "Fancy pets—that's where the money is. And you don't get called out at two in the morning. Nobody wants to do large animals anymore."

Well, this *particular* body loved working with large animals, even if that meant making less money and spending long nights treating colicky horses or orphaned calves.

She walked up to the reception desk, where a small man was speaking to the blond receptionist.

He could barely hold on to the leather leash of a young Great Dane who obviously wanted to be somewhere else. "Ernest T., down! Stay!" the man said.

The dog sighed and sank to the floor. He rolled his sad eyes up at Sarah.

"Okay, Mr. Bass, you and Ernest T. have a seat. It'll be about ten minutes," the receptionist said. She smiled and picked up the telephone beside her. "Creature Comfort Veterinary Clinic."

"Come on, Ernest T."

The dog sighed again and heaved himself to his feet. His uncropped ears flopped endearingly around his face.

Sarah walked up to the reception desk and said, "Hi, I'm Dr…"

"Watch out behind you!"

Sarah glanced over her shoulder and shrank back against the reception desk, but not fast enough to avoid a butt behind her knees from a stumpy black pig. She caught herself on the counter.

"Oh, I'm so sorry. Are you okay? Egg Roll, stand still."

The "miniature" Vietnamese pot-bellied pig stood nearly three feet tall at the shoulder and must have weighed about two-fifty. The woman he towed at the end of his leash weighed maybe one-ten. Anyone could tell who was in charge.

The receptionist punched her hold button and leaned over her desk. "Egg Roll, cut that out!" She tossed a piece of hard candy onto the floor.

The pig hesitated, snuffled, then scarfed up the treat. A moment later he collapsed into a big black blob of contentment. His owner wiped her forehead and gasped, "Thanks, Alva Jean. He hates having his hooves trimmed."

"No problem, Judy. Candy gets him every time. You better wait in room three." She picked up the phone once more. Judy nudged the pig with her toe. Still snuffling contentedly, he stood and lumbered through the door beside the counter.

A sigh of relief went up from the waiting dog and cat owners. Sarah sighed as well. The chaos felt just like home.

"No."

"But I promised when I hired her."

"Un-promise." Mark Scott leaned back in his rickety desk chair and propped one knee against the scarred edge of his elderly desk. Once the clinic was fully operational, this room would hold patients' records, but at the moment it served as a general storeroom and Mark's office.

From the far side of the wall came the pop of a nail gun. A small puff of plaster dust floated down from this side of the unprimed wallboard.

Rick Hazard sneezed, wiped his nose and eyes. "Mark, we need Sarah. She's young, she's top-notch, she's hungry, and we're getting her cheap because she wants to work large animals. She'll build that side of the practice fast. Don't act as if we've never talked about this. We've got to have another full-timer. She'll start with evenings, some weekends—fill in whenever she's needed, until the large-animal practice is big enough to occupy her full time."

"Fine, you need *her*, but you don't need a portable fluoroscope or a laser. And definitely not a large animal MRI."

"We do."

"We can't afford to buy any more equipment at the

moment, Rick. We can't afford to lease, either. She'll have to make do with what we have until the clinic generates some decent income."

"But I promised her if she'd move here—"

"Answer me this—would you rather participate in the grand opening of this clinic or appear in bankruptcy court?"

"It's not that bad."

"It's close. The cost overruns on Margot's design changes and the construction delays have killed you."

"I'm not responsible for the wettest winter and spring since the 1880s," Rick protested.

Mark longed to say that Rick was certainly responsible for his wife's continuing upgrades and changes, but he kept his mouth shut. No sense in antagonizing Margot any more than he had to, and even less in forcing Rick to defend her. "Blame the gods, blame the weather, blame the contractors. None of that changes the fact that you're skating very close to the edge of your available capital—what the hell, your capital, your wife's capital, your partners' capital, your investors' capital, your credit and every other type of financing you can lay your hands on. How can I explain this to you in terms you understand, my friend? I can't—won't—approve a purchase order for any more equipment until you at least come close to meeting the objectives in your business plan."

Rick sucked in his breath. "The small-animal area is more than meeting objectives."

"That's true, thank God. But Bill Chumney hasn't finalized the contract with the zoo or the wildlife conservation people to treat their exotic animals—"

"He will. We already have a verbal agreement. They're just waiting for us to finish building the flight cage to handle their raptors. That won't take more than a week. Bill already has one of their eagles in recovery. He's done a great job reconstructing that wing. The wildlife people will have to be impressed.''

''Wonderful. However, a verbal contract is not worth the paper it's written on. The fluorescent lights aren't connected in the large-animal surgical suite, there's no hardware on the intensive care stalls for the cows and horses, the observation cameras aren't calibrated yet....''

''Punch list problems. We'll have them done by tomorrow, close of business.''

''That's what you said last week. Give it at least a month before you bring in Dr. Marsdon, Rick.''

Rick hunkered down in his chair like a sulky child. ''The only person with no vested interest in this clinic is you.''

Mark closed his eyes and took a deep breath. ''We've been over that before. I want this clinic to succeed because that's what Coy Buchanan wants, and I work for him. Like I've said from the beginning, I never invest my own money in a project I'm overseeing. Don't want my own financial concerns to cloud my judgment.''

The door behind Rick opened, and Alva Jean stuck her head in. ''Dr. Hazard, there's a Dr. Sarah Marsdon waiting to see you.''

''Oh, God, not now,'' Rick moaned. ''She wasn't supposed to be here until tomorrow.''

''Tomorrow? Why didn't you tell me she was already scheduled?''

''What am I going to say to her?''

''Start with your punch list,'' Mark said.

The door opened again.

Sarah Marsdon was silhouetted in the light from the

hallway behind her. Mark had assumed a woman who dealt with horses and cows would look like Hulk Hogan.

Sarah's silhouette looked more like Julia Roberts.

"Hi, Rick." The silhouette spoke. "The drive from St. Paul took less time than I thought."

She came forward into the light.

More Melanie Griffith than Julia Roberts. Hair the color of well-aged honey and eyes the color of a cloudless sky.

Rick hugged her, then turned to introduce Mark. "Dr. Sarah Marsdon, may I present Markham Scott?"

She shook his hand with a firm grip. "Nice to meet you," she said.

"My pleasure," Mark responded. "Although I—"

Rick stepped in with a nervous laugh. "Mark's vice president of operations for Buchanan Enterprises. He's the money man of Coy Buchanan's company. Coy is Margot's father—my father-in-law. He gave us the land for the clinic and lent us Mark to handle the finances."

Waiting for Rick to wind down, Mark caught Dr. Marsdon's curious glance. She'd obviously picked up on Rick's nervousness. Time to step in. "He's telling you I'm the resident bad guy, Dr. Marsdon. Rick says my middle name is Scrooge."

"I'll try to stay on your good side, Mr. Scott."

"Mark—please. As a matter of fact…"

Rick jumped in. "Come on, Sarah, let me show you around." He put a hand to the middle of her back and practically pushed her into the hall. Then he turned to Mark. "Would you mind organizing some temporary accommodation for Sarah?"

Mark nodded. Sooner or later Rick would have to tell her she wouldn't be getting her equipment for a while.

He wondered how she'd react. She seemed like a nice enough lady, but he'd learned to be wary of vets. Even the nice ones exploded when they thought something stood between them and the welfare of their animal patients.

At least this one was easy on the eyes. Very easy. The sort of woman who went around stirring up male hormones without even realizing she was doing it. Not that her looks would get her one step closer to that portable fluoroscope. Mark considered himself immune to feminine wiles. And plenty had been used against him. So far none had succeeded.

He clicked on his cell phone and speed-dialed his office. "Beth? Mark. Rick's just dumped a new lady vet in our laps. Get her a suite at the motel, could you? And stock it? Ground floor, I think. Thanks."

He hung up, shut his briefcase and headed for the door. He'd be willing to bet that the job of letting Dr. Marsdon down gently was one Rick would leave to him.

"SO, HOW WAS THE WEATHER in St. Paul?" Rick said as he propelled Sarah down the hall.

"I left in a snowstorm."

"You have snow in April?"

"Won't last long, but it was a mess to drive in until I got south of Eau Claire. After that, I made great time. Drove half the night. I can't believe it's almost summer in Tennessee."

"Just wait until August."

"It gets hot in St. Paul, too."

"Not a soggy heat like Memphis, I'll bet." He opened a door onto a small operating room. "Mac, when you're finished spaying that Dachshund, stick your head in my office and meet Sarah Marsdon, our newest staff member.''

The large man in scrubs and mask who stood at the operating table grunted but didn't lift his head from the small brown dog that lay on her back.

Rick closed the door quietly. ''John McIntyre Thorn, our resident ogre. The best surgeon I have ever met, but he has the personality of a Tasmanian devil.''

''That makes two people whose bad sides I don't want to get on. You got any nice guys around here?''

''Everybody else is pretty nice. But overworked.''

''What else is new? This place is enormous, Rick, and downright palatial. You're very lucky to have this much suburban land to build a clinic on.''

Rick opened another door on a small utilitarian office. ''Margot's dad is the biggest real estate developer in these parts. He gave us the ten acres. Sit. You must be tired after your drive. Want a soft drink? Coffee?''

''No, thanks.'' Sarah sat down. ''What about zoning variances? You're surrounded by expensive mansions with acres of manicured lawns. Didn't the neighbors object?''

''That's where Mark Scott comes in. He was dead set against this project, but once Coy told him we were committed, he did the research. The land was zoned agricultural and light industrial and hadn't ever been changed to residential.''

''Like I said, lucky you.''

Rick rubbed his fingers under his eyes. ''A few of the neighbors don't approve. Most of the area residents were glad to see us—better than a fast-food joint or a chicken ranch—but a couple of people whose kids prefer motorcycles and fast cars to horses are still fighting us tooth and nail.''

"I see."

"Hey, it's just another of those handy-dandy little problems that come with the territory, right?"

Sarah wondered at the weary exasperation in his tone. His eyes were red-rimmed. He looked as though he hadn't slept in weeks. He was a far cry from the bouncy guy she'd met two years ago at the Kansas City conference, when he'd approached her about taking a job in the new clinic he was planning to build.

She shoved down her misgivings. "I'm dying to see the large-animal facilities," she said, and noted the change in Rick's color to pale gray.

"Um, yes. We're a little behind on getting everything finished." He hurried on. "Punch list things. Minor, mostly. Look, I know you must be exhausted. Go get some rest. I've got you scheduled for two to ten p.m. for the first few days, so you overlap all but the midnight-to-eight shift. But if you could come in about eleven tomorrow you could meet the day staff first. Then we can go over the whole place and go through the large-animal area. Okay by you?"

She didn't want to wait until morning. She'd never been able to hold on to her lollipop until she got out of the candy store. But something told her Rick was uncomfortable, and it was never a good idea to start a new job by making your boss uncomfortable. She tamped down her anxiety and said, "Sure. I'll need a hotel room for a week or so while I look for someplace more permanent. Any suggestions?"

"I asked Mark to book you into a good motel. Check with him."

The blond girl named Alva Jean stuck her head in the door. "Hey, Dr. Hazard, could you give us a hand with Egg Roll? He's got Dr. Bill backed into a corner."

She snickered. "He's looking at Dr. Bill like he's another piece of candy."

"Of course," Rick said, with what Sarah thought was relief. He raised his hands apologetically. "Sorry, Sarah, duty calls."

"Can I help?" Sarah asked. "I like pigs, and I'm generally pretty good with them."

"No, no, wouldn't think of it! Alva, please ask Mark to take care of Dr. Marsdon." And with that, Rick was gone. When he opened the door to the examining room, Sarah heard a cacophony of grunts, a female voice shouting, "Egg Roll, stop that!" and a male tenor shouting, "Get off my foot, dammit!"

Sarah desperately wanted to help, but Rick had told her she wasn't needed. She sat on the hard chair and crossed her arms. Great. Just great. What was that old saying? *When something sounds too good to be true, it usually is.* Rick's job offer had sounded like paradise and had come at absolutely the best possible moment. Things at home were a mess. No matter how often she tried to tell him, Gerald never understood why she was so upset with him. Neither did her family. They always took Gerald's side. In addition to her personal problem was her unhappiness in her job. No wonder Rick's offer had seemed like the perfect opportunity to start afresh.

The door opened and Mark Scott leaned in. "Hi. How about we get out of here and go see your motel? We'll have to take both cars, so I'll lead, you follow." He handed her a card. "This is my cell phone number. If you get lost, call me."

"On what? A can and a string?"

His eyebrows went up. "No cell phone?"

"It belonged to the practice in St. Paul. I've never had one of my own."

"Okay. I'll put that on my list. We'll get you one tomorrow morning. Until then, just stick close to my tail."

He turned around and left with the blithe assumption that she'd trot after him. Watching that particular tail in its well-tailored slacks, she suspected that most women did trot after him.

She intended to keep her vow. No more good-looking men. No more entrepreneurs and titans of industry. No more hard-driving A-type personalities. She'd sworn off them forever. One Gerald in a lifetime was one too many.

The next time she fell for a man, if she ever did, she'd find a nice, gentle nest-builder with a sensitive heart, who actually listened to the things she had to say. A nurturer. Someone with glasses.

Her ruminations took her to the parking lot, where she watched Mark climb into a British racing-green Jaguar sedan. He *would* drive a Jag. He'd never be able to fit his long legs under the dashboard of a Porsche.

She climbed into her black Dodge Ram truck and pulled in behind him. He drove well and made following him easy, though she'd never be able to find the clinic again on her own with all the twists and turns they took down country roads, past vines heavy with wisteria and riots of azaleas in bloom.

After a twenty-minute drive, the Jag pulled up to a shiny new motel advertising executive suites. He climbed out, waited for her to pull up beside him, and lo and behold, opened her door for her and offered her a hand. It felt cool, smooth. She was certain that if she glanced down she'd find his fingernails better cared for than hers.

"Come on. My assistant said the keys would be over the door. Bags?"

She opened the back door of her truck and pointed to a pair of bulging duffel bags. She was suddenly aware of how ratty they looked. He probably carried matching monogrammed pigskin cases—but he reached for her duffels without batting an eye.

She tried to take at least one, but he walked off before she could snag it. The man had shoulders on him. Probably one of those guys who worked out at the gym five days a week and did iron-man competitions on the weekend. No wedding ring.

She followed him down the hall, waited while he carefully lowered the bags (which she would have simply dropped), unlocked the door and stood aside. She entered, to find a tiny hall, a small living area with a couch, a couple of chairs at a round table and chairs for dining, a credenza, a small kitchen that could be closed off with louvered doors, and at the back a bedroom with a king-size bed and a bath with a whirlpool.

The thought of the whirlpool was seductive. Her arms and shoulders ached not only from the drive, but from the tension of the past few days.

The suite was institutional and bland, but still more than she had expected. "I can't possibly afford this," she said.

"The clinic is paying for the first two weeks," he said over his shoulder as he carried her bags to the bedroom. "By then, you should have your own place and can send for your things."

"What things? With the exception of books, stereo equipment, my computer and a few old pictures that mean something to me, I'm starting from scratch. New furniture, new town, new job, new apartment."

"Excellent idea. I didn't know whether you'd prefer to be on an upper floor, but this level has a small terrace—and the security is good."

"A terrace?" She hadn't noticed. She walked past him, unlocked a sliding glass door, and opened it. The motel had been built on the edge of a golf course, and acres of landscaped grass stretched down from the tiny terrace. She turned. "This is heaven."

For the first time Mark smiled. "Glad you like it."

He had a genuinely sweet smile. "You ought to do that more often."

"What?"

"Smile. Makes you look human."

"Coy says it makes me look like a gator who's just spotted an absent-minded duck."

She laughed. "He has a point."

"I had the refrigerator and the bar stocked. Could you use a drink?"

"Yeah, I guess I could. Could we sit out here?" She pointed at the two molded plastic chairs.

"If you like. I didn't know what you like, so my assistant brought over a bit of everything. Frankly, I'm amazed she got here and left again before we arrived— but then, Beth's amazing."

"I'd better go with what the natives drink."

"That would be Jack Black and branch."

"I beg your pardon?"

"Jack Daniels bourbon and branch water. Or in this case, good bottled water."

"Oh. Make it very light, otherwise you'll have to pour me into bed when I pass out."

He raised an eyebrow. She felt her face go red, as he turned away and went back into the suite. One lousy eyebrow, and she reacted like a schoolgirl.

He handed her the drink in a heavy crystal glass that clearly had not come with the motel's stock of bar glasses, and took the chair beside her. He stretched his long legs in front of him. "To crime."

"How about to secrets?"

He glanced over at her. "Huh?"

"Come on, Mr. Scott…"

"Mark."

"I doubt you generally baby-sit newcomers in your busy executive life, yet here you are playing bartender, while Rick ran from me to trim a pig's toenails. What gives?"

He took a deep breath. "You're too observant for your own good, Dr. Marsdon."

"Oh Lord, don't tell me there's no job!"

He raised a hand quickly. "No, no, there's a job. There's very much a job. You are our only full time large-animal specialist at this point. We've got a couple of part-timers, and everybody has had some experience with large animals—but we definitely need you."

"So, what's the problem?"

"The problem is the same as it usually is with any start-up organization. Money is tight."

"Is that all?"

"Oh, that is very much all. Or is likely to be if we're not careful."

"Meaning?"

"Meaning that everyone connected with the clinic is going to have to start generating income big-time or make do with a great deal less in the way of resources for the foreseeable future."

"No problem." She hesitated. "How much income? And how much less are we talking about?"

He sighed. "That's the thing. We're only now going

fully operational 24–7, and you are the low man on the totem pole, since you are the newest vet.''

''And?''

''That means we need you not only to cover the large animals, but to work small animals most evenings and some weekends.''

She sat up. ''And I sleep and eat when?''

''You'll have time off during the day and at least two—possibly three—weekends a month, but most of that time you'll still be on-call for large-animal emergencies.''

''For how long?''

He opened his hands. ''A few weeks, maybe a few months.''

''Uh-huh.'' She leaned back and peered at him. He avoided her eyes. ''I don't mind the hours, since I obviously don't have any other life yet. What else?''

''There have been a few construction problems, delays, cost overruns. Nothing unusual in the start-up phase of an operation this size.''

''Rick said that.''

''The thing is, Rick tends to make promises—all in good faith—that he may not be able to deliver on.''

''What precisely can he not deliver on?'' Her drink splashed onto her jeans.

''Calm down. We're talking a little glitch here.''

''How little?''

''At the moment, there aren't sufficient funds to equip more than one operating theater for large animals, and even that is not quite finished. We need additional lights, for one thing.''

''Is that all? I can't operate on more than one animal at a time, anyway, and we can always bring in portable lights for a few days. You had me worried. As long as I've got the diagnostic equipment and the other stuff…''

"Yes, well. Unfortunately, that is the other problem. We don't quite have all the equipment yet."

She set her drink down on the plastic table beside her. "The equipment is nonnegotiable, Mr. Scott. Why do you think I uprooted my life and dragged myself down here to work with Rick? He promised me lasers, ultrasound, magnetic imagery, fluoroscopes, an anesthesia machine—a state-of-the-art operating theater."

"And you'll get all of it, Dr. Marsdon. Just not in the next few months."

"But it's ordered, right? You're simply having a problem with delivery dates?"

"Unfortunately, no. The orders have been held up."

"By whom? You? Scrooge Scott?"

"That's my job."

"Who says?"

"The bank says, the stockholders say, the mortgage company says, and most of all, the medical equipment supply houses that require payment before they ship so much as a scalpel say."

"Then, send them the money."

"At the moment that is not possible. I'm just the messenger, doctor."

"At the moment, if I had a gun, I'd shoot the messenger, just like in the old days, Mr. Scott. I can guess what a building like that clinic costs, and the equipment I want is small potatoes next to that. Don't tell me you can't find that money, because I do not believe you."

"That's your choice. The point is, I can't until I'm certain that this place is going to fly and not turn into another dog and cat hospital where pampered pigs get their damn nails clipped!"

"I'm surprised you're paying for this place. Can you afford it?" She heard the contempt in her voice and wished she'd suppressed it, but the sort of obstruction she was running into from a man who didn't understand the problem pushed all her buttons at once.

"We're getting the corporate rate, and Rick promised you moving expenses."

"And this place is a sop to keep me pacified so that I don't pitch a fit about the equipment he promised me? A couple of thousand bucks to stave off paying a couple of hundred thousand?"

"There's no point in continuing this discussion at the moment, Doctor. We can go into the circumstances tomorrow when you're more…rested." He put his glass down and walked back into the bedroom.

"You think you'll be able to handle me tomorrow? Forget it. Rested, I just get tougher."

"Good night, Doctor. You'll find some food in the refrigerator, in case you don't want to go out."

She heard the door open and close a little harder than necessary. She picked up the crystal glass, ready to hurl it after him, then stopped. She'd only have to clean up the mess afterward.

She sat and took a swig of her drink, then coughed as it hit the bottom of her throat. She could feel the bourbon all the way down to her toes. She set the glass down, suddenly feeling guilty about yelling at Mark. She was tired, more tired than she'd realized. But she *had* counted on that equipment. She'd been promised that equipment, and Mr. Mark Scott was going to have to come up with a stronger argument than lack of funds if he expected her to accept the delay.

If only she had enough money to buy the things herself. But she didn't, even though she'd finally almost

paid off her student loans. Truth was, even if Steve
Stapleton in St. Paul had broken down and allowed her
to buy a partnership in his clinic, she'd have had to hock
her eyeballs to get the money together.

No, the thing to do was to persuade Mark that the
equipment was crucial to the success of the clinic.

She took her drink into the kitchen and poured the
rest down the sink. Pity to waste good bourbon, but she
didn't want to pass out in the Jacuzzi. She opened the
small refrigerator and found eggs, bacon, bread, butter,
sweet rolls, and an assortment of sandwich makings
with condiments. Good. She could take her sandwich
and a soda, and dine while the water washed away all
her aches and pains.

Tomorrow was soon enough to tackle Mark. Tomorrow she'd meet the staff, assess the facilities, and do
some real work. Tomorrow she'd start lining up allies
in her battle against the bureaucracy. This was one battle she expected to win, and win quickly. Mark Scott
didn't have a clue how hard—and how dirty—she could
fight. When it came to her patients, she was like a
mamma grizzly defending her cubs.

CHAPTER TWO

SARAH CALLED HER FATHER in St. Paul before she went
to bed, only to get his answering machine. She gave it
her telephone number and hung up. She supposed he'd
gone over to one of his sons' houses for a family conference on the best way to get Sarah to come back
home.

It was nearly midnight when the phone rang. Sarah
picked it up.

"At home at least you had an apartment. Now you
live in a motel," Lars Marsdon said in his clipped voice.

"Actually, this is nicer than my apartment, and the
clinic is paying for it."

"You quit your job and ran off to Tennessee because
you had a fight with your fiancé. You've made your
point, so come back home."

"Dad, I just got here this afternoon."

"So, you won't have had time to settle. They will
not miss you. Your old job is still available. Steve told
me he would hold it for a couple of days, although he
is annoyed because you walked out on him."

"Dad—" She tried to sound patient, but could feel
her heart rate increasing with every sentence. "Steve
was never going to allow me to be a partner. Then,
when I gave him notice, he got so mad he told me to
get out right that minute. I would have stayed two
weeks. The choice was his, not mine."

"This is your home. This is where your family, your fiancé, your job are. Come home where you belong."

"Sorry, but no."

"Call back when you're ready to speak sensibly." He hung up.

Sarah lay back and tried to slow down her breathing.

How soon would Lars Marsdon mobilize the troops? Would he ask all three of her brothers and their wives to call and put additional pressure on her? That's what he generally did when he didn't agree with her choices. Occasionally Peter would refuse, but the other two always went along with their father. They were all so content with their lives that they couldn't understand why she wanted more.

Sarah always wondered whether they made up their own scripts or said what Lars told them to say. Didn't matter. This time she was free, and intended to remain free.

Now, all she had to do was make Mark see things her way.

"HEY, DR. SARAH," Alva Jean Huxtable chirped, when Sarah walked in the front door of the clinic the next morning. "Mr. Scott said to tell you he's bringing you a cell phone, and there's a parking place for you around back. The staff park there."

"Oh, I didn't know."

"That's okay. It's not like we're running out of parking space in front." Alva Jean looked at the nearly empty waiting room.

"Dr. Rick said he was going to try to get everybody together at eleven so you could meet them."

"Where?"

"He calls it his conference room, but it's really our

break room. He's got a drink machine and a snack machine in there and a little refrigerator. If you bring your lunch, you better mark the sack with your name—otherwise somebody's bound to steal it."

Sarah raised her eyebrows. "Thanks, I'll remember that. Do I have a desk?"

Alva Jean shook her head. "Not yet, but there are some extra file cabinets in the storeroom. You can have one of those, if Rick says it's okay."

Sarah smiled. "Thanks. I'll ask him when I see him."

She pushed through the door to the central hall and glanced in at Mark's partially open door, but he wasn't in. For some reason, she felt a stab of disappointment. Was she so anxious to go into battle with him again? Or was there another more personal reason? Nonsense. The fact that he was tall with brown eyes that crinkled at the corners had nothing to do with anything. She simply relished a good fight with a worthy adversary. Period.

At this point she didn't even know the full extent of the battle she needed to wage.

At the far end of the hall there was a door with a smoked-glass panel in the upper half. Beside it someone had taped a small handwritten sign that read, Large Animals. No fancy brass plaques back here.

To the right, a solid door had a green lighted exit sign over it. That must lead to the employees' parking area. She'd move her truck there as soon as she'd done a bit of exploring. She needed to restock the vet cabinet in the back of her truck, anyway. One of the vet techs here ought to be able to restock for her. While she'd half watched television in her motel room last night, she'd put together a basic list of the drugs and paraphernalia she'd need.

She took a deep breath and opened the door. Then stood for a moment and stared. The room was cavernous, the central hall more than wide enough to admit an eighteen-wheeler. On the right, doors could be rolled up into the ceiling so that a big rig of cows could be backed into the slot that opened into a large fenced pen.

She opened the first door on her left. It was empty except for packing boxes and paint cans. She assumed it would eventually be her office. She'd probably have to leave room for storage shelves that would hold everything except the drugs that had to be kept double-locked and accounted for to the government.

She walked past the cow pen, and past the small stalls where cows or bulls could be kept individually so that they could be examined safely in a relatively confined space. Looked strong. Good. An angry bull or cow could do extensive damage.

Past that area on her right were three doors. She peeked through the window of the first and saw a completely padded stall—floor, walls and ceiling. The recovery area—where a large animal could come out of anesthesia without hurting itself. The next two doors opened into similar stalls, but without the padded walls. These, then, were the ones that Mark had told her weren't quite finished. Three recovery stalls—impressive for a private clinic. Many of the teaching veterinary hospitals didn't have as many.

On her right across the broad hall, she discovered the prep room where the animals could be anesthetized and readied for surgery. Through the double doors at the end of the prep room, she could see the surgery. She opened the door, but when she flipped the light switch, nothing happened. Great. She hoped no horses or cows would have to be operated on by candlelight.

The surgery seemed to contain only basic equipment. The lights, when they were hooked up, would no doubt be more than adequate, but at the moment it was difficult to tell much in the gloom.

As to the diagnostic equipment she'd been promised—one portable ultrasound was all she could see. Well, that would change.

She stood in the doorway with her hands on her hips. First priority—get the blasted lights hooked up. That was something Mark could darn well put at the top of his To Do list.

"Help ya?" A raspy voice spoke from behind her.

She jumped and turned.

"New doc, are ya?"

The man who leaned against the far wall grinned at her. He stood no more than five-two or -three and probably weighed a hundred ten pounds. His face was covered with sun-ruined skin, wrinkled like badly tanned leather, and the teeth revealed in that grin were crooked. His blue eyes were bright as a bird's.

"I'm Sarah Marsdon."

"The new vet?" He narrowed his eyes at her. "Told me you were a lady, but didn't say that you were a pretty one. I'm Jack. Jack Renfro. I'm your vet tech, your surgery assistant, and your jack-of-all-trades, no pun intended."

The slight southern accent was overlaid with a thick cockney twang.

"Jockey?" Sarah grinned back at him.

"And exercise boy and groom before I got too old and too stove up to ride. What I don't know about horses ain't been writ down as yet."

"How about cows?"

"Hate the stupid buggers, but I can handle 'em. And anything else with four feet comes into this place."

"Good." Sarah extended her hand. "What's with the lights?"

Jack blew out his breath. "Bloody contractor's supposed to have everything done here today. But then, he was supposed to finish last month, wasn't he?"

"Was he?"

"You weren't to know, of course, but we've had one muck-up after another. That woman kept trying to turn the place into a bloody palace, then the almighty rain and the mud, and delivery problems, and if that weren't enough, we have the neighborhood rowdies at night."

"Rowdies?"

"Kids. Too much time and no sense, is what I says. Don't know much about tractors and such myself, but I do know you can't run one without a carburetor. Took a week for the contractor to get a new one in and installed. Meantime we had to rent another tractor. Cost a bloody fortune."

"They stole a *carburetor*?"

Jack humphed. "As good as. Turned out the little devils hid it behind a stack of plywood, but the contractor wasn't to know, was he? Only found it a month later when he'd already bought the new one. Then there was the great plumbing caper." He sounded disgusted.

"Plumbing?"

"Contractor came in one Monday and found every bit of PVC pipe spread out over the two back paddocks. Spelled out words not fit for your tender ears."

Sarah laughed. "You'd be surprised how un-tender my ears are. Besides, I know that's annoying, but it doesn't sound as though they're really destructive."

"That bit of mischief took four men and a truck most

of the day to pick up and get the mud out. Costs money, things like that. And time we didn't have.''

''If we had an emergency, could we handle it?''

Renfro cocked an eye at her. ''That's up to you, ain't it?''

''You mean I'm it?''

''You got Dr. Eleanor Grayson comes in, but she's part-time, mostly night or when we're pushed. We're supposed to be open twenty-four hours a day, but right now, we only got a couple of part-timers on call after midnight. And Dr. Mac can muck in if you need him. Staff's good, but they're mostly used to handling puppies and kittens.''

Sarah laughed at the obvious sneer in his voice. He grinned back at her through his terrible teeth.

''Well, I says, don't ya know, if it ain't good for racing or eating, then what's the sense of it, I says.''

''Don't let the clients hear you say that.'' Sarah laughed.

''Keeps me thoughts to me'self. You worry about the cutting, Doc, I'll handle the rest of it.''

''Deal. Nice to work with you, Jack. By the way, they say I'm going to be working a good many nights and weekends, as well, until we're fully staffed. What are your hours?''

''My good lady says they run from 'kin to cain't,' but she's from Arkansas and talks funny. Don't you worry. You need me at four in the morning, I'll be here.''

Suddenly Sarah didn't feel quite as overwhelmed as she had, with the problems she faced. With an old pro like Jack Renfro to back her up, how could she fail? She glanced at her watch. ''Oh, hell, I'm late for Rick's meeting.''

Jack rolled his eyes. "Get more done without these infernal meetings of his. You run along. I'll hunt up that contractor and put a flea up his nose. You'll have your lights and that office cleaned up today." He trotted off with the rolling, bowlegged gait of a man used to having horse flesh between his knees.

"Jack?" Sarah called after him.

He turned.

"I've got a list of medications and stuff I need in my truck cabinet. It's lying on the front seat of my truck, which is, I'm sorry to say, in front of the clinic instead of where it belongs."

"Toss me your keys. I'll move it and stock it for you."

"You're a wonder. Thanks."

"MARK, MY CHILD is driving me nuts." Coy Buchanan slumped into his maroon leather desk chair in the corner office of Buchanan Enterprises. It had been specially constructed to accommodate both his height and his bulk, but it still groaned under his weight. He reached for his oversize mug of New Orleans coffee.

"Margot Hazard may be your child, Coy," Mark said from the chair across the acre or so of inlaid leather on top of Coy's desk. "To the rest of the world, she's a grown woman." *And an annoying one.* Mark didn't voice that thought.

"I'm getting to the point where I don't want to take her calls. Terrible thing to start screening out your only daughter's telephone calls."

"Switch her over to me."

"Oh, I've tried, son, believe me. She says you aren't responsive, whatever the hell that means."

"It means I don't sit up and jump through her. You pay me for *not* jumping through hoops."

"I know, I know. But couldn't you at least act like maybe you're planning to leave the ground occasionally?" Coy grinned. "Make my life one hell of a lot easier."

"As long as you don't expect me to sign blank checks."

"It's that damn animal clinic," Coy said, and gulped half the mug of coffee. He wiped his mouth. "Why couldn't Margot have married somebody like Ted Turner or Donald Trump? Even a king might have been able to afford her. But no, she's got to go and marry a veterinarian. And then try to turn him into a millionaire. Last I heard, wasn't nobody trading veterinary stock on Wall Street."

"True, but we've got investors, Coy. You are not the only one. And some of them can't afford to lose what money they've put into the clinic."

"Hell, you think *I* can?" Coy came close to roaring. "First rule of business my daddy taught me is 'Don't lose money.'"

This time Mark grinned. "You lost two fortunes before you were forty."

"Yeah, but I made 'em back, and then some. I'm getting too old for this game. I hired you to see I don't lose any more. I just want to build nice office buildings and fancy subdivisions, pay the IRS entirely too much of what I earn, and still have time to go fishing occasionally. I've got a good mind to go do that right this minute and leave you to deal with Margot all by yourself."

"You do, and I quit."

"You won't quit. You got too much junkyard dog in you. How many times I fired you?"

"I lost count after fifteen."

"And have you once ever started cleaning out your desk? No, you have not. You know I don't mean it, and you're just too damn mean to leave."

"If I ever do start cleaning out my desk, Coy, you'll know I really have quit. In the meantime, I will be pleasant but noncommittal. I will not give her or Rick carte blanche to spend whatever they like on fancy furniture, equipment or additional personnel until they're fully operational and at least breaking even. Do I have your agreement on that?"

"Sure you do."

"You'll back me up, no matter how hard Margot pleads?"

"Yeah, yeah, if I have to. But—" Coy looked sheepish "—I have to ask you for something."

"Oh, damn," Mark muttered. "Here it comes."

"I know you're supposed to be going to Houston tomorrow to meet with the Center City Commission…"

"Right."

"I'll take the meeting. For at least the next month I want you to stick close to town and spend most of your time out at that clinic."

"Coy…"

"I know it's been years since you supervised a construction project personally—at least a penny-ante one like the clinic." Coy sounded plaintive. "I need you to do this for me, son."

"Construction's almost finished. You don't want a construction supervisor. You want an on-site CFO to deal with the problems while you wine and dine and avoid Margot's telephone calls." Mark sighed. "Last time I checked, I still work for you." Mark stood. "Okay, I'll keep up with things here and check on the clinic at night."

"I wouldn't ask…"

"Sure you would." Mark walked to the door and stood with his hand on the knob. "But too much Margot, and the next time you fire me I may just go."

"I'LL HAVE TO MAKE THIS FAST," Rick said to Sarah in front of the assembled people in the break room. "This is everybody I could track down at the moment. You'll have to introduce yourself to the others when you run into them. People, this is Dr. Sarah Marsdon who is going to put our large-animal clinic on the map."

"I'll certainly try." Sarah smiled at the group. "But I'll need some help and I'll need a surgery with lights." She gave Rick a hard look.

Rick looked uncomfortable. "The lights were supposed to be hooked up yesterday. I'll check."

"Thanks." She smiled again and tried to keep her tone light and even. This was no time to air her dirty laundry. "Jack Renfro's going to harry the contractor."

"Good. I'll back him up." Rick pointed to a tall man with a gray buzz cut who stood over a coffee urn at the back of the room. "That's Dr. Mac Thorn, the other senior partner. Mac, I introduced you yesterday, remember?"

"I don't remember anything while I'm operating," he said grumpily.

Sarah raised her eyebrows. So Dr. Thorn had an attitude.

"Jack Renfro says you'll assist me if I need help in surgery," she said.

He nodded and took a sip of coffee.

"This is Bill Chumney, our exotics man. He's about to get us a very lucrative contract with the local animal refuge, to do all their vet work."

"Actually," Chumney said, "I'm a raptor man by preference, but I can handle everything from armadillos to iguanas if I have to."

"What are the laws about exotics in Tennessee? Can people keep them as pets?"

"The state is extremely strict about issuing permits to people who want to keep local fauna, or zoo animals—big cats, elephants, that sort of thing. Iguanas, reptiles, ferrets, hedgehogs, even sugar gliders—small creatures bred and sold to be pets—are okay. Sometimes Rick and Mac handle them in the small animal section, sometimes I do. And then somebody has to look after the raccoon whose mother got hit by a truck, or a possum with his tail bitten off. That's why we're anxious to get the contract with the animal refuge people signed. We'll handle all the hurt animals the public brings in. And the zoo, too, of course. They have their own staff, but it's pretty limited."

"Are you busy?"

"Not yet, but we will be when that contract goes through. That's my flight cage they're building outside by Dr. Sol's research lab." He glowered at Rick. "It was supposed to be finished, and a damn sight larger, as well. I've got an eagle about ready to try his wings. Eagles need space to get lift."

"Okay, okay. After the lights are up. I promise I'll check it out."

Rick turned back to Sarah. "Dr. Sol Weincroft isn't in today. He's actually more of a silent partner for the next few months. We're building him a wing out back for his research in return for financial support from him and the pharmaceutical companies funding his research. He'll be available in emergencies, but he's concentrating on research as much as he can. I think you may have met him in Kansas City, Sarah?"

Sarah nodded. "Heard him give a paper on his research on an equine infectious anemia vaccine."

"And he's very, very close to success. That'll be one hell of a feather in our caps." Rick sighed. "Eleanor Grayson isn't in, either. She's part-time and your backup after hours. She was here pretty late last night with a flipped gut."

Sarah knew Rick meant that one of Dr. Grayson's charges had a flipped gut—not an unusual occurrence in large breeds of dog. It was a deadly emergency requiring instant surgery—and there was only a fair chance of saving the animal's life.

"Yeah, and I've got a hip dysplasia in twenty minutes," Mac said. He put down his coffee cup and left.

"Now that the Grinch has departed," a small blond woman said, "I'm Liz Carlyle. I just graduated from Mississippi State last year. I'm on small animals, but I kind of swing where I'm needed. I really want to go into ophthalmology eventually, but I can't go back to school until I make some serious money, or until and unless my husband gets one heck of a promotion." She shrugged and turned pink with embarrassment.

Sarah thought she was very young indeed.

"That's the current veterinary staff," Rick said. "We're piecing out for the first few months with a roster of part-timers from midnight to eight. So far, there hasn't been much call that late. You've met Alva Jean, who handles the desk during the day, does the billing and such. Mabel Halliburton comes in at four, so you'll mostly be working with her. She kind of mothers us all, and she's a wonder with the paperwork. Does our ordering, backs up Alva Jean. We're still hiring kennel and cleanup staff. People keep quitting on us after a week or so. Nobody seems to want to work so hard for minimum wage.''

"Go figure," Liz whispered.

Rick glared at her. "We're going to need at least three more vet techs once we're fully up and running, but at the moment we're making do with Jack for large and Nancy here for small, and part-timers from other clinics hired on an hourly basis.''

Sarah took the sure, brown hand of the woman who offered it. "Nancy Mayfield. I do anything and everything. At the moment I've got to go get Dr. Mac ready for his hip dysplasia.''

"You're assisting?''

"Yep. I'm better at surgery than Jack. He's better at post-op. We complement each other.''

The telephone on the wall beside the door rang. Liz jumped. Rick answered it and listened for a moment. "Yeah, yeah, Mac. She's on her way.''

Nancy Mayfield grinned at Sarah and stood up slowly. Sarah saw her catch her breath. The woman stood for a moment with her eyes closed.

She's in pain, Sarah thought.

Nancy caught her eye. "Jack and I are a lot alike. He raced, I rode hunters and jumpers in the show ring. We're both too stiff to do it any longer.'' She glanced at her own strong hands. "Nothing wrong with these. It's my neck that gives me fits. Ah, well, I'd better head on out before Dr. Mac explodes.''

"We'd better all head on out," Rick said. "Sorry you couldn't meet everybody at one time, Sarah.''

"That's okay. If I see anybody in greens with an animal under his arm, I'll assume he's a staff member."

"Nice to have met you," Bill Chumney said. "Now I'm off to exercise Marvin's wings for him. This time I think he's really going to fly."

The telephone rang again, and Nancy answered it. "I'm coming!" She listened a moment, then turned to the room. "Scratch the dysplasia. We've got a couple of bull terriers who've just been hit by a car."

"Damn!" Rick said.

Chairs scraped. Bill Chumney reached the door first. The moment it opened, Sarah heard the howls from the waiting room.

"Oh, God," Liz whispered. And ran to help.

Sarah ran, as well. She noticed on her way by that Mark Scott stood in the door of his office. "Come on," she said. "We may need another pair of hands."

A broad, gray-haired woman, in a pair of disreputable shorts and a shirt that said Kiss the Gardener, sat on her knees on the floor just inside the door cradling the body of a dog wrapped in a blanket. She sobbed, the dog whined pitiably. The blanket in which it was wrapped was bloodstained.

"George is still in the car, I couldn't carry him. Please, please, they're badly hurt." She grabbed Sarah's hand. "Don't let them die!"

Sarah dropped to her knees and pulled the dog's lips back. The dog made no attempt to bite at her, which in itself showed how close to shock she was. The gums were too pale. "Nancy! Ringer's *stat*—push. And get out a couple of surgery packs and some Ketamine, in case we have to immobilize fast. Call Jack. Tell him to bring a couple of gurneys."

The dog whined again. Mark said over her shoulder, "I can carry him to OR."

Sarah shook her head. "Could do more harm than good. Go help get the other one in." She began to touch the dog gently, expecting the terrier to turn on her. "What happened?"

"They're never out of the yard! Never!" the woman sobbed. "This morning we had a new meter reader. He must have left the gate ajar." She caressed the white fur beneath her hand. "I was planting azaleas, and then I heard these brakes screech and..." She broke down completely.

"Here you go, Doc," Jack Renfro said.

Half an hour later, both dogs lay on surgical tables on either side of the small-animal operating theater. Mac Thorn worked on the large male dog, while Sarah worked on the female.

"She got a crack on the head," Sarah said to Jack. "But the X rays say she doesn't have any broken bones or skull fracture. Both her eyes look normal—pupils are the same size and responding. Not sure about internal bleeding, but if there was any, it seems to have stopped. We need to clean her up, stitch her up and watch her." She worked steadily, confidently, and in silence except for an occasional instruction to Jack.

Mac Thorn, on the other hand, kept up a running stream of curses, demands and snarls, which didn't seem to bother Nancy Mayfield a bit, but which occasionally made Sarah lift her head in astonishment. Sarah finished with her dog, left it to Jack to bed down in the ICU, and moved over to Mac while she pulled off her gloves. "Need a hand?"

"No, dammit! Blasted idiots! Let dogs run loose! Broken pelvis—have to pin it, blast it. People!"

Sarah was certain Nancy was grinning, but that was impossible to tell with her mask on. Sarah grinned back and got out of the way. She went to find the dogs' owner.

Not in the waiting room. Odd. She walked back down the hall, and heard voices from Mark's office. She pushed open the door. The owner of the dogs pushed herself out of the chair across from Mark's desk.

"Are they going to be all right?" She clutched a cup of what appeared to be coffee.

"Mrs. Jepson needed someplace quiet to sit," Mark said. "And something hot to drink."

Sarah looked at him with new eyes. So he wasn't a total dolt.

"Mrs. Jepson," she said, "I'm Sarah Marsdon. What are the dogs' names?"

"George and Marian." Mrs. Jepson began to cry again.

"They're beautiful bull terriers. And they're tough little critters, you know."

"Otherwise, General George Patton would never have kept one with him," Mark said.

"Oh, you know that? That's why my husband insisted we get one. George and Marian are our fourth and fifth." She sniffed. "They're the last pups my husband and I bought before he died."

"Marian may have some internal trauma that hasn't shown up yet, Mrs. Jepson, so we'll be watching her very carefully. But I cleaned her cuts and stitched her up. I doubt she'll even have scars, once the hair grows back."

"And George? She's never been without him. They were litter mates."

"Dr. Thorn is the best surgeon there is," Sarah said,

although she had no way of knowing whether that was true. "He'll talk to you himself..."

She stopped. That would not be a good idea. Dr. Mac Thorn's bedside manner would probably involve blasting Mrs. Jepson for something that was only marginally her fault. "Tell you what, Mrs. Jepson. When I left, Dr. Thorn was saying that he could pin George's hip and that there was every reason to believe he'd be all right."

"Oh!" Mrs. Jepson began to cry again.

Mark stared at her helplessly, then handed her a pristine handkerchief.

"It's going to be a long haul, probably physical therapy. You're going to have your work cut out for you."

"I don't care! As long as I have George and Marian back safe and sound."

She raised her head as a knock sounded on the door, and Nancy Mayfield stuck her head in. "Mrs. Jepson? Didn't know where you were. We're taking the male dog to Recovery now. If you'd like to see them for just a moment—"

"Oh, please!" Mrs. Jepson followed Nancy out, and Sarah sank into the chair that was still warm from her body.

"Hell of an introduction," Mark said. "You want a cup of coffee, too?"

"In a minute. At the moment I simply want to sit."

"Are they really going to be all right?"

"I have no idea. Looks good, but there's always something that can go wrong." She glared at Mark. "Now, about my equipment..."

"Whoa! Can we put this off until later? I'm late for a meeting downtown at Buchanan."

"Are you avoiding me?"

"No. I'll be here this evening after work. I promise

we'll talk then." He went out the door before she could call him back.

"Fine," Sarah said. "Tonight it is, Mr. Mark Scott. You can't avoid me forever."

MARK SPENT THE AFTERNOON at Buchanan Enterprises, putting out more fires. When he walked into the clinic late that afternoon he found the waiting room filled with sick pets whose owners had obviously held off until after work to bring them in for treatment. Despite the heavy-duty sound-deadening tiles on the ceiling and the upper third of the walls, Mark felt an instant kinship with Noah, who must have wished constantly for earplugs during that forty days and forty nights in the ark.

Alva Jean motioned to him while continuing to make 'uh-huh' noises to whoever was on the phone, which seemed to grow out of her ear. He pulled his electronic notebook from his breast pocket, keyed in "headset fr desk" and slid the device back into his pocket. That was the sort of simple change that wouldn't cost more than a little petty cash and should make the receptionist's job both easier and more efficient.

Alva Jean covered the mouthpiece and hissed, "Dr. Marsdon is looking for you." She rolled her eyes to leave Mark in no doubt that Dr. Marsdon was not a happy camper.

He hadn't expected her to be. Apparently, Mark was going to be dealing with Margot and Dr. Marsdon. He sighed. At least the good doctor was single, beautiful and sexy. He rather enjoyed the thought of mixing it up with her again.

He looked into the room next to his and found that the walls had been finished and painted. The paint odor still lingered, but otherwise the place was ready for storage shelving and file cabinets. Tomorrow morning he'd call and have the stuff delivered. He sighed with satisfaction.

Maybe things were coming together, after all. Lately he'd about given up hope.

He ducked into his office and shut the door. Then he shucked his jacket and hung it on the nail somebody had driven into the woodwork. An accident waiting to happen. He made another note: "hammer nails into walls." And prayed that when he got around to checking his notes at midnight he'd have some inkling of what he'd meant.

He kneaded the muscles along the tops of his shoulders and slumped into the ratty desk chair. A normal day at Buchanan. Endless conference calls, endless meetings, a Chamber of Commerce luncheon with Coy, more meetings, work with engineers on HVAC bids for a bank headquarters in Charlotte that had come in high, a surprise visit from the INS about forged green cards on a job they were subcontracting in Little Rock. More telephone calls chasing down the general contractor in Little Rock. Protestations of innocence followed by arguments that the only decent drywall workers in the entire southeast were illegal Mexican laborers.

Mark believed him—and so, for that matter, did the INS. But that didn't matter. He pulled out his notebook. "Check grncds subcon vet." What were the chances he could decipher *that* tomorrow?

His left temple throbbed, and he longed to go home to his quiet house, put on a pair of shorts and a T-shirt, pop a cold beer, and watch mindless television until he fell asleep. What a life for a man who was supposed to be in his prime.

Anyone meeting him would think he had the world

by the tail—a great job with a boss he not only respected but liked, more money than he'd ever dreamed of and an excellent reputation among his colleagues and friends.

Right. Friends. Acquaintances, more like. There simply hadn't been time to develop a life away from work, much less create anything resembling a family. He was like the new Silicon Valley computer kids who ate, slept and lived their jobs.

A far cry from the life he'd envisioned when he was eighteen, before his father's death had brought the world crashing down around his head.

At the knock on his door, he glanced up.

It opened immediately. Dr. Sarah Marsdon came in—no, marched in—and shut it a little too forcefully behind her. Mark didn't bother to stand up.

She sat down. "I'd about decided you weren't coming, Mr. Scott."

He sighed. "Mark—please. I thought we'd settled that."

"That's the only thing we seem to have settled. Now, let's talk about my equipment."

CHAPTER THREE

MARK SIGHED. "Okay. Hit me."

"Believe me, I wish I could. But let's get to my list. Bear in mind this is the *basic* equipment we need. We already have a portable ultrasound. It's a thousand years old, but it will do for the moment."

"Oh, goodie."

"However, we are missing the mobile fluoroscopy machine and the portable X ray..."

"To the tune of eighty thousand bucks or more."

"And the endoscope and laser. Shouldn't run more than about twenty-five each for the bare bones. I can share the X-ray developer with the dogs and cats for the moment, but I'll really need it to stay in my area. The small-animal technicians can come to me to develop their plates rather than the other way around. Of course, a second developer would solve that problem."

"Another twenty-five thou, if we're lucky."

"Be lucky." Sarah ticked off on her fingers. "I was promised an anesthesia machine. You may be able to find one of those from a 'human' medical supply house for about forty-five or fifty thousand."

"Oh, you're too kind."

"That leaves a portable laser, which you can probably pick up for around ten thousand dollars used, and a blood chemistry analyzer. We have an autoclave. I won't ask for a nuclear cytography machine yet, but I do need a laptop computer with Internet and fax capability that I can carry in my car so I can fax ultrasounds and fluoroscopes either back here to the office or to the vet school at Mississippi State. Oh, and the vet cabinet in my truck is too small. Jack said he'd stock the one I have, but I don't have enough room for all the equipment and medication I'll need to take with me on offsite calls. And I need keys to the Schedule 2 drug storage cabinet—both keys, please.''

''Is that all?''

''For the moment. Eventually, we really will need an MRI. And that will involve training at least one employee to use it. Oh, one more thing—a really good pair of surgical clippers for large animals. I can have one sent overnight for four or five hundred dollars. And I'll have a list of additional medications and supplies I'll need, as soon as I check what you already have.'' Sarah started to get up. ''That's it for now.''

''Whoa, there, Doctor. You've just given me a list that runs over two hundred thousand dollars.''

''That's what I was promised.''

''I'm not a miracle worker. I can't pull two hundred thousand bucks out of the air.''

Sarah took a deep breath. ''Look, I know I sound peremptory. But surely Rick had a budget for the things he promised me.''

This time Mark sank back in his chair. ''I haven't looked at the original equipment list lately. Frankly, I've been too damn busy putting out fires. The truth is that Coy Buchanan gave Rick and Margot this piece of land. He could have put up several more mansions on it and made a great deal more money. He's been in on the plans for the building from the beginning, and we've given this place every break on construction we could give.''

''But?''

''You've met Margot.''

''And?''

''And Margot has continued to make the building more and more elaborate. The changes have cost much more than originally budgeted. Then the weather, the damage we've had—it all adds up. We're at least a month away from a grand opening, when it should have taken place in February. I think Rick—no, make that everybody—I'm as guilty as he is—has been robbing Peter to pay Paul, and now Peter is presenting his bill. I'm sorry, but that's the way it is—at least for the next six months, maybe longer.''

''You do think you'll eventually be able to pull things together?''

''I'm dancing as fast as I can. Will you work with me?''

Sarah stood. ''I understand your problems, and I'll try to be as patient as I can. But remember, this is lives we're talking about, here.''

''Animal lives. Animals can be replaced.'' The moment the words left his mouth, he regretted them. He'd done something he seldom did—speak first and think second. She'd gotten to him.

From the look on her face, Sarah wasn't about to let him get away with it.

''Tell that to the teenage girl who loses her very first pony because we have to take it four and a half hours away to Mississippi State for colic surgery. You might as well say you should avoid an expensive procedure to save your grandmother because she's old and ill.''

''A grandmother is a human being, and most people

don't have but two. You can't put a price on human life."

"You certainly *can* put a price on animal lives, Mr. Scott. Farmer A knows precisely what his prize Angus bull is worth. If we screw up through negligence, or because we don't have the right diagnostic and operating equipment, we'll have to pay that price. You might add that to your two hundred thousand."

"That's what we have liability insurance for."

"Liability insurance won't cover that teenage girl's heartbreak. Do you think Mrs. Jepson would prefer to have the value of George and Marian so she could buy a pair of puppies to take their place?"

"No, but she *would* replace them."

"Not replace them. She'd bring other dogs into her life, but she'd never forget them or stop grieving for them. And that's not one bit different from the way you feel about your grandmother."

"Both my grandmothers are alive and very well, thank you."

"Dammit!" Sarah snapped. "Don't play games with me. So long as you don't see the value of animal lives, you and I will never be able to communicate." She walked out of his office.

"Hey..." he said, "I didn't mean..."

The woman always put him on the defensive, made him say stupid things he would never say to anyone else. The problem was, he liked her. He wished he could give her everything she wanted. But there was no way—not if the clinic was to survive. Drat Margot Buchanan, anyway. If she hadn't been able to wrap Coy around her little finger, if she hadn't been able to con Rick... Hell, if Mark hadn't been in Texas building a mall for three months last year, he could have headed her off. Now his job was doubly difficult.

Because Sarah Marsdon stirred his blood.

Even in the loose scrubs he could see the outlines of her body. He liked the way she moved with an easy swing that was more than a little cocky. He grinned. She might have been put on this earth to complicate his life, but at least the complications made him feel more alive than he had for years. Now, if he could only figure out some way to accommodate everybody's needs without either bankrupting the clinic or giving himself an ulcer, he'd be fine.

Maybe for some lonely people animals did fill an unfillable gap in their lives, but that still didn't compare with the loss of a grandmother, say, or a father.

Or did it?

Suddenly, his mind flashed back to the only animal he'd ever owned. Okay, so Mickey had been different. But when Mark and his mother had been forced to move into the apartment after his father's death, he'd done what everyone had told him was the best thing for Mickey—he'd given his dog to Uncle Greg, who had a farm and young children for Mickey to play with. Uncle Greg had told Mark he'd always be welcome to visit the big black Labrador when he was home from school.

He'd only visited once. Seeing Mickey, playing with him, then driving away had been too painful to endure a second time. Mickey—now long dead and buried under the wild dogwoods at Uncle Greg's farm.

He hadn't allowed himself to think about the dog for years. Hadn't trusted himself to think about Mickey. How come he still felt as deep an ache of emptiness as he did when he thought about his father's wreck? That was stupid. They weren't the same thing at all. Were they?

Obviously the point was that he must never allow himself to care that deeply about anyone or anything again, whether it was a Mickey or a father. Building the walls to keep out the pain of inevitable loss took too much effort.

He took out his notebook and reached for the spike impaling a half-dozen telephone messages. Both his temples throbbed. How could such a beautiful woman have such a devastating effect on him?

SARAH POPPED the top of a diet soda with so much force that it spewed all down her front. Obviously Mark was one of those people who simply didn't recognize the relevance of animals in people's lives. The kind of person she used to despise. Now she simply felt sorry for them. She'd long since learned that animals gave their humans far more than they took.

Mark's attitude might be fixable. Once she was settled and knew her way around, she would try to convince him to come with her when she went to the local old folks' home with one of the visitation dogs, or to a Special Cargo class, in which developmentally delayed children rode horses. Simply watching a sheepdog herd sheep wouldn't do it. He'd be impressed with the dog's skills, but not with its ability to provide emotional support.

She'd lay out her strategy carefully. It might take a few months, but before she was through, she'd have Mark as passionately committed as she was to Creature Comfort and its clients.

As she finished her soda, Bill came in, got himself a

drink, opened it and drank deeply. Then he plopped his body down in the chair opposite Sarah's.

"So he's screwed you, too."

"I beg your pardon."

"Scott. I've been out supervising the workmen finishing up my flight cage. He cut back the dimensions. He told me we'll enlarge it when there's more money, but I know he's hiding money that we could use right this minute." He sounded on the verge of angry tears.

"What makes you think he's hiding money?"

"He's noted for it. He's overcautious, and in this case, he's not really committed to the clinic."

"He doesn't want it to fail, surely."

"Who knows? Maybe he's got his own agenda. We go under, he and Buchanan sell this place to a medical group or bulldoze it and put up apartments."

"Bill, that doesn't make any sense. I'm just as annoyed about his tightfistedness as you are, but I don't think he has any deep and sinister plot. He probably thinks he's doing the right thing. I don't agree with him, and I intend to change his mind, but he does have a right to his opinion."

"Oh God. I can't believe he's conned you, too." Bill threw his empty can in the general area of the trash can and stomped out.

She finished her soda, picked up Bill's can, and tossed both into the trash container. Then she went to find her next appointment.

A monumental woman in a flowered print dress stood behind the examining table with a gigantic black-and-white Maine coon cat, who began to yowl the instant Sarah walked in the door. The cat sounded hoarse. "Mrs. Pulaski, the desk says that Sweetums has a cold."

By THE TIME Mark worked through the telephone messages, his stomach was rumbling.

So was the weather, as it turned out. His cubicle was so insulated that he didn't hear the thunder until he walked into the hall. The yaps and meows seemed to have increased in volume to vie with the cracks of thunder and flashes of lightning—although the waiting room was nearly empty.

Alva Jean on the desk had been replaced by Mabel Halliburton, fiftyish and comfortable. She cocked a motherly eye at Mark and said, ''You look like you been rode hard and put away wet.''

''I was hoping it didn't show.''

''Well, it does. Go home, have a nice glass of wine and a decent dinner. Can you cook?''

''Can but don't. My idea of a gourmet feast is takeout Chinese.''

''Then take out. You need a good woman, Mark. Somebody to look after you.''

Mark laughed. ''My mother gives me a decent dinner most Sundays when she's not traveling. That's as close to a good woman as I'm likely to get.''

Mabel shook her head and picked up the ringing telephone. ''Creature Comfort Veterinary Clinic,'' she trilled as she waved her fingers at Mark.

Damn! He'd forgotten to order that headset. He'd call Beth first thing tomorrow.

He stood for a moment in the doorway of the clinic and watched the rain sluice down. The wind drove it against the building and the cars. He looked at the flapping tarps that covered the remaining piles of building materials and fence posts, and hoped that whatever was underneath stayed dry.

The temperature had dropped about thirty degrees

since he'd arrived at the clinic several hours ago. A night for neither man nor beast, as his grandfather would have said.

He took a deep breath and raced toward his car, clicking the button on his remote door lock as he went. As he yanked the door open, he saw a flash of dirty gray that looked like the head of an old mop skitter behind his front wheel.

"What the—"

The mop slid farther forward, flattened under the car. Some damn animal must have gotten loose from its owner. The last thing he needed was to drive over somebody's pet tabby.

Rain ran down under the collar of his coat and dripped off his eyelashes. He was about as wet as he could possibly get. He hunkered down, and saw only the end of a matted behind. Didn't look like anybody's pet anything. But whatever it was, was shivering and soaked, much like Mark, himself.

He moved around to the front of the car and squatted to look under the bumper—and came nose to nose with a small, wet, gray face with shoe-button eyes rimmed in white.

A dog. Something resembling a dog. A terror-stricken little creature. Mark called to it. It stayed flat. He could see the water pouring under its belly. He couldn't drive off with the thing under his car.

"Come on out of there," he said.

The button eyes held his. The shivering continued. Damn thing must be half frozen. No way could that matted coat provide any protection.

Lightning flashed, and the dog whimpered, turning its head slightly in the direction of the flash.

It was wearing a collar. Oh God, it *was* somebody's

lost pet. Long lost, judging from the condition it was in. He'd heard that abandoned dogs tended to go feral, became frightened of human beings. Maybe this one was too cold and too wet and too frightened to run.

But probably not too frightened to bite Mark's hand if he reached out for it. And it might be rabid.

For a moment he considered going back into the clinic and hunting up Jack Renfro or one of the kennel cleaners to capture the pup. But it might disappear in the meantime. The animal might not be Mark's problem, but he couldn't leave the poor thing to suffer.

He took a deep breath and reached out a tentative hand. "Come on, boy," he whispered. "Nobody's going to hurt you."

He expected the dog to snarl or back away. For a moment nothing happened, then it began to wriggle its body forward toward Mark's outstretched hand.

Mark ignored the water streaming into his eyes. Suddenly the only thing that mattered was that he win this creature over. He kept talking.

The dog kept inching.

Mark was afraid that if he made a grab for the dog, it would spook, so he kept up his soft patter, kept his hand out there while the rain ran down his arm.

"We'll both wind up with pneumonia," he whispered. The rear end of the small body gave an answering wriggle—as though the dog were trying to wag a tail that was no longer there.

The small triangular head had almost touched Mark's knee. He reached down and touched the wet fur between the ears. The little dog sighed softly and came all the way out to lean against Mark's leg.

"What the hell am I going to do with you?" he asked

as he stroked the pitiful body. His hand felt lumps under the matted fur.

Ticks. The dog was covered with them, buried deep in his fur. Mark hated ticks. He'd had to pull them off Mickey after they'd spent an afternoon in the woods. Pulled them off himself, as well. Fat, bloated, disgusting things. He closed his eyes.

"Okay, up you go," he said. "But if one of those things comes off on me, you're in big trouble."

The animal couldn't have weighed more than eight or nine pounds. When Mark lifted it, he felt its ribs and heard its heart fluttering. Mark held it against his chest.

He walked back to the clinic, pushed the door open with his hip and walked in.

"Car won't start?" Mabel asked as she looked up from her registration sheet. "Oh my God, what on earth…?" She came around the counter at a run.

"Stray, found him under my car. Can you take him?"

He held the dog out, but it struggled to remain in his arms.

"Wait, I'll call Dr. Marsdon."

Two minutes later, when Sarah reached across the steel examining table to take the dog, he whimpered again and buried his head under the shoulder of Mark's jacket.

Mark cupped him possessively. "You're scaring him."

"I know," Sarah said. She came around the table. "Hey, sweetie, it's okay." She stroked the small body.

Her gentle voice, the soft hand that touched his chest as she reached for the dog, made Mark's whole body tense.

She took the dog and set it carefully on the table.

"Hand me some of those towels over there," she said, pointing to the corner of the room.

Mark complied. She began to dry the dog gently. It cowered on its belly, eyes never leaving Mark's face.

"We've got to get these ticks off," Sarah said. "Lord knows how much blood she's lost."

"She?"

"She. Didn't you check?"

"Who could tell under all that matted hair?"

"Well, she's a she, and..." Sarah raised the corner of the dog's mouth. "Her gums are pretty red. That's a good sign. It means she's not as anemic as I thought she might be, with all the fleas and ticks."

"Fleas?" Mark began to feel itchy at the very suggestion.

Sarah glanced up. "Don't worry. They prefer dogs when there's one available. Just hold her, while I take some blood and fecal samples for a workup."

The dog cowered deeper against him. He put a hand protectively around her head.

Sarah sighed. "I won't hurt her, I promise. But we need to see whether or not she has heartworm."

She picked up a needle and syringe. Mark tensed.

"Oh, come on," Sarah said as she stuck the needle into the flesh of the dog's neck and drew a vial of dark blood. "See, that wasn't so bad, was it?" She disappeared from the room for a moment with the vial.

When she came back, she said, "We can get quick results on the heartworm test. In the meantime, give me a hand bathing her. She trusts you. After that, we'll get the vermin off, trim off all that hair, then we'll give her another bath—and by that time we may see what kind of a pup we've got here."

"Pup?"

"Probably less than a year old. Mostly Jack Russell terrier would be my guess, but with something furry mixed in. Maybe Lhasa apso or shih tzu. Whatever gave her all this hair, it's got to go."

"So do I," Mark said. "She's in good hands."

"No, you don't," Sarah said. "She's your responsibility. Some idiot abandoned her or lost her, and she's found you. You try to walk out that door, buster, and I will personally lock it and throw away the key."

"All I did was find her."

"That's all it takes. Give me those scissors—we need to cut this collar off her and start cutting some of the worst stuff off before we stick her in the washtub."

"If she's lost, we can call her owners."

"No address on the collar. I've got Mabel checking the want ads we keep on the computer—but the dog doesn't have a registration tag, and I can't feel a microchip under her skin. There may not be owners looking for her. Somebody may have simply tossed her out with the garbage. People do it all the time." Sarah's voice was suddenly hard.

Over the next hour, the pup had a flea and tick bath, and was personally deloused by Sarah—and Mark, at Sarah's insistence. Then the matted hair was snipped, clipped and shaved. Finally the little dog had another bath, but this time the bathwater was clean and not crimson from her blood.

Jack Renfro stuck his head in the door, as they were toweling the dog off for the second time. "The test says no heartworm. Lucky."

"Thank God," Sarah said. "But we'll give her her shots and start her on dewormer and flea stuff and everything else she needs. Bring me a couple of cans of dog food and a water dish. She's been damn patient with us, but I suspect she's starving, and I know she's dehydrated.''

"Shouldn't we have fed her first?" Mark asked, rubbing the small head with the towel.

"Judgment call. I wanted to see what we had to work with.''

Mark guessed that Sarah wanted to see whether the little dog was too sick to be saved. He gave a small prayer of thanks that apparently the tiny dog wasn't.

She was, however, hungry. She devoured a can of food and drank half a bowl of water, while Sarah and Mark looked on, smiling like happy parents.

"She's really a precious little thing," Sarah said as she stroked the newly fluffy white head, with its black circles around the eyes and over one ear. "How could anyone toss her out to die like that?"

She glanced up at Mark, who saw tears in her eyes.

"She would have died, you know. If not tonight, then tomorrow or the next day. Run over by a car, eaten by a coyote or a bigger dog. Or she'd have starved to death eventually. It makes me so angry!" Sarah said.

"If the people who owned her couldn't look after her any longer and couldn't find a home for her, why wouldn't they take her to the Humane Society?"

"Because people have this crazy idea that letting an animal, a pet animal like this, out into the world to fend for itself is all right. I would love to throw those people out into a totally unfamiliar environment and see how well they do.''

"Harsh.''

"Not really. We understand what we're doing. They—'' she touched the pup ''—don't.''

"So what happens now? You put her up for adoption?''

Sarah stared at him. "Why? She already has an owner—you."

"Oh—no, you don't. I do not have time or room in my life for a dog. She's probably not housebroken, she's probably sick, and I'm away all the time."

"Take her with you. She can stay here during the day if you like, then you take her home at night."

"Why not let her stay here all the time, and find somebody else to take her?"

As though she understood that her fate was being discussed, the pup wriggled over, sighed, and laid her head on Mark's gloved hand. Her ragged little rear wagged gently as she closed her eyes.

"There, you see—" Sarah said. "She is *your* dog. Besides, somebody has to pay for all the treatment we've given her—isn't that what you say, Mr. Scott? If she's your dog, she's your responsibility, and you get the bills."

"Whoa."

"No whoa. You brought her, you worked with me, you saw what we did. It all costs money—isn't that what you say? That we have to make money? Well, Mark, you have just spent about two hundred bucks, and by the time I get through loading you up with all the things you're going to need for her when she goes home with you tonight, you will have spent a bunch more." She rubbed the pup's ears. "Sweet baby, Mommy loves a paying client."

Sarah raised her blue eyes, and batted her eyelashes at him in a parody of sweet innocence.

For a moment he hesitated, then he began to laugh. The pup woke up for a moment to stare at him, then obviously assumed everything was fine and went back to sleep.

"Okay, Doc, I'll pay the freight. But I still can't manage a dog."

"Didn't you ever have a dog?"

He glanced away. "Yeah, once."

"I'll make you a deal. I'm off in about—" Sarah glanced at her watch "—twenty minutes. Good thing it's been quiet tonight. Dr. Grayson can take over from here. If she needs me, she can page me. I think it's stopped raining, so we'll get the pup a new collar and leash. You can take her out to go to the bathroom, while I collect what you'll need for her. Then I'll follow you home and help you get set up."

"What about food? I just realized I haven't had anything to eat."

"Me, neither. We can order a pizza. Deal?"

"You, Doctor, are a monster, you know that?"

"Where animals are concerned, you bet. Deal?"

"Yeah, at least for tonight. Deal. And you can order your clippers. After tonight, I realize you do need them. But I'm not agreeing to keep this thing."

"Thanks. Stay here. I'll send Mabel in with a collar and leash." Sarah walked out of the examining room and softly shut the door behind her. "But you will, Mr. Mark Scott," she murmured to herself smugly. "You will. You're the proud owner of a dog." She pumped her arm up and down. "Yes!"

CHAPTER FOUR

"MARK'S LETTING YOU get away with this?" Mabel said as she hefted the bag of kibble and a few cans of dog food. "And here, I thought he was such a hard-nose."

"I sandbagged him," Sarah said happily as she checked the plastic animal carrier at her feet. "Yeah, this is the right size. She should be happy to have her little den to crawl into when she's frightened. Tomorrow we can get her a regular wire kennel to keep in his office here, and whatever else I can figure out to spend his money on."

"Dr. Marsdon, you are a devil," Mabel said, grinning.

Sarah lifted her eyebrows. "I was hoping to keep that a secret for a couple of days." She glanced around the now empty waiting room. "Here are my car keys," Sarah said, and tossed them to Mabel. "Stick that stuff on the back seat of my truck, if you don't mind, while I brief Eleanor on what's going on in ICU. You have my new cell phone number if you need me, don't you?"

"Sure, but Dr. Eleanor's able to handle most things—she's as good with the large animals as she is with the small."

Sarah glanced up at Mabel. "Why is she only working part-time? Seems as if she'd be a partner in her own clinic by this time."

Mabel sighed. "Long story. Lost her husband, lost her confidence, I think. She's finally coming out of her funk, though."

"She doesn't seem to lack confidence now. I watched her work with Dr. Thorn. At any rate, I need to brief her on what's happening with the animals. Then I'll pick up our new dog owner and his pup. And off we go to her new life." Sarah laughed. "And his."

THE RAIN HAD STOPPED and a watery new moon hung high, barely bright enough to reflect in the pools that rimmed the parking lot at the clinic. Mark felt the little dog quiver in his arms when he tried to put her down on the asphalt.

"She's afraid you're going to throw her away," Sarah said.

"I ought to. Little scrap of ratty fur like this," he said, but the softness in his voice belied his words.

"I don't know where you live, so I'll follow you again," Sarah said. "I've got your stuff in my truck."

Before he could shift his car out of park, the little dog had scooted across the seat so that her read rested on his knee. "You're going to have to learn to ride in one of those carrier things," he said as he caressed her head. "But not tonight. How the hell did I get conned into this?" He glanced in his rearview mirror at the headlights of Sarah's truck. He knew damn well. He'd been suckered by a better con artist that he'd met in some time. Considerably better than some of the manipulative subcontractors he dealt with.

He hated to admit it, but it was those darn blue eyes of hers. And those darn black eyes of the pup in his lap. An unbeatable combination.

Well, he'd keep the pup tonight, and tomorrow the

clinic could start searching for a permanent home for her. He obviously couldn't spend the time with her that would be necessary to get her over her fear. She needed someone who could be with her all the time, give her a fenced yard to play in. Maybe a couple of kids to play fetch with.

He realized he was driving one-handed while he scratched the pup's ears with his other hand. Okay, so he did have a fenced yard, small though it was. But no kids, no time, no experience, and absolutely no desire to take this creature into his life.

He poked the remote garage door opener, waited while the door swung silently up, and then pulled into his two-car garage. Sarah's truck pulled into the empty space beside him. He shut the garage and opened his car door.

"I should have known you'd be one of those people who never stores stuff in their garages," Sarah said as she climbed out of her truck. "Neat freaks always give me the willies."

"Not a neat freak. I don't *have* stuff," Mark said. The pup began exploring the corners of the garage.

"I think she needs to go out," Sarah said.

Mark opened the side door that led to the yard, and a motion sensor light came on. As he walked out, a stream of water from the gutters ran down his neck. He jumped and cursed. Instantly the little dog dropped and flattened herself against the paving stones.

"Hey, you scared her—don't do that," Sarah admonished.

He picked up the dog gently and took her to the back-yard, where he let her off her leash and watched her investigate the interesting smells until she finally did her business. It was like having a baby, except that the pup could walk on its own and didn't use diapers. He definitely was not used to scooping poop, and he doubted the expensive yard crew that did his gardening would appreciate stepping in it. He wondered whether he could pay them extra for the service.

"Come on, sweetie," Sarah said, dropping to her haunches and clapping softly. "Let's go see your new home."

Twenty minutes later Sarah knelt on the quarry tiles of Mark's largely unused gourmet kitchen and watched the pup nibble at her dry dog food. The lights overhead reflected on Sarah's still-damp hair and turned it to antique gold. Mark longed to reach down and touch it, to see if it felt as silky as it looked.

"What's her name?" Sarah asked.

He drew back his hand without touching her. "How should I know?"

"She's your dog."

"She is not."

"Sure, she is. What are you going to call her? Dow Jones?"

"How about Merrill Lynch?"

"Yukk."

"Ameritrade? Paine Webber?"

"None of the above. She's not a stock certificate."

"How about Phoenix? She's definitely been reincarnated."

Sarah sat back on her heels. "Better, but I always see the Phoenix as this huge, ugly bird with a really loud voice and big claws." She touched the pup, who moved over to lean against her knee.

"The way she slides along the ground, I ought to call her Lava."

This time Sarah laughed. "Not Lava. How about Pudding?"

Mark hunkered down beside her. "Here in the south, that would be Puddin."

"Oh, brother. I can hear it now. 'Isn't 'um the sweetest ole puddin?'"

"I refuse to have a dog called Pudding. How about Nasdaq?"

"You're kidding, right?"

Suddenly the little dog shook the entire length of her body in sheer delight and let out the faintest hint of a bark.

This time both Sarah and Mark laughed out loud. Mark stood and reached a hand down to Sarah. "Nasdaq it is."

She took his hand and came to her feet close to his chest. They grinned foolishly at one another for a moment. Slowly, the smiles subsided. Their eyes locked.

Mark could feel his heartbeat against his chest and see the answering pulse in Sarah's slender throat. He felt as though he'd suddenly been struck dumb. Dumb and breathless. Sarah's blue eyes were deep enough to drown in, and that's what he longed to do.

He slid his arm around her waist and pulled her to him, bent his face to hers, felt the touch of her lips like flaming velvet against his mouth. She felt good in his arms—not soft and boneless but lean and supple. A woman who would bend to him only if she chose. Suddenly, fiercely, he wanted her to choose. He wanted her body beneath him, wanted to ignite the passion he sensed beneath that cool exterior. Wanted—

The doorbell buzzed—an ugly *brap* sound that went on until he couldn't ignore it.

Neither could Nasdaq. She cowered between their

feet, her body flattened against the tiles, her eyes staring up imploringly.

"Damn!" He released Sarah. "Must be the pizza."

The instant he released her, Sarah sank to the floor again and gathered Nasdaq's shivering body into her arms. "It's all right, baby," she crooned, knowing that it had very nearly not been all right. "Now, you listen to me, dog," she continued, "I am starting a new life. I have sworn off males. I have just dumped one man who tried to run my life. I am not about to take on another."

Nasdaq listened attentively with one ear perked, the other drooping slightly.

"I swear you understand. I don't think you've had puppies yet, but I'll bet you've done some fast running to escape the boys, haven't you."

She panted eagerly.

"Pizza," Mark announced from behind her.

"Great, I'm starved."

"You want a glass of wine?"

"Not when I'm officially still on call, and I do have to drive home."

Mark wanted to tell her that she didn't have to drive anywhere—not on his account, but he couldn't quite bring himself to suggest she stay. The moment they had shared seemed forgotten, as she casually accepted her pizza.

Nasdaq sat at their feet expectantly, but when Mark pinched off a bit of pizza to offer it to her, Sarah put her hand over his. It felt incredibly warm. And insistent.

"No, you don't. She's probably had too much food for her stomach as it is."

"So she's going to throw up?"

"Possibly, but I doubt it."

She was reaching for another piece of pizza when the telephone rang. "Oh, heck." Sarah grabbed for her shoulder bag, dug into its depths and answered the phone. "Dr. Marsdon."

She listened for a moment, then said, "Okay, I'm on my way." She clicked off the phone. "Well, Mr. Scott, you got your wish. We're going to see whether we can make do with what we've got. We just had a client roll in with a walking horse with a bad case of colic. Dr. Grayson thinks we may have to do an emergency bowel resection. God, I wish I had that ultrasound!" She grabbed her purse. "Open your garage for me."

"Sure. But can't Eleanor handle it?"

"It's a very complicated and delicate surgery, and recovery rates aren't that good at the best of times. We may even need to call in Mac Thorn." She knelt to rub the dog's head. "Look after our girl. See you tomorrow."

Mark stood in the garage and watched her drive away. Nasdaq sat at his feet—no, *on* his feet. Rain had begun to spatter the road once more.

"Okay. One more bathroom run, and then you get in your nice new carrier and go to sleep. That's what I'm going to do."

As a precaution, he laid papers around the carrier in the corner of the kitchen, and put Nasdaq into it before he latched its door. He hadn't taken two steps before she began to whine—softly at first, then with increasing insistence.

"Be quiet. That's your new house. Get used to it." The whining increased to a low wail.

He turned out the kitchen light. "Go to sleep," he said in what he hoped was his authority-figure voice.

She didn't seem to be impressed. He listened to her

cry while he brushed his teeth and stripped for bed. Then he gave up. "How can one little dog be so much trouble?" he said as he opened her door. She trotted out in obvious triumph and followed him into the bedroom.

"I do not share my bed with nonhumans," he said. "You stay down there on the carpet, or I'll put you back into that carrier thing and put a pillow over my head to keep out the sound. You got that, dog?"

She wagged her tail and jumped up on the bed.

He removed her.

This time she stayed down. He turned off the light and cradled his pillow, wishing it were Sarah Marsdon. She'd probably be up all night. He sincerely hoped *he* wouldn't be.

He rolled over onto his back. He hoped she wouldn't need that fluoroscope.

Without warning, lightning flashed through the room. Two seconds later the thunder crashed. "Close," Mark said, just as Nasdaq landed on his stomach in a quivering ball. He stroked her gently. "It's okay, girl. You're all right with me."

He started to shove her off the bed. "Oh, what the hell," he said, and rolled over with the little dog cradled against his stomach. "Maybe all I'm good for is to keep you from being frightened."

She nestled against him and laid her head on his arm. She smelled of fancy flea shampoo and just the faintest aroma of Dr. Sarah Marsdon—a blend of disinfectant, hand lotion and newly ironed cotton. Hardly an expensive perfume, but its effect on him was the same. He found himself thinking of Sarah and recalling that kiss—even though it hadn't even been much of a kiss. Given the chance, he could do much better.

He *would* do much better at the first opportunity....

To AVOID having to take Nasdaq into the offices of Buchanan Enterprises, Mark spent a good hour in the morning on his cell phone and his Internet connection at home, while the dog ran around the backyard. However, by the time she came inside, her paws were matted with mud, which she proceeded to deposit on the kitchen floor.

Mark's house cleaning service wasn't due for another three days. He cleaned Nasdaq, cleaned the floor, and then cleaned himself again. If he was going to spend all day working at the blasted clinic, he knew he'd better go casual and take a suit with him in case something came up that he had to attend to. He tied his shoes, while Nasdaq lay on her stomach gazing up at him. It took him a second to realize she was shaking again.

She was afraid he was going to leave her. He'd heard of dogs who had separation anxiety. As a matter of fact, one of Mark's acquaintances had brought in a doggie psychologist to condition his deaf Dalmatian to stay at home alone.

Mark had thought the guy was nuts—considerably crazier than the dog, which was, after all, a dog, and thus incapable of complex emotional responses. He had managed to avoid telling the guy—a fairly important client—what he thought.

A good thing, considering the quivering heap of fur at his feet. Crow was not Mark's favorite dish, but if Nasdaq couldn't learn not to be afraid all the time, she'd be miserable.

He did not want her to be miserable. He wanted her to be the happy, muddy, cheerful little bundle he'd glimpsed out the window this morning. As a matter of fact, how much he wanted her happiness amazed him. Damn it, she wasn't even his dog. The clinic would probably find her a suitable home today. Then she'd be out of his life.

A small voice in the back of his consciousness whispered, *Over my dead body*. He ignored it.

When they reached the clinic, he had to carry Nasdaq through the waiting room. She must have recognized the place because she'd refused to get out of the car. She brightened when Alva Jean came from behind her desk and made a fuss over her, but the moment Mark put her down, she sank into her pudding position again.

"Your new headset should arrive today," he said, picking up the dog. "Where's Dr. Marsdon?" he asked over his shoulder. "How'd the colic go?"

"She's probably gone home," Alva Jean answered, and raced to pick up the telephone.

He opened the door of his storeroom office and flipped on the light. It took him a second to see that there was a long lump covered with a red, wool horse blanket on his ratty sofa.

Nasdaq gave a single bark, wrenched out of his arms and jumped onto the sofa.

"Go way, dog." Sarah's voice was muffled.

She began to emerge from the blanket, and blinked in the light. "Oh, it's you. You go way, too."

"It's my office."

"It's got the only sofa in the place. We need a place to bunk when we have to stay here all night. Put that on your list."

"You've been here all night?"

She sat up and raked her fingers through her uncombed hair. Her eyes were red-rimmed, her lipstick was only a vague memory, and her skin looked blotchy.

To Mark, she looked beautiful.

"We didn't finish the surgery until almost four, and then we took turns watching until the mare was on her feet. I think Eleanor's asleep in Rick's desk chair. I found the sofa first." She yawned.

"Can't have been very comfortable. I think Rick had that sofa in his first waiting room."

"I can sleep anywhere. It's a trick you either learn in school or you keel over from exhaustion. However, that's why I'm dead serious about the bunk room."

"One bunk room. Any ideas as to where we put it?"

"Don't ask me questions at this hour and in my semi-conscious state." She scratched the dog's ears. "How's my girl doing this morning?"

"She tracked mud all over my kitchen floor. I had to mop it."

Sarah snickered. "Poor baby! Never mopped a floor before, I take it?"

"I have probably mopped more floors than you have seen, Doctor, but not recently." He sank into his desk chair. "Seriously, the moment she thought I was going to leave her, she did her oozing act again. I can't take her with me everywhere. What can we do?"

Sarah stretched her arms above her head and her legs in front of her. Mark gulped at the rise of her breasts under the thin surgical scrubs. He didn't think she was wearing anything under the top. He was supposed to be thinking dog psychology, not male libido, but God, Dr. Marsdon was sexy in the morning!

"We'll set her up a wire kennel in the corner, put some toys in it for her. It'll take awhile, but if you leave for short periods and come back without making a big deal of either going or coming, I think she'll grow less scared of being alone."

"You don't sound too certain."

"All dogs are different, but I think she is a one-man dog. And at the moment, you are that one man."

"But she needs a family, kids..."

"So have some."

"Sure. Memo to self—produce wife and children by noon today."

"Why don't you? Have a family, I mean?"

"Why don't *you?*" he asked.

"I very nearly did. And I still hope to, someday." She stood. "Now I am going home to my nice big whirlpool, where I'll probably fall asleep and drown." Nasdaq groaned. Instantly, Sarah leaned over and scratched her ears. "I'll be back, girl. I promise." She glanced at Mark. "I'll leave orders to have you set up in here for doggie nursery school on my way out."

"When will you be back?"

"I'm going to catch a few hours' sleep, then start looking for an apartment or a small house to rent. Be back around four this afternoon. If you're still here, I'll see you and Nasdaq then." She began to drag the blanket toward the door.

"Hey, how's the horse?"

"Thought you'd never ask," she said over her shoulder. "It was bad, but barring infection or another blockage, she should make a full recovery." As she closed the door softly behind her, she leaned in and said, "No thanks to you and our lack of equipment. Bye."

Sarah opened the door to Rick's office softly. Dr. Eleanor Grayson slept with her hands folded over surgical greens stained brown with dried blood. Her feet were neatly crossed at the ankles. She looked completely peaceful. Sarah envied her. She shut the door gently and went to check on her patient once more before she left for home.

"Hello, Sarah." A female voice spoke from behind her. She turned to meet a small, dark woman dressed in impeccable linen slacks and a silk shirt. "Remember me? Margot Hazard—Rick's wife. We met in Kansas City."

Looking down at Margot's outstretched right hand with its long manicured nails, Sarah felt even tireder and grubbier than she had before. She managed a smile and took the extended hand. Margot's handshake was soft and tentative—only a momentary touching of fingers.

"Hard night?" Margot said. She started toward Rick's office.

"Um, there's somebody asleep in there," Sarah said. Margot raised her eyebrows.

"Eleanor Grayson. We were up with a colic all night."

"And?"

"Successful surgery, I think." Sarah pushed her hair out of her eyes. "I was just going home to get some sleep, myself."

"Oh, dear, I am sorry. I dropped by to see Rick on my way to the Symphony auxiliary meeting. Any idea where he is?"

Sarah shook her head. "Probably in one of the examining rooms." She widened her eyes in an effort to keep them from shutting completely and stifled a yawn. "Sorry."

"Not at all. We're glad to have you. Now we can really start pushing the large-animal section."

Sarah took a deep breath. "That would be a whole lot easier if we had more equipment—nuclear cytography and ultrasound and lasers.'' Speaking to the managing partner's wife was probably dirty pool, but she had a suspicion that a word in Margot's ear might do more to loosen the purse strings than a word in Rick's.

"I know. It's just awful. Don't worry. I'm working on Daddy. He always gives me what I want."

"I get the feeling Mark Scott is the one who needs to be won over."

Margot's face clouded. "Mark is Vice President for Obstruction, as far as I'm concerned. He doesn't realize we have to put on a really big show, or we'll look like just another clinic and not the biggest and finest this side of Mississippi State University. He's bound and determined to nickel-and-dime this place to death."

"So I've noticed."

"Noticed what?" Rick came out of the small-animal operating room at the far end of the hall. He wore surgical greens, as well, but his were immaculate and so starched that they would probably stand on their own. "Hey, Margot."

She offered her cheek. "I missed you at breakfast, darling."

"I told Mac I'd help him this morning. He's got some kind of personal thing to attend to." Rick kissed his wife perfunctorily and nodded at Sarah. "Good job last night."

"Thanks."

"Mark is up to his old tricks, Rick," Margot said with some heat. "You really have to speak to him."

"He's right, Margot. We have to pull in our horns until we can generate some decent revenue."

"Nonsense. Daddy's got enough free capital to finance this place for five years."

"Well, he's not going to, and even if he would, I wouldn't let him."

"Don't be silly. We'll spend whatever it takes to make this place the best in west Tennessee. I keep telling you, darling, we can't simply be the best, we've got to be the trendiest and look the chicest."

"It isn't a beauty parlor."

"It is exactly like a salon. We want everybody who is anybody to bring their animals here for everything from grooming to parvo, and don't you forget it." Margot sounded like a mother disciplining a child for poor manners.

"Well, I'm off before I fall down," Sarah said brightly, and ran for the parking lot.

She was more than willing to use any ally to get what she wanted for her animals, but *trendy* and *chic* were definitely not her idea of a veterinary practice.

CHAPTER FIVE

SARAH CAME AWAKE instantly when the telephone rang. "Oh Lord," she said. "Don't let that mare have taken a bad turn— Hello?"

"Dr. Marsdon, I hope I didn't wake you?"

The voice was cheerful, female and young, although it was hard to tell how young. She glanced at the clock. One o'clock in the afternoon. The lined curtains at the motel windows kept out every bit of light. It might have been midnight. "No, I'm glad you woke me."

"This is Elizabeth Marelli, Mr. Scott's personal assistant. He asked me to give you a call."

"Wake-up calls? I am impressed."

Cheerful laughter from the phone. "Even *he* doesn't go that far. He asked me to check into some rental houses for you, since you don't know the city all that well yet."

He did, huh. "Anxious to get me out of here so he doesn't have to pay the bill for a whole two weeks?"

"Oh, no, nothing like that!" The woman sounded genuinely horrified. "He was just trying to be helpful. Let's see, he gave me a list of your requirements…"

"What requirements?" She didn't remember discussing them with Mark.

"Mark realizes you'll probably want to buy a house in six months to a year, and maybe you'd like some land at that point, so he asked for a six-month lease

renewable for six more. Now, let's see. Three bed-
rooms, two-and-a-half baths, great room, dining room
or dining area, up-to-date kitchen, good heat and air,
gas water heater, washer and dryer—preferably close to
the master bedroom. Security system, microwave, dish-
washer and trash compactor in the kitchen, fenced back-
yard, enclosed double garage. He thought you probably
wouldn't want much yard in the rental since you
wouldn't have a great deal of time to garden. I thought
maybe an enclosed courtyard. I hope that's all right?''

Stunned, Sarah managed to choke out something that
sounded affirmative.

''Good neighborhood...of course. Ten-minute drive
from the clinic...I'm afraid I didn't manage that. The
houses I've found you are at least fifteen to twenty
minutes away. And oh, yes, no more than one-fourth of
your monthly salary including utilities.''

''That's an impossible assignment, Mrs....''

''Miss. Call me Beth, everyone does.''

''Well, Beth, I certainly didn't ask Mr. Scott to send
you on a hopeless mission.''

''Oh, it wasn't hopeless. I've found two places that
fit the bill. I really prefer one over the other, but, of
course, you'll be making the decision. Shall I pick you
up to look at them? Say, in half an hour?''

''I guess so.'' They hung up.

Sarah sank back on her pillows. Her stomach rumbled. Hunger. But she was more annoyed than hungry.
The nerve of the man! My God, he was doing precisely
what Gerald had done in Minnesota! Mark hadn't actually bought the damn house, but in some ways his
intrusion was worse. At least Gerald had planned to live
in the house he bought *with* her. Mark had his own
house, complete with dog, so he had no business decid-

ing what kind of house she should live in. Did he think that the kiss last night gave him the right to choose a home for her?

She'd tried to forget that kiss, but the memory kept coming back.

She could still see the look in his eyes the moment before he reached for her—that serious straight-on gaze that raised her temperature about a hundred degrees. The moment before everything changed.

Probably not for Mark. But for her. She couldn't look at him without feeling her blood pressure soar. The trick was to not look at him.

Fortunately this little house-hunting intrusion on her privacy should temper whatever feelings she might have been developing for him!

She considered calling him to blister his ears. No, better wait until she could do it face to face. She should have told Beth that she wouldn't be looking at any houses today, thank you very much—but that might get Sarah in trouble with her boss. And she needed Rick's support if she was going to get her equipment.

She dressed in her clinic clothes—jeans and running shoes with thick soles. Beth probably wore suits, hats and gloves, she thought. She fixed herself a sandwich, ate it at the kitchen counter. The phone rang. She hoped it was Beth canceling her appointment.

No such luck.

"It's Nels."

Sarah sat on the stool at the kitchen counter and propped her chin with her free hand. Big brother Nels—calling, no doubt, on his father's orders.

"Hi. How are you?"

"Fine, fine. The thing is, Sarah, the whole family

misses you. We think you should come home where you belong.''

"In other words, Dad told you to call and pressure me, right?''

"No, no, not at all. But we've always stayed together. We belong in Minnesota. It's not good for our little sister to be so far away. What if you need help?''

"Nels, I appreciate your concern but why on earth should I need help?''

"All the crime down there. It's not safe.''

"And Minnesota is so crime free.''

"In Minnesota you have brothers to protect you.''

"Give me a break, Nels! How many times have you and the others been with me when I've gone out on a call at midnight on a back road in a blizzard? These people don't *have* blizzards.''

"They have tornadoes.''

"Nels, I know you mean well, but this is a pretty silly conversation. We have tornadoes in Minnesota, too. I love you dearly, but it's time I was out on my own. Tell Dad I'm not coming home. And thanks for calling. Give my love to the others.''

She'd barely hung up the telephone before it rang again. Surely not another one!

"Hey, big sister, it's your baby brother.''

"God, Peter, is Dad running a roster? I'm supposed to get a different call every five minutes?''

"Huh?''

"He told you to call, right?''

"No, no he didn't. I called to tell you I think you're doing the right thing. I always thought Gerald was a jerk and not nearly good enough for you.''

Sarah sat down on a bar stool and began to laugh.

"What's so funny?''

"Is this Dad's idea of reverse psychology?"

"Man, I never did understand you."

"Sorry, Peter. Everybody's been calling to warn me of dire consequences if I don't come home immediately. I thought you were going to do the same thing."

"Oh. Dad did try to get Mary Ellen to call, but she very sweetly told him it was none of her business." He chuckled. "Then she told him she thought you were doing the right thing and maybe we ought to move, too."

"That must have thrilled him."

"Let's face it, I can be an engineer pretty much anyplace. She did go a little overboard when she mentioned Alaska. That wife of mine has a truly weird sense of humor. Although it might not be such a bad idea."

"You think Minnesota's cold? Listen, Peter, flowers are blooming all over the place down here. If you're going to run away from home, try North Carolina or Texas or someplace warm."

"What? And give up my beloved snow-blower? You must be kidding."

"Seriously, Peter, I'd love having family around, you especially. I just don't want to come home to do it."

"Yeah, I understand. Anyway, I got to go back to work. Hang in there. Maybe Mary Ellen and I can come and visit this summer."

"Please try. I ought to be in my house by then. People down here say the summers are miserable, but they've never dealt with blackfly, so what do they know?"

"Anyway, Sarah, call me."

"Thanks, Peter. Give my love to Mary Ellen, and thank her for standing up for me."

By the time the bell rang at her door, Sarah had

worked herself up into a minor snit. She took a deep breath. None of this was Miss Efficiency's fault. She opened the door.

Beth was every bit as elegant as Sarah had supposed, and a good deal younger. Probably a few years younger than Mark, as a matter of fact. And a real beauty. One of those women from lipstick ads in *Vogue*. Rail thin, with a short skirt, three-inch heels and a mass of red-brown hair cut in the new wispy look that gave the impression it hadn't been combed for days.

"Hi, I'm Beth." The beauty stuck out an elegantly manicured hand. "Shall we go? I can bring you back here to your car afterward."

Sarah grabbed her purse and followed, wishing she'd at least put on real slacks and a decent shirt. So much for making a statement.

"Now, I'm taking you first to the one I really don't like as much," Beth said as she drove her Audi out of the parking area. "The setting is nice, but the yard's a bit large for one person with a full-time job. And I don't think the neighborhood's as stable, although it's not easy to find rental property that's affordable in nice neighborhoods."

As she chattered on, Sarah watched her. Once she got over feeling dowdy, she realized that Beth was probably a perfectly nice woman who tried to do a good job— with any assignment Mark gave her. She wondered briefly if there was anything romantic between them.

"When did he give you this…assignment?" Sarah asked, hoping she'd kept the snarl out of her voice on that last word.

"He called from the clinic first thing this morning." Beth grinned at Sarah momentarily before turning back to her driving. "He told me about Nasdaq. I'm amazed you were able to persuade him to take in the stray, even temporarily. He's never been a dog person. Nor a cat person, come to that.''

''Why do you think that is?''

''Too busy, too focused. No time left for involvements. Too competitive—''

That last word made Sarah sit up straight.

''He hates to lose.''

''I got that impression.''

''Here we are.'' Beth pulled into the driveway of a town house.

Fifteen minutes later, as they pulled away to visit the other, Sarah said, ''I have to admit, I'm impressed.'' *Hated* to admit was more like it.

''Whichever one you choose, I'll arrange to have it professionally cleaned and your furniture delivered. And I have the address of a house cleaning service to take over on a weekly basis, or biweekly if you prefer. It's the best and most reasonable in town.''

''How did you get so efficient?'' Sarah asked.

''I have a degree in business administration from Penn State. In another five years, I'll be a VP at some other company.''

''Not Mark's?''

''Oh, no. I could never move up quickly enough in the same company. I'll have to job hop. I've only been with Mark eighteen months. I'm finishing up my Master's—and he gives me plenty of time to study and take time off for practicums. Then I'll move up to the next rung of the corporate ladder with another good line to my resume and a glowing recommendation from Mark.''

''Very ambitious.''

''I expect to be a CEO before I'm forty.''

"What about family?"

"I'm an army brat. I've moved all my life. I have no roots. Anyplace is much the same to me. What matters is the job. I'm learning a great deal from Mark. Of course, I do think he's terribly fiscally conservative, but that's not surprising considering his background."

"Why is that?"

"Sorry. I don't usually talk out of school. I've probably said too much already. I am, among other things, a *confidential* assistant."

She said it with a smile, but Sarah realized Beth meant what she'd said. No pumping the assistant for info about the boss. And no way to tell whether the two of them had a thing going or not.

"Now, this is the one I think you'll like," Beth said as she pulled into the driveway of a brick duplex. The house was probably twenty-five or thirty years old, but had been well maintained. The street was a cul-de-sac shaded by old trees. "The owner lives in the other half of the duplex," Beth said as she climbed out of the car. "But she travels a good deal, so she won't bother you." She pulled out a key and opened the front door.

The house was perfect! It had everything Mark had asked Beth to look for, including an enclosed courtyard, with roses already in bloom, trailing over the fence.

"I thought you'd like a fireplace in the great room, although Mark didn't mention that," Beth said. "It does get cold in the winter, you know—although nothing like Minnesota."

By the time she checked the walk-in closet in the second-floor master bedroom, Sarah was seething. She was faced with a major dilemma. She could take the place—which, as Beth said, she could afford—and admit to Mark that he could run her life, or she could cut off her proverbial nose to spite her face and tell him to stick it in his ear. The house—not the nose.

She leaned against the kitchen counter and folded her arms. "Okay, Beth, this is the way it is. I didn't ask Mark to send you out house-hunting for me, and I'm not sure I appreciate his doing it without asking me."

Beth's face registered dismay.

"Not your fault," Sarah continued. "I have this thing about people making my decisions for me. And his gloating at my expense really annoys me. So you can see I'm torn."

"But you like it, don't you?" Beth asked. "Why does it matter who did the legwork? What matters is the outcome, isn't it?"

"It's not that simple. Maybe it ought to be, but at this point if I had Mark standing right here in front of me, I'd probably slap him silly."

"But why?"

"First, for presuming to work out my requirements, as you call them, without checking with me. For all he knows, I could be looking for a mansion an hour outside of town or a log cabin in the woods with an outhouse."

"Don't be silly. Nobody wants an outhouse."

"That's not the point, and you're much too bright to not know what I'm talking about."

"Okay, so he is a little pushy," Beth said. "His heart is in the right place."

"And second," Sarah continued, "for sending you out on this errand for him instead of giving you work that you're obviously more than qualified to do."

"This *is* work I am qualified to do. Listen, Sarah— if I may call you that—I get my kicks pulling rabbits out of hats. You said this was an impossible task. Well, I haven't had an impossible assignment in months—not since Mark started spending too much of his time on this clinic for Mr. Buchanan. I was frankly bored to death until Mark's call this morning. I like being indispensable, and perfection is a turn-on for me. I'm sorry that you think we're intruding.''

"Please, don't get upset. I do appreciate your efforts. I am annoyed at Mark, but I'm not annoyed enough to turn down this house. I am, however, going to convince myself that you did it, not Mark. That way maybe my orneriness won't kick in quite so bad.''

"Hey, whatever floats your boat.'' Beth turned to look out the French windows into the courtyard. "It is nice, isn't it. If I cared about things like houses, I'd love it.''

"Where do *you* live?''

"I stay in a one-bedroom high-rise. But I *live* in the office.''

"Now, that I can relate to. Speaking of which, I have to get back to the clinic. Can you drive me home?''

"Sure. What about this place?''

"Yes, I want it for six months. What do I have to do?''

"Not a thing. I'll take care of the paperwork tomorrow, fax you a copy at the office, you sign it and fax it back. I can set up an account to pay the rent directly out of your salary so you won't have to bother with it. The rest of your recurring bills, as well, if you like.''

Sarah laughed. "No, thanks. I'd like to be able to buy my own bubblegum without Mark's knowing about it.''

As Sarah climbed out of Beth's Audi, Beth leaned across the seat. "He's really a good guy, and very smart about a great many things. He's not too good with people.''

"That's an understatement," Sarah said as she watched the Audi drive out of the parking lot. She'd have to do something nice for Beth—a good bottle of wine, maybe.

She decided to avoid Mark until she'd had time to process what he'd done. On the plus side, he'd gone out of his way to find her a house. On the negative, he'd done what corporate executives so frequently do— he'd given his assistant the job. Like buying a birthday present for his wife because "if you pick it out, she'll love it."

A cop-out, in Sarah's opinion.

But in reality, there wasn't any reason he should have bothered at all. She decided to explain to him calmly and rationally that she liked to make her own choices. She'd be assertive, not aggressive.

MARK SIGHED WITH SATISFACTION and scratched Nasdaq's ears. The pup sighed back and snuggled into a tighter circle on his lap. So Dr. Sarah had liked the duplex. Good old Beth. She always delivered the goods.

There had been a subtext to Beth's announcement over the telephone that he hadn't quite understood. It wasn't what she'd said, precisely, but a hesitancy about the way she'd said it. Odd. Beth was usually straightforward and didn't think twice about challenging him when she thought he was wrong.

He wasn't wrong this time. He'd done his good deed for the day. He could hardly wait for Sarah to come in. She'd probably be bubbling over with pleasure and gratitude. She could never have found a place like that on her own.

"Come on, Nasdaq old girl," he said, and slid the

dog off his lap. "Time to see if Dr. Sarah has come in yet."

He slipped the leash on Nasdaq's collar. He'd already discovered that she knew how to heel. As a matter of fact, she followed his steps so closely he'd tripped over her in the parking lot and damn near taken a header. That had resulted in another episode of what he'd come to call her "oozing," and he'd had to spend ten minutes convincing her she'd done nothing wrong.

Reassured now, she trotted through the back door into the delivery area behind the clinic, as Sarah's truck pulled into a staff parking space. Mark waited. He knew he was wearing a silly grin. He'd always enjoyed watching his mother open her presents from him, even when they were worthless trinkets. It was one of the few pleasures he'd had as a child. His father had valued only expensive gifts—things Mark could never afford to give him.

"Evening," he said pleasantly.

"Thank you and please don't ever do that again," Sarah said quietly.

"Huh? I thought you liked the place. Beth told me you took it."

"Of course I took it. It's perfect. *She's* perfect. Mark, I know you thought you were just being a nice guy. I may be crazy, but I prefer to make my own choices, set my own parameters and make my own decisions. I tend to turn nasty when someone tries to take my sovereignty away. Can you understand that?"

"Certainly." He felt his face shut down, his jaw tighten.

"And I also understand that the sooner I am out of that rented suite in the motel, the sooner I start paying my own rent and the less money the clinic is on the hook for."

"That had nothing to do with it."

"Of course it didn't." She started to walk past, then stopped and bent. "Hello Nasdaq," she said, and scratched the dog's ears. She straightened, gave Mark a long, hard look and strode in the back door of the clinic.

Mark stared after her. "Of all the ungrateful..." He looked down at the dog. "I will never understand women, definitely not that *particular* woman. Come on, Nasdaq, let's go home and lick our wounds."

His pager buzzed, and Mabel's tinny voice said, "Mark, Mr. Buchanan's on your private line. He says he needs to speak to you."

"Oh, hell," Mark whispered, and went back into his office to answer the call.

"THE MARE seems to be recovering well," Eleanor Grayson told Sarah as she turned over the chart to her. "Gut is functioning. She's sore, but we're keeping her on Bute. So far, she's just standing there in her stall looking miserable."

"Thanks, Eleanor," Sarah said. "Did you get any sleep?"

Eleanor shrugged. "I bedded down in one of the padded recovery stalls after Rick came in and claimed his office." She yawned. "They're really pretty comfortable."

"I'll remember that."

"I'm going to have a cup of coffee so I don't fall asleep on my way home. Then I'm going back to my apartment to sleep the sleep of the just. Call me if you need me."

"Mind if I join you? I could use a jolt of caffeine myself."

The two women got their coffee and sank into chairs in the conference room with cavernous sighs. Eleanor looked at Sarah and began to laugh.

Sarah joined her. "I'm not sure whether this is exhaustion or hysteria."

"Exhaustion."

"I can't thank you enough for assisting last night, Eleanor. I would have hated having to call Jack back over here that late."

"Anytime. You're good."

Sarah leaned forward and templed her fingers over the steaming coffee. "May I ask you something? If it's none of my business, tell me to shut up."

"Sure. Ask away."

"Why did Rick come all the way to Minnesota to hire me and pay my moving expenses, when he already had you on staff? You should be working full-time, not just filling in."

For a moment Sarah thought Eleanor wouldn't answer. Then the woman took a deep breath and leaned back in her chair. "I didn't want the pressure."

"Oh, come on—you handled the pressure fine last night in the OR. You were great."

"Thanks. Maybe I can handle it now. When Rick hired me in February, I was working part-time at one of the downtown emergency clinics, always assisting another vet. I wasn't in the best shape."

"What happened? A case go bad on you? Make you doubt yourself?"

Eleanor laughed and ran her finger around the rim of her coffee cup. "Not quite that. I can talk about it now, and that's largely because Rick and Margot and everybody here have been so supportive. Their combination of 'poor baby' and butt kicking seems to have done the trick. You're new to Tennessee. Do you know Franklin?''

"No."

"Small town outside of Nashville. Pretty much a twin to this one. Wealthy. Lots of horses, fancy farms, lots of work for vets. My husband Jerry and I met in vet school and put ourselves in hock for as much as the bank would give us to set up practice together in Franklin.''

Sarah had an idea what was coming. She really didn't want to hear that Eleanor, whom she was beginning to really like, had an abusive husband or a bad marriage. "It's okay if you don't want to talk about it," she said.

Eleanor smiled at her. "No, actually it helps to talk about it. Jerry was a great guy—big and handsome and funny. He was the one that made the practice successful. Everybody loved him. Then he started having balance problems. He put off going to the doctor—you know guys. When he did, they found a tumor. They thought it was a meningioma…'' She looked up at Sarah enquiringly.

Sarah nodded. "Sometimes recurring, but usually not malignant.''

"Unfortunately, they were wrong." She looked away and put her hand over her mouth for a moment.

Sarah could see her chest rise and fall.

When she spoke again, her voice was tight. "He took eighteen months to die.''

"Eleanor, I'm so sorry.''

"That's not all. Jerry hadn't been able to work, and I was looking after him almost full-time. We hired a couple of part-time vets, but they couldn't really build a relationship with the clients, so by the time Jerry died we were even more in debt. Then the IRS came calling, and after that the insurance people refused to pay for some of his treatment, and the hospitals and doctors sent bill collectors. Oh, it was fun, let me tell you. My only choice was to sell the practice for what I could get, pay the bills I could, and declare bankruptcy. The last sensible decision I made was to get out of Franklin, walk away from everything, and come to Memphis. I probably would have ended up on the street if Rick hadn't tracked me down, banged on my door and practically forced me to work at that emergency clinic. Then, when this place opened he wanted me to work full-time, but I knew I wasn't ready. You know, after I came to Memphis, I slept around the clock for an entire week!''

"Depression," Sarah said.

"Absolutely. But also sheer exhaustion. I never want to be that tired again." She drank the remains of her coffee, took her cup to the sink, washed it and put it back on the shelf. "And now that you know the saga of Eleanor Grayson, I'm going home and maybe sleep for another week."

As the two women made their way down the corridor back to the large-animal section, Sarah said, "Thanks for telling me. And believe me, after last night I'd say you have every bit of confidence back."

As Eleanor walked away, Sarah saw her massage the tops of her shoulders. All vets did that, because they always ached from too much tension or from the effort it took to get less-than-grateful patients to cooperate.

"HAVE YOU HAD anything to eat?" Mark asked several hours later when he met Sarah in the hall coming back from the bathroom.

"I had a sandwich about four-thirty," Sarah answered. Her stomach rumbled.

"It's nine o'clock now. I haven't had dinner, either. How about I get some takeout Chinese and bring it back to share? Is that intruding on your decision-making capabilities?" He grinned sheepishly.

"Not if you let me pick the menu."

"Deal. Just so long as you don't include egg fu yung. I hate egg fu yung."

"Memo to self—no egg fu yung."

"You're laughing at me."

"I certainly am. Now, if you'll excuse me, I have a couple more clients to check out before evening office hours are over and I can get some sleep."

"On my sofa?"

"Unless you managed to create that bunkroom sometime today."

Mark shook his head. "Even I can't work that fast."

"Put Beth on it. She can."

CHAPTER SIX

SARAH STOOD IN THE HALL outside the window of the mare's padded recovery stall and watched her. So far, so good.

There was a steaming pile of manure in the corner. Ordinarily one of the pickup night crew would have removed it, but both she and Eleanor had agreed that in this case, evidence the mare's gut was functioning outweighed the need for speedy cleanup. Sarah walked across the wide aisle to the cleaning closet, picked up a manure fork and bucket. There was no reason to leave the mess any longer.

The mare barely looked up from her hay, when Sarah came into the stall and scooped the pile into the bucket. She patted the mare's rump and slid her hands along the flanks. No sweating. Actually, a textbook recovery so far. She crossed her fingers.

As she slid the bucket into the aisle, she heard the double bell that was her call sign, and then Mabel's voice. "Dr. Marsdon, telephone call."

She shut the stall door, picked up the extension on the wall, and answered, "Dr. Marsdon."

"Sarah, darling."

She leaned back against the wall, felt the flood of adrenaline rush over her and closed her eyes. "Hello, Gerald."

"Sorry to call you at work, but I don't have a home number for you."

Sarah thought. "I...uh...don't have a permanent address yet."

"Good. I'm hoping you won't get one, darling," he said. "You've made your point. Don't you think it's time to come home so we can get on with our lives?"

"Excuse me? Who's this 'we'? You and me, or you and my father? I'm surprised he didn't give you my home number when you talked to him."

"I didn't ask him. That would have put him in a bad position."

"Gerald, I have a new job. I can't simply walk out on my contract—even if I wanted to, which I don't."

"Come on, Sarah. We can certainly make some arrangements with the people you work for to let you out of your contract. Steve would take you back in your old job."

"How do you know that? Have you talked to Steve? Please, tell me you didn't ask him to take me back."

"A couple of casual conversations."

She ran her hand over her hair.

"Tell the people at your new job that you have family commitments." He laughed cheerfully. "In a sense, that's exactly what you have."

"No." No arguing, no excuses. Once she started arguing, she'd have to justify her decisions all over again, and Gerald would make them seem trivial.

"Sarah, darling, what's wrong with giving the woman I love an early wedding present? I truly thought you'd love the house."

She took a deep breath and turned to lean her forehead against the wall. "Gerald, a present is a book or even a piece of jewelry. Not a mansion I'd never seen in an area I didn't want to live in."

"Why didn't you just tell me that?"

"Gerald, you had put down earnest money on that house." She heard the edge of hysteria in her voice and stamped down on it hard. "A lot of earnest money."

"I'd rather lose the money than you."

"Did you? Lose the money, I mean? Or did you go ahead and buy the house, anyway?"

"Of course I bought the house, Sarah. It's a great house. If you'll just come back, I know I can convince you to like it as much as I do, to live in *our* house, marry me."

"I am buying my own house down here, Gerald. A house *I* chose." That wasn't exactly true, but she wasn't about to let Gerald know that.

"You know I can't move my business down there. You can come home to another job tomorrow. Your career is portable. Mine isn't."

"And you make more money than I do."

"I didn't say that, but, yes, it's true. I do make more money than you do." He still sounded patient, reasonable, but his tone had changed ever so slightly.

"Gerald, the house and your career aren't the only problems. You and I haven't been on the same wavelength for a long time, but we were both too stubborn to admit it. I'm not the right woman for you."

"Sarah…"

"You'll find someone else, Gerald. Someone who loves you as you deserve. Find a woman who appreciates being given mansions to live in and diamond rings, and who will give you two-point-three children and go to PTA meetings and cook gourmet meals and run the altar guild at church."

"Sarah, you're getting hysterical."

"All the things you wanted. A woman who prefers dresses to jeans, who doesn't have manure on her shoes or blood on her hands, who doesn't have to drag out of bed at three in the morning to dismember a dead calf to save a heifer."

"I never asked you to give up your career."

"No, just to cut back on it so I only worked from nine to five on cats and dogs—that is, until I got pregnant. I'm so sorry, Gerald. This is truly all my fault. We should have talked the problems out long before this. We've both been dancing around the issues because we're too damn stubborn to admit we made rotten choices."

"So now I'm a rotten choice?"

"No, but you're the wrong choice for me, and I'm the wrong choice for you."

"When I tell your father—"

"Don't you dare call my father!"

"I like your father and he likes me. More than you do, apparently."

"Gerald, I'm sorry."

"Sarah, I'm trying to understand. For God's sake, call me back when you've had time to think about what you're doing. We can still salvage this thing." He waited a beat. "But don't take too long."

The line went dead.

She looked at the phone in surprise. "He hung up on me!"

"Such bad manners."

She caught her breath and swung around. At the end of the hall, Mark leaned against the door holding a large white bag.

"Dinner's here."

"How long have you been listening?"

"Not nearly long enough to know what that was about. Come on, this stuff is getting cold. Assuming you're not too angry to eat."

She threw up her chin. "I am never too angry, too sick or too anything to eat. I do, however, need to wash my hands."

She ducked into the rest room, lathered her hands to the elbow and began to scrub as forcefully as if she were preparing for surgery. She raised her head and saw her face in the mirror. Her cheeks and nose were red; tears coursed down her cheeks. Sorrow? Grief?

Would she regret not having Gerald around? Probably. But not because she loved him. She realized now that she'd never loved him. She was...fond of him. When had she realized that wasn't enough? Not when he'd driven her out to that blasted mansion and presented her the keys. That had merely been the last straw, the final revelation.

"I deserve to love the man I marry and have him love me back," she said to her reflection. "I deserve fireworks and cannons firing. Convenience isn't nearly good enough. If I can't find a man I really love—whatever love actually feels like—I swear I'll be an old maid."

Her reflection ignored her. She tore out too many paper towels, then wiped her hands and her face. No way would she allow Mark to see that she'd been crying.

She took a deep breath, squared her shoulders and went to dinner in the conference room.

Mark had opened all the little white boxes and set them on the table, then laid out paper plates, napkins, chopsticks and a couple of bottles of soda.

"My, just like a restaurant," Sarah said as she sat down.

"Dig in. I'm starved. You have no idea how difficult it's been to wait for you."

He looked at her curiously. Obviously, he wanted to know about the telephone call, but she had no intention of enlightening him.

"You assume I can use chopsticks?" she asked.

"You can use a scalpel. Chopsticks shouldn't be a problem."

She laughed and started in on the food. She was starving.

"You want to talk about it?" Mark asked, after they had finished the first round of Mongolian beef and Pork Chung King.

"Breaking up is hard to do, as they say in the song."

"That's why you came south?"

"One of the reasons."

"And he wants you back?"

"He says he does—but it's ego, not love."

"What makes you think that?"

"I'm actually not that lovable."

"Really? I hadn't noticed."

MARK HAD BEEN SURPRISED at the stab of jealousy he'd felt when he'd heard the few snatches of Sarah's telephone conversation. He'd known he should just turn around, go back to the conference room and wait for her, but he couldn't help himself.

"Rick said you finally accepted this job because you'd had a fight with the vet who owned the practice you worked in," Mark said casually as he forked over another egg roll. He glanced up at her as he bit into the corner of the little packet of soy sauce. "God, I hate these things—"

She reached across the table, took it gently from between his teeth and carefully tore it apart at the small black square in the upper corner. It was a simple gesture, and Mark doubted Sarah realized how intimate it was, how it made him feel.

Then she handed it back. As he took it, their fingers touched for an instant, their eyes locked, and Mark felt his blood pressure respond.

She looked down, then picked up a shrimp in her chopsticks and ate it, chewing carefully. She refused to meet his eyes.

"My fight with my boss Steve was only one of the reasons I came down here, but it was a valid one," she said eventually. "I wanted a partnership, I deserved a partnership. Even my dear old mossbacked boss admitted I deserved a partnership. But he refused to give me one."

"Money?"

"I could have gotten a loan. It's a small practice, mostly cats and dogs. I wanted to expand the large-animal side, start doing more with the horse barns in the area of the clinic, work with the few remaining cattlemen. Steve's approaching retirement. He didn't want to bother, even if it meant an enormous increase in profit. We'd been disagreeing about it for almost two years."

"Why now?"

"A lot of things came to a head all at once. Gerald began crowding me to set a wedding date, and Steve told me in no uncertain terms that he intended to leave the practice to his wife's nephew, who isn't half the vet I am and never will be."

"Turning down a qualified partner with money is bad business practice."

She laughed. "And a cardinal sin in your book."

"Absolutely. Makes no sense. Why did you continue to work for this moron?"

"He's a dear man, really, and a good vet, if a little old-fashioned. I learned a tremendous amount from him. I kept thinking we could work it out. I tend to hang on like a bulldog. I don't give up or quit easily on people, or situations, or anything else."

"I've noticed."

"I guess that's why I became a vet. No matter how bad things get, I keep thinking I can fix them." She shrugged and scooped up fried rice expertly.

"Sometimes you can't."

"No. And finally, finally, after having trumpets blaring at me and banners telling me 'This won't ever be fixed,' I got the message."

"And turned your life over completely in an instant."

"That's another thing about me. I'll fight and fight and fight until there isn't a thing left to do. Then I cut my losses and walk away."

"Without a backward glance?"

"No. Plenty of backward glances. But in my line of work, you lose more often than you'd like. If I couldn't walk away, I'd be no good the next time I faced a crisis. There's a great cartoon somewhere about that. There's this fire-breathing dragon, and on the ground is an empty suit of armor. The caption says, 'Sometimes the dragon wins.' I have a framed copy of that cartoon somewhere in the stuff I haven't unpacked."

"Did the dragon win this time?"

"That remains to be seen— Where's Nasdaq?"

"Asleep in her crate."

"Both of you survived your first day together. I told you it wouldn't be so hard."

"She can't go with me to Buchanan Enterprises. And I have to spend most of the day there tomorrow. It's not fair to leave her alone all day in my house, and not fair to burden the already overburdened staff of this place with her. She needs a home, a family that is there for her all the time. Children. I'm not cut out to be a pet owner."

"I thought you liked her."

"I do like her. I simply do not have room in my life for an animal or any other encumbrances at the moment. It's not fair to her."

He saw Sarah's face cloud, and her mouth—that mouth that he had discovered was so kissable—snapped shut.

"Fine. I'll see what I can do. Thanks for dinner. Now I have some patients to see." She walked out of the conference room.

Leaving him the mess to clean up. He made a small plate of pork and beef scraps and added a little fried rice. That couldn't hurt Nasdaq, surely. She'd undoubtedly been living on worse without serious damage to her digestive tract. He cleaned up the rest, put it neatly into the paper sack, wiped down the conference table, and took the sack with him when he went to give Nasdaq her snack.

She greeted him immediately and joyously, inching forward on her belly, her stubby tail wagging wildly. He set the paper plate down in front of her and watched her sniff, then eat fastidiously.

"You've stayed a lady, haven't you, girl." He stroked her fur, soft and clean, while she snuffled contentedly over the scraps.

When she was finished, he put the paper plate in with the rest of the trash and snapped Nasdaq's leash on her collar. "Come on, girl, let's go put this mess outside in the garbage so we don't get ants or worse."

Nasdaq scampered ahead for two steps, then looked up at him and moved to his side without taking her eyes off his face.

"Somebody trained you. I wonder what happened to make them want to get rid of you."

Dusk had faded into early evening while he'd been eating with Sarah. The floodlights in the area behind the clinic went on at dusk and stayed on until morning, but there were still areas where shadows hung over the piles of lumber and poles waiting to fence the paddocks and the walkway to Sol Weincroft's laboratory wing. He had bent to let Nasdaq off her lead, when she suddenly stiffened and growled, her body at full alert. She began to bark, darting frantic glances up at him, obviously afraid to move away from him, but longing to go after whatever was out there. A raccoon, probably.

He heard the scrabble behind the woodpile, what sounded like an expletive, then silence. Raccoons did not curse.

He shoved Nasdaq back inside the door, and hoped she'd have sense enough to stay in the hallway and not wander up to the front of the clinic.

"Come on out!" he called. "I know you're there." He wished he had a big flashlight. He started toward the lumber at a jog.

"Come on. You don't have anyplace to run. The gate's closed."

He started around the pile of wood, glimpsed a flash of black shiny fabric that glinted in the parking lights, and heard more than one set of feet scrambling away from him.

Suddenly, from above him he heard a male adolescent voice pitched high and scared. "Kenny, don't!"

Without warning the pile shifted. Mark barely had time to lift his arm before he was hit with rolling, tumbling eight-foot fence posts. He stumbled, stepped on a post that rolled beneath his foot, went down on one knee and both felt and heard a numbing crack against his temple.

As he struggled to stand, he heard another voice say, "Oh, man, you've hit somebody!"

He heard running feet and glimpsed several figures racing to climb the gate at the end of the parking lot. He ran his hand over his temple; it came away wet and warm. His stomach roiled.

He had to lie down.

"MARK! MARK! For God's sake, Jack, don't try to move him!"

He heard Sarah's voice, but it sounded both far away and much too close.

He sat up. "I'm fine. Give me a hand."

"No!"

"Look, I'm fine. Just got my chimes rung. I never went out."

"You're bleeding. You could have a concussion, a compression fracture—anything. Jack, get a gurney, *stat!*"

"Don't be an idiot. Give me a hand, Jack."

Mark felt Jack's arm under his own. Jack might be small, but although it had been twenty years at least since he'd ridden Thoroughbreds on the track, he'd stayed in shape. Mark felt himself lifted to his feet easily.

"You're the idiot," Sarah said. She slipped her arm around him.

"Wait a minute," he said, as the world began to spin. "Dammit!"

"Okay. Just a little dizzy there for a minute."

Even in his dazed state he relished the feel of Sarah's soft body against his. He could feel her breath against his throat, smell that half perfume, half medicine smell of hers that drove him wild. She reached her left hand across his chest, pulling him against her.

Now that he was up, his head was clearing rapidly, and his balance was already pretty good, but he wasn't about to let Sarah see that. He realized Jack knew, for he heard the little man snicker once before he relinquished the task of supporting Mark completely to Sarah. *Must remember to thank Jack,* he thought.

"Let's get him into the recovery stall," Sarah said. "He can lie down on the padded floor, and we'll have good light."

Mark heard Jack slide open the doors of the cell. He allowed Sarah to slide him gently down. He closed his eyes against the bright lights and wished the throbbing in his head would stop so he could enjoy the closeness of her body. He heard her murmurs, felt the cool cloths against his pounding head, Sarah's gentle fingers probing the scalp.

"I don't think you need stitches," she said. "Scalp wounds bleed so badly. It looked a whole heck of a lot worse than it is. Good thing, too. I don't want you to sue me for practicing medicine without a license."

"Ha, ha. Ow! Watch it."

"It's just a butterfly bandage, tough guy. How on earth did this happen?"

"Don't really know. Kids, I think. I couldn't get a good look at them. How'd you know to look for me?"

"Nasdaq ran down the hall barking, with her leash still attached. I couldn't figure out why you'd let her loose, and when I couldn't find you, I went out in the parking lot—and found you. Okay, that should do it. I do think I should drive you to the emergency room, have a real doctor check you out."

"You are a real doctor. Besides, I was never unconscious. My head hurts like hell, but that's all."

"That and a gash and a goose egg the size of Rhode Island," Sarah said.

"We ought to call the police," Jack said. It was the first time Mark realized Jack was still with them. "Bloody little buggers. Could have killed you."

"What can the police do? I have no idea even how many of them there were. I definitely can't identify them, and I think when they realized they'd toppled that stack of poles they were more scared than I was."

"Stupid blighters. Parents give them too much freedom and too much money. Ought to have to work for a living like I did."

"I agree." Mark sat up, then put his head down on his knees for a moment.

"You need to go to the emergency room. I'm not kidding," Sarah said.

"Forget it. All I need is a couple of aspirin and a good night's sleep."

"Not alone. First of all, you can't drive. Second, somebody needs to wake you up every couple of hours to see how you respond."

"Not me, luv," Jack said cheerfully. "My old

woman'll have a fit if I'm later than twelve-thirty getting home.''

Sarah sat beside Mark and sighed. "I guess I'm elected. Mabel will have to call Mac if we have any emergencies the temps can't handle— Come on, Jack, let's get him to my truck.''

"We can take my car.''

"Oh, no. I have no intention of being responsible for your Jag. Jack, if you can handle Mark alone, I'll go tell Mabel why I'm leaving, and collect Nasdaq.''

Mark found that once he had his feet under him, he was fine. "Thanks, Jack," he said.

The little cockney grinned at him. "Thought you'd like having the doctor cuddling up to ya. Beats a gnarled ole piece of leather like me any day.''

Mark slid into the passenger seat of Sarah's truck and leaned his head against the rest. A moment later his door opened, and a squirming bundle of fur landed in his lap, stood up and began kissing him on the nose.

"Hey, down, blast it.'' Nasdaq instantly sank into a crouch on his lap, but her stumpy tail continued to wag. He stroked her. "You're a lifesaver, girl, you know that? Remind me to buy you a steak tomorrow.''

"Memo to self—get Beth to buy steak?'' Sarah said as she slid into the driver's seat.

"That's getting a bit old, Doctor.''

"I'm just getting started. Hold on to your wounded head. This truck is not nearly as smooth a ride as a Jag. Are you certain you don't remember anything that could identify those kids?''

"I think somebody called one of them Kenny. I doubt that's going to be much help. Oh, and one of them was wearing a shiny dark jacket.''

"Gang jacket?''

"In this neighborhood?"

"In St. Paul the gangs have invaded every neighborhood."

"I guess. Not very different from what we called in my day 'fraternities.' We did one hell of a lot of drinking and some other things I'm not too proud of, but I don't recall vandalism or assault as part of our initiation rites."

"I can't see you as a fraternity boy."

"Oh, I was every bit as wild as the rest of the poor little rich kids." He sat silent for a moment. "At least, until my senior year."

"What happened then?"

"Life changed," he said.

He realized that Sarah had glanced over at him, surprised at the bitterness even he could detect in his voice. She didn't pursue the subject.

"CAN YOU UNDRESS yourself?" Sarah asked as she guided him to his bedroom.

"I can, but I don't think I'm going to." He sank onto the edge of the bed and bent over to untie his shoes. A wave of dizziness washed over him. "Whoa!"

"Lie back, I'll do it." She knelt as his feet. The light reflected in her silky golden hair as it fell forward. He leaned back and closed his eyes, aware with every fiber of his being of her fingers as she slipped his shoes off. The intimacy of having her touch his feet was incredibly erotic.

"You wouldn't happen to have an ice pack, would you? Or a package of frozen peas?" she asked.

"Huh?"

"Works beautifully, although I doubt this household runs to frozen vegetables."

"It does run to an ice bag, Miss Smarty," he answered. "Sometimes my knee swells after a tennis match."

"I'll get it. Where?"

He kept his eyes closed. He felt the way he used to after a fraternity party when he'd had too much beer. Not really drunk, just a little disjointed. "Cupboard over the refrigerator. You may not be able to reach it."

"I'll manage."

He heard a *thud*, and felt Nasdaq's body cozy up beside him.

"Nasdaq, down." Sarah's voice was stern.

"Let her stay." Mark stretched his arm out, and the little dog snuggled into it and against his side.

"Sure."

Mark thought he heard her chortle, but he didn't open his eyes to check for a smile. He heard her rummaging in his kitchen, and in a few minutes she came back.

"Here you go." She put the ice bag gently against his skull and plumped up a pillow to hold it in place. "Better?"

"Didn't know you cared."

"Professional courtesy. Besides, better the devil you know than the devil you don't know. If you kick off, Mr. Buchanan might replace you with an even stingier bean counter. I'd rather break down your defenses than have to start over with some new sort of animal."

"Oh, thank you, Doctor," he whispered. Talking made his head hurt.

She sounded amused, and he was probably a sight to see. A grown man stretched fully clothed on his bed with a ratty dog under one arm and an ice pack on his head. He felt extremely vulnerable and defenseless—not a feeling he relished, and one he'd managed to avoid in recent years. Nobody, but nobody, came into his bedroom these days.

"You may have a shiner, you know."

He groaned. "Just what I need."

"Is there anyone I should call? Family?"

He started. "God, no. Don't, whatever you do, call anybody. Coy's in Texas. He's likely to get on his jet and fly back if he hears I've had my head bashed in. He tends to blow things out of proportion."

"Is he family?"

"Same as. I definitely wouldn't call my mother. She tends to freak out even worse than Coy. Besides, I think she's still on a cruise in the Mediterranean."

"You think? Don't you know where your own mother is?" Sarah sounded incredulous.

Mark knew he sounded defensive when he answered. "We don't keep tabs on one another. She's remarried to a very nice guy. They're retired and travel a lot. Hell, I'm a grown man. I don't need my mother calling me every day to check up on me."

"Your father?"

"Dead. Long dead."

"But..."

He heard her sigh.

"Okay. You're right. It's just that in my family, everybody wants to know what everybody else is doing every minute of the day."

"We are not that sort of family." He closed his eyes as a signal that the conversation was ended. His headache had settled into a dull throb, and he had to admit the ice pack felt wonderful. Something settled close to him. He'd have preferred Sarah—she was a good deal taller and not nearly so hairy. He chuckled.

"What?"

"Nothing. Go away. I'm fine."

"I'll bed down on the couch."

"Go home. Please."

"Nope. Shut up and sleep."

He felt the comforter at the foot of the bed being drawn up over his chest. Gently. Erotically. Hell, the damn woman could probably feed him oatmeal and make it an erotic gesture! He was so tuned in to her, but obviously she felt nothing for him but professional compassion.

He opened his eyes in time to see her glide out of the room. In the light from the kitchen her hair was the color of old gold, softly burnished.

"MARK?"

He lifted one eyelid. His head hurt like the devil, and for a moment he had no idea where he was or how he'd gotten there. Then he remembered. "What?" he asked muzzily.

"Who am I?"

He smiled lazily and raised a hand to touch the long strand of hair that had fallen across her forehead. "My nemesis."

"Be serious."

"Dr. Doolittle, I presume."

"Who are you?"

"I am the bean counter extraordinaire who makes your life impossible."

"Right. You're fine. Go back to sleep."

"I'm sloshing."

"You need to go to the bathroom?"

"No." He pointed at his head. He could feel the melted ice moving as he moved his head.

"Okay. Be right back." She took the bag from his forehead.

Nasdaq raised her head for a moment, then lay back down.

In a moment Sarah returned and settled the fresh pack in place. "Want some more aspirin?"

"Nope."

She moved away.

"Hey, don't I get a kiss good-night?" He must be concussed. He'd never said a stupid thing like that before in his life.

"Sure." She came back to the bed, bent over and gave him a chaste kiss on his forehead.

Before she could move away, he reached up, wound his fingers through her hair and drew her face down. She didn't resist. He lifted his head and kissed her mouth. Her lips felt soft and yielding, half parted, and tasted sweetly of ginger. For a moment she was there fully with him, as involved in that kiss as he was, and then he felt her stiffen as she pulled away.

"Now I know you're concussed," she said. "Go to sleep. Tomorrow you won't even remember this."

The hell I won't, he thought as he lay back.

SARAH STRETCHED on the maroon leather couch in Mark's austere living room. She had no idea where he kept his linens and extra blankets, so she hunkered down with her jacket across her shoulders. She wasn't cold. Actually, she was so far from cold that it frightened her.

Mark had kissed her twice—and twice he'd made the hair on the back of her neck stand up. Was this what people meant by "rebound"?

Surely people didn't rebound further than they'd

bounded in the first place, and she'd never felt this way with Gerald, who always removed his glasses and folded them into their case before he kissed her.

Mark had nice hands. She could still feel his fingers interlaced in her hair, moving along her cheek, caressing her with gentleness and yet with a kind of proprietary maleness that told her he knew how to handle a woman. She ached to feel those hands on her body.

Of course, she told herself, he wouldn't remember kissing her, or, if he did, he would never admit it. They'd be back to where they'd been before—adversaries, a pair of dogs squabbling over a bone that he wanted to keep and she wanted to use. How could a man who turned her on—and he certainly did do that—be such a horse's rear about the things she needed?

For an instant she wondered whether she could use his obvious desire for her to manipulate him. The moment the thought went through her head she dismissed it. If she'd learned anything from her father, it was that she hated manipulation. Her father was a master. She'd long ago sworn not to emulate him. No. She'd have to get what she wanted without using her sexuality on Mark. That meant she had to keep their relationship strictly business—friendly but professional.

From the sensations his kisses caused in her midsection, she was afraid that wouldn't be too easy to do.

CHAPTER SEVEN

"YOU STILL KNOW who I am?" Sarah asked two hours later.

Mark groaned. "The woman who keeps waking me up and reminding me my head hurts. Can't you just let me suffer in peace?"

"As soon as I redo your ice bag. You're sloshing again."

"Yeah, and this time I do need to go to the bathroom."

"Okay. Take it easy sitting up." She took the ice bag and offered him her hand.

He was certain he didn't need it, but he took it nonetheless. Any contact was better than none. He sat on the edge of the bed, gave himself a moment to let his stomach settle, then pulled himself to his feet, using much more leverage on her hand than he really needed. He stood swaying, with his arm around her shoulders and her arms around his waist.

"You need lights?"

"It's my house, remember. I know my way around in the dark."

"If you say so."

He might not need help finding the bathroom, but that didn't mean he had to let her go quite yet. He could probably prolong this physical contact only a few seconds more before she'd begin to get suspicious, but he intended to enjoy it for as long as possible. She was tall, but he was taller. Her cheek fit against his chin. He'd seen her in short-sleeved greens and knew she had muscles, but here in his arms all he could feel was the softness of her breast, the curve of her hip, her thigh against his.

She pulled away, as he knew she would. "Onward and upward."

He wasn't certain about the onward part, but he'd certainly been aware of the upward.

"I'll let Nasdaq out while you're gone," she said.

Hearing her name, the dog jumped down and trotted through the kitchen.

"What time is it?" Mark asked when he'd settled back on the bed with Nasdaq beside him.

"About four in the morning."

"God. Look, I'm obviously fine. Why don't you go home and get at least a few hours of sleep? Or use my guest room. It's within yelling distance if I start having a fit."

"I'm fine where I am. And I'd rather go home after I make certain you've had a decent breakfast. Call it professional courtesy."

"Then, stay here with me." He patted the bed beside him and moved over a few inches, while Nasdaq grumbled at the disturbance.

"Not a good idea."

"Great idea."

"I'll stick to the sofa, thanks."

Watching her walk away from him was becoming physically painful. He wanted her badly, much more than a man with a concussion should want anything. But desire apparently overrode even pain.

WHEN HE OPENED his eyes, he knew despite the closed curtains that it was morning. Nasdaq was licking his face and demanding to be let out. He ran his hand down his cheek, felt the heavy beard under his fingertips, and realized he was still fully clothed. Suddenly he remembered. He sat up and looked through his door. Then he got to his feet. The headache was practically gone, but he could feel the lump under his hairline. It was only mildly tender now.

He checked the living room. Sarah wasn't asleep on the couch. Gone home, obviously. He let Nasdaq out and went to dig out the coffee beans from his freezer.

Then he heard the shower running in his bathroom, and his heart lifted. He wondered what would happen if he opened the door, stripped and joined her. Maybe she'd be glad to see him. He looked at the bathroom door. If he tried the knob, would it turn, or would she have locked him out? He realized he didn't want to know.

The shower stopped as the coffeemaker began to sputter. He let Nasdaq in, and went to find his shoes. As he reached the door to his bedroom, the bathroom door opened and Sarah came out.

"Oh!" She jumped when she saw him. "I thought you were still asleep."

She was toweling her damp hair and wore the baggy top to her surgical greens. She was half in and half out of her jeans. He caught a tantalizing glimpse of black panties above very long legs and bare feet.

"I'm awake."

She draped the towel in front of her. "How's your head?"

"Fine."

"Good." She yanked her jeans the rest of the way and zipped them quickly.

"I'm making coffee."

"Great. You mind moving? I left my shoes in the living room."

"Sure. I'll wait in the kitchen. Then I could use a shower and a shave."

"I'll just get a cup of coffee and leave you to it."

As she passed him, he caught her arm. "You said I had to have a good breakfast, remember?" She looked up at him. He could see the pulse in her throat throb. He pulled her around to face him, but she ducked away. "Go take a shower. I'll make toast."

Damn. The woman was an eel. But he'd swear she felt the same attraction he did. What was so wrong with acknowledging it? They were both adults, free of other commitments.

Or maybe he was the only one who was emotionally free. He had no idea how attached she'd been to that idiot she'd been talking to last night, but she'd been willing to marry the guy.

KEEPING HER professional distance was getting harder and harder. Sarah found cups, bread and all the makings for a simple breakfast as she listened to the water running in the shower. What would he think if she were simply to drop her clothes again and join him?

He'd probably be appalled. And then he'd think she was trying to seduce him into buying her the goodies she wanted for the clinic. He had that kind of mind. In any case, he'd never be certain whether she was interested in him, or in the expenses he could sign off on.

Obviously, the only thing to do was to get the equipment she wanted first, and then see what developed between them. That way he'd be certain she wasn't simply doing it for business.

"SIGN THIS," Beth said, and handed over a legal document to Sarah. "It's your lease agreement. I've already paid the first and last months' rents and damage deposit for you. You can repay it to the practice in increments over six months. And here are your keys—front door, back door, storage room. The cleaning crew is in today at the owner's expense, and you and I can do a walk-through before you move in. I can arrange to have your furniture delivered whenever you let me know. Give me twenty-four hours' notice."

Sarah signed where indicated. "Actually, the little I have won't arrive until early next week. I need to buy almost everything."

"Let me know the details. I'll have your stuff sent to your door and arrange for someone to meet the truck. And if you'll tell me what sort of furniture you like, I can arrange to rent the bare necessities like beds, bureaus and couches for a couple months so you have a chance to shop."

"Beth, do you do this for everyone Rick hires?"

Beth looked surprised. "Of course, and for Buchanan, too. Why?"

"Because I don't know how you have time to go to the bathroom, much less eat, sleep and do the rest of your job."

"Well, neither the practice nor Buchanan hires that many people. The turnover is extremely slim at Buchanan, and most of Rick's people already lived in town. And, of course, I take care of a lot of stuff on my car phone—I have a hands-free option."

"I still don't know how you manage everything."

"I have a staff of four secretaries, two clerks and a paralegal. Mostly I delegate to them what Mark delegates to me. Simple."

Sarah suspected that was as much hard information as she was going to get. Beth might be a whiz kid, but she was a closemouthed one. Sarah wondered not for the first time whether Beth was more to Mark than an assistant.

"And in case you're interested—and I think you are—Mark and I are just friends, nothing more."

"Now you do mind readings, too?" Sarah asked.

Beth laughed. "You have what I think is called a 'speaking countenance.' Everything you think is written right there for anyone with half a brain to see. Plus, I know the effect Mark has on women from three to ninety-three. He's not my type."

"Who is? Ming the Merciless?"

"Not until after he takes over the universe. Then he might be worth cultivating. I much prefer the top man."

Sarah's eyes widened. "I hear Coy Buchanan is very attractive for an old guy."

"He's not old!" Beth snapped. "Oh, drat. Sign your lease, Sarah, and let me get back to work. And if you ever breathe a word of this conversation…"

Sarah patted Beth's shoulder. "Okay, Wicked Witch of the North, I promise to keep your secret."

"Besides, he doesn't know I'm alive. Have you met him?"

"Not yet."

"He's big and rough, and he can be ruthless and foulmouthed. He's also as cuddly as a baby bear." Beth held up a finger. "Mention that, and I'll have to *kill* you." She reached for her papers, shoved them into her alligator briefcase and stalked out, leaving Sarah smiling.

So the impervious Beth wasn't so impervious, after all. Coy Buchanan must be over fifty—more than twenty years older than Beth—but that didn't seem to have kept her from…what? Being attracted?

More than that. Sarah wondered whether Buchanan had an inkling that this brilliant and beautiful woman was smitten. Probably not. Men could be such dolts. Maybe she could do a spot of matchmaking while she was keeping her mind off Mark.

Sarah glanced at her watch. Only four hours until she had to be back on duty. That couch of Mark's might be comfortable to sit on, but not to sleep on. She ached. She decided to use the Jacuzzi, to which she might well become addicted.

The telephone rang, just as she'd barely gotten comfortable. She struggled up and went dripping into the other room to answer it.

"Dr. Sarah? This is Alva Jean. I'm sorry to bother you, but Dr. Rick says we need you."

"What's the problem?"

"Big new client. Bought some cows at the sale today in Collierville. He's got them loaded and wants to bring them by right now to be tested and vaccinated."

"How many?"

"About twenty, I think." Alva Jean dropped her voice. "Dr. Rick says to tell you he and Dr. Mac will be happy to help, but he thinks you ought to meet this guy, and maybe we can get more of his business, you know?"

"Right. I'll be there in twenty minutes. Ask Jack to assemble the testing supplies for me, will you? And to get as many people as he can to help unload those cows and move 'em from the pen to the headstalls and back.''

Rick was right, of course. She had been brought down to develop the large-animal practice, and a new client with twenty cows would be a good start. Cattlemen talked. Word would get around that the new lady vet from Minnesota did a good job. At least, she hoped that's what would be reported.

MARK'S CAR was not in the parking lot, but Nasdaq was curled in the corner of her open crate asleep, when Sarah stuck her head into his office. Mark had said he'd be at Buchanan all day, so why did she feel disappointed?

Rick met her at the door to his office. ''Thanks for coming, Sarah.''

''No problem. Don't they generally have a vet come to the sale barns to test the cows?''

''He's on vacation. And this is a new man from Arkansas. Somebody at the sale barn recommended us. Have to send the guy a case of beer or something.''

''What do they need?''

''Pregnancy, tuberculosis, brucellosis—the usual. Vaccinations, the whole shebang.''

''He's not here yet?''

''Due any minute.''

Alva Jean opened Rick's door. ''There's a big van pulling in the gate. Must be him.''

''Showtime,'' Rick said.

''What about Mac? Can he help?''

''He had an emergency. Rottweiler hit by a car. He's splinting a broken leg, but he said he'd help the minute he could.''

She and Rick shoved through the broad door side by side into the large-animal area.

Jack looked up from arranging his supplies on the side cabinet. "He's backing the truck up now."

"Got the chute ready to hook to the trailer?" Sarah asked.

"Yeah. He's bringing his own people to help."

"Good. We can run the cows down his ramp into the pen. Should be pretty straightforward."

Jack pushed the button to raise the big overhead door at the back of the loading area. From the maneuvering that the driver had to do to line the open-sided livestock van up properly, Sarah suspected that he was not very well practiced.

She walked up to the cab of the truck. "Hi. I'm Dr. Marsdon."

"Harry Vollmer," the driver said. "Just bought these heifers. How long's this gonna take? I got to get on back to Arkansas this evening."

"We'll do our best. Depends on how well the cows cooperate." She looked at the back of the van. "I can see a possible problem, Mr. Vollmer. You seem to have a gap beside the back door on the right. It's too short to mesh properly with the top of the chute into our pen."

"Hell, I been unloading cows out of that thing forever. I just kind of stand behind the door and yell at 'em."

"Un-huh." Sarah glanced at Jack, who stood beside the gap with his hands on his narrow hips and his eyebrows raised. "I've always found it's amazing how small an area a cow can squeeze through when it's excited."

Vollmer opened his door and climbed down. "Aw,

they ain't gonna do nothing.'' Three Hispanic men climbed out of the rear of the truck and stood smiling at Sarah. ''Don't none of them boys speak no English,'' Vollmer said. ''But they understand gestures well enough, don't you, boys.'' The men smiled at him.

''That blighter's a silly fool,'' Jack whispered. ''There is no way he can hold that trailer door tight against the chute if one of those cows decides to run over the top of him.''

Sarah sent up a silent prayer, then turned to Vollmer. ''Mr. Vollmer, the pen is set up inside the clinic and the chute's attached. You can open the back doors. I suggest you have your men back you up.''

''You worry too much, sweet thang,'' Vollmer said. ''I been doing this for years.'' With a flourish he reached over and lifted the latch on the back gate of his trailer.

Sarah had been expecting heifers. What she saw first was the biggest Santa Gertrudis cow she'd ever laid eyes on. It had a head like a Cape Buffalo and the shoulders of a bull rhinoceros. And it was absolutely furious.

The cow erupted from the back of the trailer, knocking Vollmer, his men and the gate back against the doorway. Vollmer flew back at least five feet to land on his seat, while the gate he had so cavalierly opened crashed against the side of his trailer where his head had been only seconds before. Sarah dove over him and dragged the trailer door back to cover the gap.

''Get up here!'' she yelled at Vollmer. ''I can't hold this damn door alone!''

He simply stared at her openmouthed as the stampede continued. She prayed that the steel rods that fenced the pen would hold, and that nobody was on the inside of the pen—the cow side.

The tumult seemed to last forever, but was, in fact, over in minutes. Finally, silence inside the trailer told Sarah all the cows were out. Vollmer had struggled to his feet and was brushing off his jeans. He refused to meet her eyes.

"Shut those damn doors!" Jack called from inside the room.

Sarah looked around. Vollmer's men had taken shelter inside the rear seat of the truck. Now they climbed out and came slowly toward Vollmer.

"Shut those doors, you bastards!" Vollmer shouted. That, at least, they seemed to understand.

"See? Told you they wouldn't do nothing," Vollmer said.

Sarah simply stared at him and walked in through the side door.

A few minutes later, Mac, all six foot six of him, clomped into the area. His greens were streaked with blood, and his graying hair was pasted flat against his head with sweat. "What the…" he said.

"Heifers," Jack said dryly.

"Of *course* they are," answered Mac. "In a parallel universe. Well, Dr. Marsdon, how can I help?"

The actual testing went fairly smoothly, once they got into the rhythm. Two hours later Sarah could barely raise her arms. Neither Mac nor Rick had recent experience palpating cows for pregnancy, so Sarah took care of that, while they did the brucellosis checks and the inoculations.

"All pregnant but one," she said as she pulled off her twentieth set of gloves.

"Good." Vollmer risked a smile. "You do a right nice exam for a pretty woman, ma'am."

She bit back a reply. Don't offend a potential client, she told herself and hoped Rick noticed what lengths she was willing to go to, to capture business.

"Now we just got to get these ole gals loaded back in my trailer, and I can get off home," Vollmer said with a hearty laugh and a slap on the nearest bovine rump. The bovine in question moved out of reach. "Lucky they're all settled down now. Won't be no trouble at all to get 'em back inside."

This time Sarah intended to keep control of the situation. The humongous cow, obviously the leader of the pack, was casting angry glances at the trailer.

Within fifteen minutes all but the big Santa Gertrudis were loaded. The tension in Sarah's stomach began to subside. It was almost over. Jack prodded the beast to no avail, then prodded her again.

She exploded up the ramp, kicking at Jack's head as she went. At the top, she swung her huge head, bashed the trailer door and knocked Vollmer's man to the concrete.

In a flash she'd swapped ends. In another flash she dove through the opening between the top of the chute and the bottom of the trailer door. She landed a good three feet inside the clinic but outside the pen.

"Hell! Watch out!" Mac yelled.

Jack vaulted over the rail into the safety of the pen. Mac followed. Rick stood in front of the charging cow like a bird caught by a cobra.

"Rick! Jump, dammit!" Mac yelled.

Rick feinted left. The cow swerved right. Her shoulder caught him a glancing blow, but that was enough to spin him like a top and throw him hard into the side of the wall.

Sarah grabbed the cattle prod and went after the cow. "She's heading for the door to the hall," Sarah shouted. "She's going to knock herself out." She was three steps behind the cow and running hard, but it was obvious the cow would reach the hall door before Sarah did. If she hit it, she could shatter the door, and probably shatter her stupid skull.

The cow hadn't slowed a step. Two yards, a yard, then two feet. Collision was inevitable.

Then, as if by magic, the hall door opened.

"Mark, jump!" Sarah shouted.

"Blast!"

She saw him flatten himself against the wall. The cow never broke stride. It was a wide hall, but Mark would be lucky not to be crushed.

"Look out!" Sarah shouted.

"Alva Jean!"

The cow paused at the far end of the hall.

"Thank God," Sarah breathed.

Then the cow swung right, bashed the double doors and ran full tilt into the reception room. Sarah heard the screams, and reached the reception area in time to see Alva Jean drag a woman carrying a poodle behind the reception counter.

The cow stopped, then turned to stare out the double glass doors at the front of the reception room. The doors that led outside.

"Oh, no," Sarah said.

Sarah knew the cow couldn't recognize clear glass. All the animal could see was freedom. If she hit those doors full force, they'd explode. "Get down!" she said.

Then she looked outside. Eleanor Grayson was walking up the front walk, reporting for her shift, and dead in the line of sight between that cow and freedom.

For a moment the cow stood snorting. Sarah didn't dare breathe.

"Alva Jean, punch the button and close the front gates," Sarah whispered. "We've got to keep her off the highway."

"Uh-huh." Alva Jean didn't move.

"Alva Jean!"

"Oh." She punched.

Now Eleanor stood directly outside the glass doors. Sarah saw the expression on her face change from incredulity to horror.

The cow backed up a step, pawed like a bull, lowered her head.

And charged.

Eleanor yanked the glass door open and flattened herself against the wall beside it. Her timing was perfect. The cow charged past her without touching the glass, soared over the front steps and headed for the front lawn.

"Are those gates shut?" Sarah asked.

"Uh-huh."

"Good. Then, let's go get her."

Twenty minutes later, Sarah led a happily tranquilized Santa Gertrudis cow back around to the rear of the clinic, into the cow pen, then up the steps into the waiting trailer.

As Vollmer watched his men shut and lock the gate, he turned to Sarah. "Honey, I ain't never seen nothing like that."

She was expecting him to say that he'd never give her another chance, either, but instead he said, "You got my business from here on out."

She forced herself to smile as she shook his hand. "Mr. Vollmer?" she said. "Promise me you'll get those extensions welded on before you come back."

He laughed and shook his head. "You got my word on it, honey."

As they watched Vollmer drive sedately through the now-open front gate, Mac asked, "Would anyone care to go get drunk?"

"I think I already am," Sarah answered. "Mark, are you all right?"

"Let's see. I have a black eye, a knot on my head, my foot has been stepped on by a fifteen-hundred-pound crazy cow, my ribs have been crushed, and I have lived through terror no man should have to endure. I'd say I'm fine."

"Jack?"

"Right as rain, Doc."

"Rick?"

"Oh, dear, that could have been a disaster if Eleanor hadn't thought on her feet and gotten the front doors open in time."

"I'd give her and Alva Jean a bonus," Sarah said. "If Alva hadn't closed that gate, we really would have had a disaster."

The group walked back down the hall toward the conference room.

"Is it possible, I wonder," Mac asked, "to identify the animal your steak comes from? I'd truly like to barbecue that cow."

"Vollmer's the one who ought to be barbecued," Mark said.

They all sank into chairs around the conference table.

"Don't blame him, people," Sarah said. "Blame me.

It's all my fault. I could have gotten somebody killed tonight.''

''Your fault?'' Mark asked. ''How is any of this your fault?''

Sarah took a deep breath. ''I knew when I saw that trailer setup that we had a recipe for disaster, but Rick wanted Vollmer's business so much that I decided to take a chance.''

''So it's my fault?'' Rick asked.

''You had no way of knowing. But I did. And I took a chance, anyway.''

''It all turned out all right,'' Eleanor said. She went to the refrigerator in the corner. ''I suppose you all want sodas. I'm so dry I can hardly speak.''

They all agreed. Eleanor served. Sarah waited while everyone drank deeply.

''It's not bourbon, but it'll have to do,'' Mac said, looking morosely into the top of his can of diet soda.

''We'll be the laughingstock of the cattle industry when this story gets out,'' Rick said.

''Any publicity is good publicity,'' Mark said. ''Or so I've been told. Frankly, Sarah, I think everyone did a superb job, including you. I had no idea those things could grow that big.''

''She's outsize even for Santa Gertrudis,'' Sarah said. ''And pregnant.''

''Now I am going home,'' Mac said. He stood and began to shuck the top of his bloody greens, which were now overlaid with dirt and manure.

''How's the rottweiler you were working on?'' Sarah asked. ''Broken leg, wasn't it?''

''He'll live. Thank you for your concern, Doctor.'' He smiled tiredly and walked out.

"I'm going home, too," Rick said. "I promise, Sarah, I'll never try to second-guess you again."

"Sure you will, boss," Sarah said. "But the next time I'll put up more of a fight."

"I'll go congratulate Alva Jean and see if anybody is still up there waiting to be seen," Eleanor said. "Good job, Sarah." Eleanor left and the door closed behind her. Mark leaned across the table. "I've never seen you in action before. Impressive."

"May you never see me in action quite that way again in this lifetime. I screwed up."

"No."

"Oh, yes, I did. If anyone had gotten hurt. If that stupid cow had cut her throat catapulting herself out of the front door, that would have been my fault and no one else's."

"Stop it. You wrought triumph out of possible disaster. Cut yourself a little slack. Nobody blames you. They blame that ass Vollmer."

"He is an ass, but I'm an idiot."

"You're just hungry. When was the last time you ate?"

"I forget. What time is it now?"

"After seven. Want me to go get takeout again?"

"How are you feeling?" she asked.

"Fine. Other than the stares I got at work today about the bruise under my eye, I'm perfectly well. The cow missed me, although I didn't realize I could suck in my gut that far. And I think I went up on point like a ballerina to get my toes out of her way. I didn't know this job would be this dangerous."

"It can be very dangerous, no kidding. My patients don't understand anything except that they hurt and they're scared. Most of them are big, and some of them are mean."

"Why do you do it?"

"Because *they* can't. They're our responsibility, and even if they try to kill us, we have to try to cure them. God, I don't think I've been this tired since vet school."

"I'll go get us both some food. What are you up for? Pizza?"

"Do you know, I haven't actually sat down to a real meal in a real restaurant since I came to this benighted town and started work?"

"Take an hour off. Hand over to Eleanor. I'll take you out for a steak."

"I'm too tired and too dirty, and I left early last night, remember? Thanks for the offer, but I'd better take a raincheck. I can exist for months on peanut butter crackers out of the vending machines. I did it in school."

"Your stomach is older now." He covered her hand with his. "You're a good vet, Sarah Marsdon."

Before she could answer, he'd gotten up and gone out. She dropped her head onto the table. One good night's sleep, that's all she needed.

She didn't realize she'd been asleep until the intercom buzzed. "Dr. Sarah?" Mabel had come on duty. Alva Jean had gone home.

Sarah shook her head. "Yes, Mabel?"

"That pig is here."

"Pig?"

"Egg Roll. He's apparently cut himself on something. He's bleeding all over the floor."

"Can he walk?"

"He walked in."

"Get him into room one. I'll be right there."

Egg Roll seemed annoyed, but not in much pain. His

owner, on the other hand, was frantic. "He must have stepped on a piece of glass or a broken bottle or something."

"When did this happen?"

"Just now. We were out for our evening walk, and all of a sudden I see these little bloody footprints. Oh, dear heaven." She sank to her knees and cradled Egg Roll's fat little head in her arms. "Is he going to be all right?"

Sarah knelt. Egg Roll glared at her from under the folds of fat over his eyes and snuffled. When she picked up his front hoof, he began to struggle and squeal.

"You're hurting him!"

"Hold him, please, if you can. I have to see how bad this cut is." Egg Roll began to exert all his strength to get away. Sarah hung on doggedly. Finally, she stood and called Mabel. "Send Jack in here, will you? I need another set of hands."

With Jack holding Egg Roll down, Sarah managed to look at the foot. "He's got something in there all right. Between his hooves. Looks like it might be a shard of some kind of bottle—beer, maybe." She took her forceps and gently pulled.

Egg Roll squealed. His owner sat on her haunches and moaned.

The moment the glass was out, Egg Roll shut up.

"Okay, Egg Roll," Sarah said. "Some antiseptic and a good bandage, and you'll be as good as new."

Ten minutes later Egg Roll limped out, but stopped at the desk and looked up at Mabel expectantly.

"Alva Jean always gives him a mint," his owner said.

"Oh." Mabel unwrapped a candy and tossed it. Egg

Roll caught it in midair, turned and limped out on the end of his leash.

Sarah leaned on the counter. "More days like this I do not need."

"Mark said he'd be waiting for you in the conference room."

"Huh?"

"He brought dinner."

"Thank God." She stopped to wash her hands and shove her hair out of her eyes, then she opened the conference room door and gasped with astonishment.

CHAPTER EIGHT

IN THE CENTER of the table, a solitary candle burned. It was stuck into the top of an empty soda can. A paper-towel place mat had been set with plastic knives and forks. She came in and sat down at the single place.

Mark materialized at her elbow. "Good evening, madame. My name is Mark, and I'll be your waiter tonight. May I offer madam her choice of beverage?" He held up a can of diet soda as though it were a wine bottle.

"What vintage?"

"April."

"Excellent choice." She grinned.

"I have taken the liberty of choosing madame's dinner tonight. We have the *biftek* on a bun with *fromage*, and the extra large *pommes frites*, to be followed by *les* Twinkies."

"Perfect, Mark. Won't you join me?"

"Don't mind if I do." He sat opposite.

"I think this is the nicest thing anyone's done for me since I got here."

"My invitation for a steak still stands. When are you off?"

"Friday night, I think. But I'm going to be moving into my new place if my stuff arrives."

"I'll..."

She grinned. "I know. You'll bring take-out."

"I was going to say, I'll bring champagne and roses."

"Mark, I'm not sure the champagne and roses are a good idea," Sarah said. She put down her partially eaten cheeseburger and refused to meet his eyes.

"Why not?"

"It's not a good idea to consort with the enemy."

"I'm the enemy? I thought we'd gotten way beyond that."

"Not when it comes to my equipment, we haven't." She looked up at him. "Did you think I'd back off? I won't, you know."

"What has one thing to do with the other? I find you attractive and interesting. Am I mistaking your reaction?"

"I am concentrating on my career. I am not ready for any sort of dalliance."

"Because you're still in love with that jerk in Minnesota?"

"Mark Scott, my private life is none of your business, but for your information, I am not in love with him. I don't think I ever was. But that doesn't mean I'm going to plunge into some sort of meaningless—"

"Whoa! Stop right there. Who said anything about meaningless?"

"It can't be anything else, as long as we're at loggerheads over the running of this place."

"You seem to be doing fine without your blasted equipment," Mark snapped.

"I've been lucky. So far nobody has needed laser treatment or a spinal tap. I refuse to go digging around in some Thoroughbred's spine without benefit of a fluoroscope, at least—preferably an MRI."

"Mississippi State has the equipment."

"Right. They do. And they're five hours away. And besides that, you're advertising this place as state-of-the-art. What art? Neolithic cave paintings? So long as we don't have the specialized equipment to handle problems, we're not state of anybody's art. Nobody's going to trust us with big contracts if we can't provide the best care possible. And we're putting animals at risk if we say we do things and we can't deliver."

"I keep telling you, you'll get your equipment as soon as we're certain this place can pay its way and at least preserve capital for its investors. I'm willing to compromise and cut you some slack on actual profit."

"I'm not interested in the investors! All they've got riding on this place is money. We're talking life and death."

He drew back, his face hard. "Investors are what got this place up and running, and they deserve to know that their investment isn't being poured down a hole. It may be only money, Doctor, but it's money that a great many people cannot afford to lose."

"I get the feeling Coy Buchanan can stand to lose millions without even noticing."

"Hardly. You don't have a clue about construction loans or bid processes, or how close to the edge even big outfits like Buchanan have to work. Coy is only one of the investors in this clinic. The majority are ordinary, middle-class people who got talked into this because Rick Hazard has a golden tongue and because they love animals—their own and other people's. Some are retirees who are trying to hang on to enough money to keep them out of nursing homes, or pay for a home if they have to move to one—and maybe, just maybe, leave their children enough money for a down payment on a decent house or college tuition."

"Don't tell me people didn't realize this was an iffy investment from the start. A veterinary clinic isn't Consolidated Edison or IBM."

"No, but it's not pork bellies or gold futures, either—or it shouldn't be. And with me around to look after things, it won't be. Don't you understand, Doctor, that I'm the one who has to keep all the balls in the air and make certain that not one of them hits the ground? I'm doing the best I can, and if that means you have to sweat out six months without a neutron whatsit, that's a damn sight better than having to go crawling back to some penny-ante practice in Minnesota where the guy doesn't even want you as a partner."

Sarah caught her breath. "You fight dirty."

"When I have to. Try to understand, Sarah, I'd give you the moon with a fence around it if it were up to me, but it's not. I'm a bean counter, I'm a hatchet man, I'm the guy who knows it's right to say 'no' when he wants to say yes. I'm already moving heaven and earth to try to find the bucks to get you at least part of what you want...."

"You are?"

"Hell, yes. But do you have any idea how close to the edge Rick is skirting? What do you want to spend money on first? Your MRI, or Alva Jean and Jack Renfro's salaries, not to mention your own?"

"It's that bad?" Sarah whispered.

"Not yet, but it could be. Hell, the business plan said we'd be in the red for a year. Everybody knew that going in. But with the cost overruns for construction..."

"The destruction, you mean. The kids."

"That's only part of it. Overruns are a fact of life, but we've had more than we bargained for. We're barely staying afloat, and with a lot of luck we'll make it without having to cut staff or services. If we do, we start a downward spiral that could sink us.''

Sarah sighed. "None of this changes anything, Mark. I understand, and perhaps in a way I agree, but I still know that we need these things. We're going to be expected to have them.''

"Then, bring in more business, Doctor, and I'll buy them for you in a heartbeat.'' He sank into the chair. "In the meantime, I guess champagne and roses are a poor substitute.''

"Put the money in a piggy bank. Maybe we'll have to use it to pay the staff next week.''

He grinned. "Not next week. Maybe next month, but not next week.''

"Okay. You win, for now. Why don't you take Nasdaq home, Mark. At least one of us can get some sleep for a change.''

"There are better sleeping companions than Nasdaq.''

"She's your best bet for tonight.'' Sarah smiled to take the sting out of her words. "She could use a good run, even though Alva Jean took her out a couple of times, and I think everybody on the staff has been in to play with her. She's not suffering by being here.''

"It's still not the best solution for her,'' Mark said. "What happens when I have to travel—and believe me, I do, often at a moment's notice.''

"You do what most people do—board her at your vet's. That's why we have kennels. It's not home, but it's not the Black Hole of Calcutta either.''

"The point is, my home is not really any home.''

"Well, tonight it is. Go get her. See you in the morning.'' She picked up her trash and stuffed it into the sack. As she reached around him to throw the sack away, he caught her.

"We're not enemies, and you know it," he said gently.

"Mark..."

He bent to kiss her. Gently, softly, he brushed her lips with his. He turned her so that her body fitted against him. One hand ruffled her hair and stroked the nape of her neck, the other encircled her waist.

When he deepened the kiss, she opened to his questing tongue and met it with her own.

In an instant gentle became urgent. His hand drifted down her cheek, across her shoulder and down, cupped her breast. His palm slid gently back and forth across her nipple.

She sighed against his mouth. Her hips pressed against him, her arms encircled his neck, her fingers dug into the tops of his shoulders. He pressed her back against the wall, his thigh between her thighs, his free hand cupping her bottom, holding her against his erection, feeling the slow circle of her hips against him.

His palm slid down her midriff and reached for the button of her jeans. She offered no resistance, but whimpered softly as he began to slide her zipper down. He wanted to touch her, caress her, feel the softness between her thighs.

He was losing control but it didn't seem to matter. Nothing mattered except Sarah against him, the heat of her mouth, the sweet hot taste of her, the hard, swollen buttons of her nipples against his chest.

Beside her, the interior telephone buzzed. Sarah jumped.

"Ignore it," he said against her mouth.

"I can't," she said the same way.

"I won't let you go."

Her eyes opened. "Want to bet?" She slipped away from him, under his encircling arms, twisted to face the telephone and picked it up. "Dr. Marsdon," she gasped.

He put his arms around her waist, felt her lean against his shoulder as his fingers slid down her belly.

"Sarah, are you all right?" Mabel asked.

"Fine...Oh God."

"Sarah?"

She wrenched away from him, yanked at her jeans, then held a hand in front of her to keep him at bay. "I'm fine—" she cleared her throat "—just fine."

"Sorry to bother you. I know you're exhausted, but we just had an English bulldog come in. She's in labor. There's a pup hung up in the birth canal. She's going to need a cesarean."

Sarah took a deep breath. "Be right there." She dropped the phone into its cradle and leaned against the wall. "Emergency. Go home, take Nasdaq. I'm busy." She opened the door and started down the hall. "And thanks again for dinner."

Mark leaned his head against the doorjamb while he tried to get his breathing back to normal. Maybe Sarah could switch on and off like a water spigot. He couldn't. His entire body ached with longing for her.

He hadn't felt this sort of thing for a woman since high school. Hell, he'd never felt like this about any woman, even then. He wanted her—to bury his face in her hair, to feel her open and warm and waiting for him. He wanted to take her to the moon—way beyond the moon. Beyond the galaxy, even. He wanted to transport her to someplace where no other man would ever be able to reach her.

He sighed and went to get Nasdaq.

"I DON'T KNOW why on earth they bred English bull-dogs so that they can't deliver their pups normally," Nancy said.

"Because that's the look the showring judges pin the blue ribbons on," Sarah said. "Now their loins are so narrow and the pups' heads are so big that they can't possibly handle a normal delivery. Scalpel, Nancy."

"Right here."

"Everybody ready? Towels? Whelping box?"

"Ready, Doctor."

"Then it's showtime."

Sarah made a single incision. Nancy began swabbing the blood away. Sarah reached in, found the first pup and brought it out. She handed it off instantly to Nancy, who cut and disinfected the cord, then wrapped the pup, who was already coughing and sputtering, in a towel and began to rub it fiercely.

"Okay, that takes care of the one that was stuck. Look at the size of him! No telling how many there are. I hope no more than four," Sarah said. Again she reached inside, and again she brought out a puppy. She repeated the process twice, each time handing off to Nancy. Sarah could hear the puppies mewling and whimpering in the assistant's capable hands. "We're running out of time," she said as she reached for the final pup. This one lay small and limp in her hands. "Damn!" she said. She turned the baby upside down and shook it, then reached into its mouth to clear it of any obstruction. "Come on, drat you, breathe!" She lay the pup down on the table and began CPR on its tiny chest.

"Here, let me take over," Nancy said. "You go ahead and close."

Sarah glanced her thanks and finished working on the

bulldog. She irrigated, then began to close up the incision. She worked quickly and smoothly.

"How's she doing?" Sarah asked her anesthesiologist.

"Fine so far."

"You can switch her to oxygen. I'm just about finished." She bandaged the mother, then turned the rest of the task over to Nancy. "How's the little one?"

"Breathing, thanks to you, but she's pretty small."

Sarah stroked the small head with one gloved finger. "We'll have to supplement the feeds if we want her to thrive. She'll never be able to compete with her siblings."

"Momma's waking up," Nancy said to Sarah.

"Okay, let's move her in the whelping box with the pups. But she's so heavy, somebody needs to watch her so that she doesn't roll over and crush one of them. Where's the owner?"

"In the waiting room, probably pacing."

"Call him in."

The owner was in his mid-fifties, balding, square and beefy—and he looked so much like his English bulldog that Sarah nearly laughed out loud. He was mopping his balding head and his sweaty face.

"Is my sweet baby all right?" he whispered.

"Come see," Sarah said.

He looked into the box. "Oh, sweet baby, Daddy is so proud of you! Five babies! Oh, you're such a good girl!"

The bulldog looked up at him, then put her head back down and closed her eyes. All five of the little blind pups had now found a teat and were slurping fiercely, their tiny paws scrabbling rhythmically against their mother's side.

"Is she going to be all right?"

"She should be," Sarah said. "Cesarean sections are pretty hard on a dog. I do hope you weren't planning on breeding her on her next heat, were you?"

The owner looked horrified. "I'm no puppy mill, Doctor. My sweet baby is my best friend. I'd never do anything to hurt her." He looked down at her with tears in his eyes. "I just wanted to breed her once because she's not as young as she was—well, who is? And I couldn't bear to lose her, but I thought if I could have one of her daughters, well, maybe I could, you know, endure being without her when the time came." He stroked the brown head. "Not that I ever want it to, sweet baby."

"I'm glad you feel that way. And you know, I'm sure they'll all be beautiful pups, but if I were you, I think I'd hang on to that little runt. She's small, but she's one tough little cookie. I think she'll do you proud." She patted his shoulder.

"Thank you, Doctor." He reached a tentative finger down and touched the downy head of the tiny pup. She immediately turned around and latched onto the tip of his finger. He laughed. "Look at that, would you! Doctor, you may be right."

Sarah gave her staff a thumbs-up sign and walked out into the hall.

THE REST OF SARAH'S shift was amazingly quiet. Too quiet if the clinic wanted income. She walked into the stall of the mare who had had colic surgery and leaned her head against the horse's shoulder to inhale the smell of clean horseflesh and feel the warmth that never ceased to seep into her bones and relax her.

"Old lady," she whispered to the mare, "what am I

going to do about the money man?'' The mare shifted her weight and leaned in to Sarah. "I understand his problems, but I wish he'd let up a little, see the benefits instead of the cost.'' Sarah scratched the mare's ears and got a small sigh for her trouble.

"The problem is that he makes my hormones go nuts the same way yours do when you see a really sexy stallion. But I can't just ignore the consequences and let nature take its course. You just enjoy the experience and get a foal out of it. It's not nearly as simple for me.''

She gave the mare's ears one final scratch, checked the incision, which was healing nicely, and walked back to Mark's office, where she took possession of his desk chair. She leaned back, let her head fall against the back of his chair, and allowed her mind to drift. Unfortunately, the thoughts that came did not give her the peace she sought.

Sighing, she got up, walked into the small-animal ICU to check on the progress of Mac's rottweiler—and almost fell over Mac. She could swear he'd said he was going home.

He slept on the floor on a double air mattress that was used for large dogs. Beside him slept the rottweiler, her splinted leg and hip stuck out at an angle. Sarah smiled and shut the door softly. So much for Mac Thorn, tough guy.

She ran into Jack on her way to her truck.

"I'll walk you out,'' he said, and took her arm.

He came to her collarbone, but she could feel the sinews in his hand. "No need.''

"So long as those little blighters are running about causing trouble, I'm walking you out, Doctor.''

No blighters, no incidents on her way home. She fell

into bed, less exhausted than on previous nights. A bad sign—less exhaustion meant less business.

WHEN SHE WALKED IN the following afternoon and checked with the front desk, Alva Jean handed her an envelope.

"Party time!" she said cheerfully. "And Egg Roll is in room three waiting to have his dressing changed."

"Thanks." Sarah walked down the hall while she opened the envelope.

Before she got to the examining room, the door to Rick's office opened and he stuck his head out. "Thought I heard you." He pointed at the envelope. "Party, tomorrow night, my house. Celebration!" He wiggled his eyebrows.

"What are we celebrating?"

"The animal refuge signed the contract. We are now the official veterinary service for their sick and injured animals. Bill is over the moon about it."

"That's great."

"He's in the back playing with his eagle as we speak. I was just on my way to give him a hand."

"What's the prognosis?"

"Good about health. Guarded about his ability to fly again, although Bill swears he should be able to."

"And if not?"

"He'll wind up in a teaching program for kids."

"Great. After I take care of Egg Roll, I'll go see Bill and give him my congratulations."

The new contract should give the clinic some extra money, and she knew darn well where she expected those dollars to go.

Thirty minutes later she walked out into the backyard to find Bill, Rick and Mark all standing outside the newly completed flight cage, watching an immature bald eagle hop around and flap his wings.

"Fly, damn you!" Bill snarled. The eagle regarded him with angry yellow eyes.

Bill was the exact opposite of the sleek birds he adored: only five foot seven and almost completely round. He smoothed his thinning hair over his scalp and blew a long breath.

"I know he can do it if he tries," Bill said plaintively. "The wing is healed, the bones are knit perfectly. We've exercised those wings to build up the muscles. He should be ready. He's been spreading and flapping for a week. He's waddling around just to torment me. I swear, I don't think he's got the balls to try."

Sarah laughed. "I don't think it's testosterone, Bill. He's so used to not being able to fly, he may simply have forgotten how to lift off. Don't they usually learn out of a high nest?"

"I don't happen to have any thousand-foot cliffs handy."

"You do have a perch pole. There ought to be a ladder around somewhere. Maybe if we set him up there and coax him with food, he'll fly down to get it."

"And if he flops, then we'll know," Rick said. "You did a great job, but it's always iffy with birds who've been shot—you know that."

"I ought to. I've failed often enough. Fly, drat you!"

Mark found a ladder left lying beside the back door by one of the painters. Bill opened the door and shooed the annoyed eagle out of the way. The eagle flapped wildly, but did not take flight.

"Can you manage?" Mark asked.

"He weighs about twenty pounds, but he's my baby, and I'm the one with the leather glove."

Bill spent five minutes chasing the bird on foot before he managed to snag it in his net. He climbed to the top of the perch pole, while Marvin protested with infuriated shrieks. When Bill set him carefully into the nest box, Marvin jabbed at him with his beak.

"Bill, watch out!" Sarah shouted, as the bird's beak missed Bill's ear by less than an inch.

Bill came down the ladder faster than he'd gone up. He left the ladder in place and backed out of the cage. The bird sat and stared at him malevolently. "Okay, Marvin, fly or flop." Bill picked up a piece of raw liver from a bucket and tossed it into the cage.

The eagle cocked his head, turned his back and ignored them all.

"Come on, Marvin!" Bill urged. "You can do it!"

After a few seconds, the bird turned around, stared at the liver, then launched himself. The flight was clumsy, but it was flight—real flight.

"Yes!" Bill said. The others clapped him on the back.

"Look," Sarah said. Liver in beak, Marvin lifted off with a great flapping of wings, and took his prize back to the nest box.

"Thank God," Bill said, and burst into tears.

The other three left Bill leaning on the wire of the cage, cajoling the bird into another flight.

Sarah followed Mark into his office and shut the door behind her. He realized she was there and reached for her. She eluded him artfully.

"Down boy. This is business—absolutely all that there is going to be between us."

"Ever, or just until I come through with your equipment?"

She recoiled. "I can't believe you said that."

"I was kidding, dammit!"

"Didn't sound like kidding. But about the equipment…"

"I'm working on it."

"We've just signed a big contract. Big enough so that Rick's having a party to celebrate. Surely that gives us enough money."

"It certainly helps, but we're still a long way from profitability."

Sarah took a deep breath. "Fine. Just don't get between me and Coy Buchanan at that party." She walked out.

Mark sank into his chair. Nasdaq hopped up on his lap and curled into a ball. Mark looked down at his navy trousers and sighed as he scratched her ears. He knew Coy wouldn't cough up another dime at this point.

Still, something would have to give if Mark wanted Sarah to stop considering him an adversary.

CHAPTER NINE

"SLUT!" a raspy voice shouted.

Sarah blinked. A large scarlet macaw sat on the shoulder of a broad woman with a flat face and embarrassed eyes.

"I'm so sorry," she whispered. "Wilbur, behave yourself with the nice doctor."

"*Fat* slut!" the parrot said decisively.

"Wilbur, stop that!" The woman turned to Sarah. "My ex-husband thought it would be funny to teach him to cuss. Normally Wilbur only does it when he's nervous and upset."

"He's very beautiful. What's wrong with him?"

"He just has to have his bill trimmed, is all."

The parrot rotated his entire head so that he looked at Sarah upside down. "*Fat, fat* slut!"

As Sarah reached for a towel to wrap him in so that she could safely trim his beak, he began to bounce up and down on Mrs. Johnson's shoulder while he whined, "Fat slut, fat slut, fat slut."

"Does he say anything else?" Sarah asked as she gathered him up.

He squawked wordlessly as she snipped off the sharp point of his bill, although Sarah knew it was no more painful than trimming fingernails.

"You don't want to know," Mrs. Johnson said. "That's why he's my *ex*-husband."

Her next patient was as quiet as the macaw had been noisy. So was her owner, a fragile lady who might be any age from seventy to ninety. At the moment, she and the big Siamese queen on the table looked very much the worse for wear.

Sarah checked her chart. "Mrs. Morrison? How can I help Ping Ping today?"

Mrs. Morrison covered her face with her hands and began to sob. Ping Ping looked up at the sound, and Sarah realized the cat was blind. Her eyes were milky, but her ears stood up alertly, and she uttered an unmistakable Siamese squall. Mrs. Morrison's tiny veined hands began to stroke her fur tenderly.

"I want you to put her to sleep."

"I see." She took a deep breath. "Do you mind if I check her over first?" Sarah listened to the cat's heart, felt all over her body, stroked her sleek hair that had been brushed to a high sheen. "May I ask why?"

Mrs. Morrison snapped, "Can't you see? She's blind! And she's old." The tears coursed down Mrs. Morrison's cheeks. "Like me."

"She's blind, all right, but she has whiskers. Does she bump into things?"

"Of course not! She finds her way perfectly in my house. She never goes outside."

"Her heart and lungs are strong. Is she eating?"

"I wish I had her appetite."

"Then why…"

"I've sold my house. I have to move into a retirement community."

"And they won't take cats?"

"Oh, yes, they'll take cats—I wouldn't have gone anywhere that wouldn't, but my daughter says she'll be so unhappy in a new place and she won't be able to find her way around."

"I see." Sarah stroked the Siamese, who began to purr like a well-oiled Ferrari. "Well, Mrs. Morrison, I'm afraid you've come to the wrong person."

Mrs. Morrison blinked. "But..."

"How old is she?"

"Fourteen."

"Siameses can happily live to eighteen or twenty. Her heart and lungs are strong, she's eating, her coat is beautiful, she's in good flesh, she seems perfectly content. Frankly, I have no intention of putting down a perfectly healthy, happy cat. I'm sorry."

Mrs. Morrison opened her eyes wide. "But my daughter says..."

Sarah wanted to say *the hell with your daughter*. Instead she said mildly, "Your daughter isn't a veterinarian. If Ping Ping were in pain, or sick, or dying, I'd be the first to put her out of her misery. But, Mrs. Morrison, this—" she reached down and scratched behind Ping Ping's ears "—is a healthy middle-aged cat. And if you want her put down, you'll have to find somebody else to do it."

"Oh, you mean it? Really?" Mrs. Morrison scooped Ping Ping up in her arms and buried her face in the soft caramel-colored fur. "She doesn't have to die?"

"Not on my watch. You can ask your daughter to call me if she wants confirmation."

Mrs. Morrison drew herself up to her five-foot-nothing height, and her eyes blazed. "Don't you worry about that. That daughter of mine may have made me sell my house, but I'll be damned if she'll make me get rid of my cat." She opened the door to the kitty carrier that sat on the table beside her. "Now you just come along, Miss Ping Ping. You and I are about to take back control of our lives.''

Grumbling, the cat entered the cage, and only yowled once when the door was shut.

''Want me to carry her to the car for you? She's quite an armload.''

''I carried her in, Doctor, and I'll carry her out.'' Mrs. Morrison raised her chin. ''I can't thank you enough. You've given us both a new lease on life.''

''Hang on to it,'' Sarah said. ''And don't forget to bring Ping Ping back in November for her shots.'' She leaned against the door and laughed. ''That's one for our side!''

Mark stuck his head out of his office door. ''What's one for our side?''

''I have just cost this clinic at least seventy-five dollars and I couldn't be happier about it.'' She started down the hall toward examining room four.

''Hey, wait a minute—'' Mark reached for her arm.

''I am fast coming to the conclusion that most families are generally a bunch of interfering control freaks whose sole business in life is to make you happy the way they want you to be happy, and the hell with what you want for yourself.''

''What brought that on?''

''A cussing parrot and a blind Siamese cat. Now, if you'll excuse me, I've got a Chihuahua with a severe allergy to grass.''

THE IDEA that people could actually swim in an outdoor pool at the end of April was almost beyond Sarah's comprehension. The Hazard's pool was heated, but even so, she'd never have been able to do this in St. Paul. When she'd first arrived at Rick's party, she'd planned

PLAY THE
Lucky Key Game
and get

HOW TO PLAY:

1. With a coin, carefully scratch off gold area at the right. Then check the claim chart to see what we have for you — **2 FREE BOOKS** and a **FREE GIFT** — **ALL YOURS FREE!**

2. Send back the card and you'll receive two brand-new Harlequin Superromance® novels. These books have a cover price of $4.99 each in the U.S. and $5.99 each in Canada, but they are yours to keep absolutely free.

3. There's no catch. You're under no obligation to buy anything. We charge nothing —ZERO — for your first shipment. And you don't have to make any minimum number of purchases — not even one!

4. The fact is, thousands of readers enjoy receiving books by mail from the Harlequin Reader Service®. They enjoy the convenience of home delivery...they like getting the best new novels at discount prices, BEFORE they're available in stores...and they love their *Heart to Heart* subscriber newsletter featuring author news, horoscopes, recipes, book reviews and much more!

5. We hope that after receiving your free books you'll want to remain a subscriber. But the choice is yours — to continue or cancel, any time at all! So why not take us up on our invitation, with no risk of any kind. You'll be glad you did!

YOURS FREE!
A SURPRISE MYSTERY GIFT

We can't tell you what it is...but we're sure you'll like it! A **FREE GIFT—** just for playing the LUCKY KEY game!

Visit us online at
www.eHarlequin.com

FREE GIFTS!

NO COST! NO OBLIGATION TO BUY!
NO PURCHASE NECESSARY!

PLAY THE
Lucky Key Game

Scratch gold area with a coin.
Then check below to see the gifts you get!

336 HDL DC60
135 HDL DC6G

YES! I have scratched off the gold area. Please send me the 2 Free books and gift for which I qualify. I understand I am under no obligation to purchase any books, as explained on the back and on the opposite page.

NAME	(PLEASE PRINT CLEARLY)

ADDRESS

APT.#   CITY

STATE/PROV.   ZIP/POSTAL CODE

🗝🗝🗝🗝 2 free books plus a mystery gift   🗝🗝🗝🗝 1 free book

🗝🗝🗝 2 free books   🗝🗝🗝 Try Again!

(H-SR-OS-07/01)

The Harlequin Reader Service® — Here's how it works:

Accepting your 2 free books and gift places you under no obligation to buy anything. You may keep the books and gift and return the shipping statement marked "cancel." If you do not cancel, about a month later we'll send you 6 additional novels and bill you just $4.05 each in the U.S., or $4.46 each in Canada, plus 25¢ shipping & handling per book and applicable taxes if any.* That's the complete price and — compared to cover prices of $4.99 each in the U.S. and $5.99 each in Canada — it's quite a bargain! You may cancel at any time, but if you choose to continue, every month we'll send you 6 more books, which you may either purchase at the discount price or return to us and cancel your subscription.

*Terms and prices subject to change without notice. Sales tax applicable in N.Y. Canadian residents will be charged applicable provincial taxes and GST.applicable provincial taxes and GST.

simply to sit and watch others cavort, but after five minutes she longed to dive in herself.

Margot Hazard kept an assortment of suits for guests who had not brought their own. Sarah pulled on a plain black maillot and took a big beach towel from the stack in the pool house, walked across to the deep edge, checked for bobbing heads and dove in.

She broke the surface and began a long, slow crawl toward the other end of the pool. After a couple of strokes she noticed that someone was keeping pace with her, and turned her head.

Mark smiled at her. "Race you? Down and back?"

"I warn you, I was on the swim team in college."

"So was I."

Halfway back toward the deep end, Sarah realized that Mark was not only in much better physical shape than she was, he was a better tactician. He was waiting at the wall when she pulled up beside him.

He wasn't gasping. She was.

"Where's all the southern gentleman stuff I've heard so much about?" she managed to choke.

"Surely you didn't want me to hold back simply because you're a girl?"

"'Woman' to you, buster. I haven't done this in a while. You obviously have."

"I try to get in a few laps every week. Keeps me sane."

"Relatively speaking."

"What do you say we stop competing and just enjoy the water?"

"Sounds good." She pushed back from the wall without realizing that Bill was right behind her. They connected without damage, but she sank instantly. Before the top of her head had gone underwater, she felt a strong arm around her, as Mark pulled her up sputtering against his bare chest.

Instantly she was aware that the length of their bodies had melted together. She didn't dare look down at her nipples, which were already erect from the water, and which were now undoubtedly swollen, as well.

That wasn't the only body part that was reacting.

She pulled an arm's length away from Mark, and continued to tread water with one hand on the rim of the pool.

"Come home with me," he whispered.

"Now? And miss the steaks?" She tried to keep her tone light, but she thought she sounded as though she had swallowed a mouse.

"Afterward."

She shook her head. "I'm on call early tomorrow. I have to check George and Marian."

"I'll drive you over at five a.m. if that's what you want."

Heaven help her, it was very much what she wanted. She shook her head and pushed away from the wall. "I've got to get dressed."

"Come home with me." He began to swim slow circles around her.

"Not yet." Where on earth had that come from? "Not yet" meant there was a possibility. "Not yet" was a marker that could be called, an IOU for something that she still was not certain was a good idea.

Her body thought it was a good idea. It was screaming at her to pull off that swimsuit, climb into her jeans and T-shirt, and drag Mark off into the woods behind the Hazard house.

"Come home with me," he whispered.

Sarah closed her eyes.

"Come home with me."

She ducked under his arms and swam for the ladder.

"Down, woman," she whispered as she walked barefoot into the pool house to change. Nancy, who was walking past, glanced at her in surprise.

"Sure, Doc, whatever you say."

Sarah felt her face flush. She was reduced to talking to herself in public. Anyone with half an eye could see that there was something going on with Mark. And there couldn't be. At least, not until the equipment had been acquired. And maybe not even then. Mark was all wrong for her. Another Gerald. Another Dad. A manipulator—a nice one, but still a manipulator who didn't understand her drive to run her own life.

Ten minutes later she came out dressed, her wet hair in a French braid. The evening was drawing in and growing chilly. She was glad she'd brought a jacket. She could smell the heavenly aroma of steaks on Rick's grill, and see his ruddy face above the leaping flames. He wore shorts, a T-shirt that read Creature Comfort and an apron with the words Kiss the Cook.

She walked to the bar that had been set up on the far side of the pool and asked the uniformed barman for a diet soda, then looked back at the crowd. The staff of Creature Comfort wasn't large, but with wives and children the group tonight was a fair-size one. With steaks for everyone, a barman and a server, it must have cost a pretty penny.

Certainly morale was important, but Sarah could have put that money to much better use—

"Hey, sweet thing, don't think I've met you yet."

Sarah turned toward a tall, broad man with a shock of silver hair, a neatly trimmed gray beard, and the face of a cowboy who has spent his life riding the range.

"I'm Coy, Margot's daddy." He stuck out a big brown hand and enfolded Sarah's fingers. His eyes, hazel and warm, crinkled at the corners. But he didn't look like a man who could be trifled with.

She introduced herself. No wonder Beth had a crush on him. He had that Clint Eastwood force of personality that couldn't be diluted by age.

"Nice party," she said lamely.

He grinned. "Margot always puts the big pot in the little one." He grinned at her confused expression. "Old southern saying. Haven't a clue what it means." He rumbled a deep belly laugh.

"Daddy? You come on over here and sit down so I can serve you a plate," Margot said from behind Sarah. She gave Sarah a social smile and slipped her hand under her father's arm. "Rick's got the best steak all picked out for you. Well done, just the way you like it."

Margot must have had a lot of practice protecting "Daddy." Sarah had no idea how long he had been a widower, but a good-looking rich man like that must be like catnip to every female between eighteen and eighty.

Margot apparently had no intention of sharing Daddy with a stepmother who might put other demands on his time and his pocketbook. Poor Beth. She was going to have to work hard to get past Daddy's little darling.

"Neat, wasn't it?" Beth whispered.

Sarah could hear the edge of anger and—what, contempt?—in her voice. "Very."

"I just wish he'd see through her, but he won't. I've tried to make her like me, but her antennae go up every time she sees us together. And he's so damn dumb."

"Well, she's not at the office every day, is she?"

"No. That's the only hope I've got."

"Keep it up. He seems like a man who deserves something more than a daughter."

"You got that right."

"Steak's on!" Rick shouted. "Come and get it."

Sarah avoided sitting with Mark. She sat with Mabel Halliburton, Sol Weincroft, who talked nonstop about his research into the Equine Infectious Anemia vaccine, and Liz Carlyle and her engineer husband.

Sarah was aware with every molecule of her being that Mark watched her from the far side of the pool. She found herself laughing a little too loud, sitting a bit too straight, making certain she held her stomach in. She kept losing track of the conversation.

As soon as she could, she took her plate and dishes to the trash barrel and went to say goodbye to Margot and Rick.

"Oh, leaving so soon?" Margot asked.

"Yeah. We've barely gotten started," Rick said.

"Sorry. I guess I'm still not adjusted to my schedule. Lovely party, Margot. Thanks for having the swimsuits."

"Of course, dear, although I probably should have bought a few larger sizes."

Ouch! Sarah smiled and went to find her truck.

Mark met her at the parking area. "Running out?"

"Yes. And not with you."

"Sure about that?"

"Absolutely sure. It's not a good idea to mix business with pleasure. Leads to all sorts of complications. And you don't want to capture a girl on the rebound, do you?"

"You warned me you're not a girl, and I'll take you on the rebound or any way I can get you."

"Not tonight. I'm spending my first night in my new

house. I think I ought to spend it alone. Go back to the party.''

''At least kiss me.''

''With everybody watching? I don't think so.''

She ducked under his arms and climbed into her truck. ''Have fun.''

''Not without you.''

Her cell phone rang before she pulled out of the driveway. ''Dr. Marsdon.''

''Dinner tomorrow night in a real sit-down restaurant with tablecloths?''

She laughed. ''All right, Mark. You're on. But I warn you, I'm an expensive date.''

''Try me. I'll pick you up at your new house about seven.''

''Fine.''

She hung up and turned on the radio to hear Carole King's ''You Make Me Feel like a Natural Woman.'' She sang along at the top of her lungs.

MARK REALIZED when Sarah walked in the door to the restaurant the following night that he'd never seen her in a dress. Certainly not a sexy little black number that skimmed her curves and ended just at her knee. He went to meet her. ''You've grown.''

She showed her foot. ''Three-inch heels will do that to you.''

''Do we actually have to stay and eat?'' He reached for her.

''You promised me dinner. Besides, wouldn't they look at us strangely if we turned around and left?''

''I promised you dinner before you came through that door and my hormones started dancing a jig. If you had let me pick you up at your new house, we might never have gotten this far.''

Sarah smiled. ''Riiiight. Also I'm on call tonight for emergencies. I hope I won't need my truck, but if I do, I don't want to have to drive halfway across town to my house to pick it up.''

''There will be no emergencies.''

Sarah sat down and looked at the white tablecloth, the candlelight, and the enormous menu that the waiter put into her hands. ''I hope you're right. Feed me enough champagne and caviar, you might overrule my good intentions.''

''How about a good white wine and something very French?''

''Sounds great, but only one glass of wine, I'm afraid.''

''You're on call. I remember.'' He tried to put on a long face, but realized he was smiling.

The soft candlelight gilded her hair, and when she looked up at him from beneath those long, dark lashes, her eyes were the deepest indigo. When she began to nibble at her shrimp remoulade, he couldn't catch his breath for watching her lips.

''So how are George and Marian?'' he asked, simply to make conversation and cover the silence that stretched too long.

''The bull terriers? Marian's fine. George has developed a bit of fever, but that's to be expected. He's on antibiotics. Mac says he should be past the worst by Tuesday. Marian can probably go home tomorrow, although whether she can manage without grieving for George is hard to say. How's Nasdaq?''

''Having separation anxiety. I refuse to hire Mabel to baby-sit my dog.''

"Nasdaq's still afraid you won't come home. Give her time."

"I still say she needs a family."

"Mabel's looking," Sarah said, although she didn't think Mabel was looking very hard.

The waiter set Greek salads down in front of them.

"Marvelous! I love olives," Sarah said, and dug in—just as her cell phone began to shrill.

"Don't answer it."

"I have to." She dug it out of her evening bag, held a whispered conversation, then dropped it back into her purse.

"Sorry, Mark," Sarah said. "I seem destined never to eat a well-prepared dinner in a decent restaurant. I have to go. It's an emergency. I hope I can find the place. The directions weren't too good."

"I'll drive you."

"No, really, stay and finish your dinner."

"Don't be ridiculous. You're not going in those clothes, are you?"

"I'll change in the truck."

"And either have a wreck or cause one. Come on." Mark threw a couple of bills on the table and spoke to the waiter, as Sarah rushed out in front of him.

"I'll drive," he said, when he caught up.

"Thanks. Here are the directions—" Sarah handed him her keys and a slip of paper.

He switched on the dome light and read them. "I know where this is, but we'll be at least half an hour getting there, even if I break speed limits."

"Do the best you can." Sarah was already rummaging in a beat-up gym bag on the back seat. "And keep your eyes on the road." She switched off the dome light, as Mark backed the truck out.

He didn't want to watch the road. He wanted to watch Sarah. She was wriggling out of her little black dress. Then she took off her shoes and stripped off her panty hose.

"Eyes front, buster," she said as she caught him glancing over at her.

"You're asking a lot, Doctor."

They pulled up to a traffic light, and an eighteen-wheeler stopped beside them in the outside lane. Mark looked up and caught a glimpse of the driver's startled expression and then his wolfish grin. He had an instant desire to smash the guy's face, but Sarah merely lifted her hand and waggled her fingers at him.

As the light turned green and they moved off, the trucker flashed his lights at them several times.

"You made *his* day," Mark snapped.

"I've got on more clothes than I'd have on at a beach."

"It's not the same. Believe me, it is not nearly the same." He could feel the heat on the back of his neck spread to his loins.

"Can't you go any faster?" Sarah asked as she leaned over the back seat to rummage once more in her bag.

"Hell, I have to drive the speed limit. No cop would believe this."

He turned his head to find his face inches away from an extremely shapely bottom in a pair of black lace bikini panties. He nearly drove off the road.

"Hey! Watch it!"

"I'm trying not to," he whispered as he pulled the car back off the shoulder.

She wriggled and swore, and the next time he dared

to look at her, she wore shapeless greens and was tying her running shoes.

He turned into the gates of Smallwood Angus Farm, drove past the columned mansion, and around to the barn in back. A tall man in jeans and a maroon pajama top covered with black hearts stood at the door of the barn. The smell of cow manure hit Mark when he parked and opened his door. Sarah didn't seem to notice.

"Got the calf out already, Doc," the man said to Mark.

"I'm Dr. Marsdon," Sarah said mildly. "You're Mr. Andrews?"

"Right."

"How badly is the uterus prolapsed?"

"You better come see."

As they walked into the barn, another man raised his head from one of the stalls at the far end. "I got the calf in here."

"Where's the cow?" Andrews asked.

"Hell, she run right over me. She's out in the back lot."

"How'd you let her do a stupid thing like that?"

"I had my hands full with this calf."

"Damn," Sarah whispered. "We don't have much time to put that uterus back in place."

"You the doc?" the second man asked. He didn't look convinced, especially when he saw Mark standing behind her in his elegantly tailored sports jacket and slacks.

"Dr. Marsdon," Sarah said. "Now let's catch that cow, shall we?"

Mark could hear the exasperation she was trying to conceal.

She turned to Mark. "Stay here. This is a pretty messy business."

He followed her to the rear door of the barn. Outside, a large black cow wandered around the small lot nibbling at grass. She seemed utterly unconcerned that she was trailed by a mass of bloody flesh.

"Quiet now," Sarah said. "Get a rope around her head. Whatever you do, don't spook her."

"Sure. We done this a million times," the smaller man said.

"Right."

"Easy, now, old girl," said Andrews as he inched closer to the cow, who raised her head for a moment before continuing to munch.

The two men approached the cow casually. She allowed them to get within two feet of her, then, without warning, bucked and bolted.

"No!" Sarah shouted. "Oh God!"

The bloody mass now lay on the ground, detached from the cow.

"Damnation," Andrews snapped. "Earl, I warned you not to spook her."

"Wadn't my fault."

"She done stepped on it and tore it right out." Andrews sighed. "Well, we got us a fine little calf, anyway, and she's not a young cow. Probably woulda culled her this year, anyway."

"Bring me a pistol," Sarah said quietly. "Now!"

"Hell, woman, I can shoot one of my own damn cows."

"Either you do it or I do it, but somebody does it right this minute."

Mark had never heard Sarah speak in that tone. Earl, the one who had caused the problem in the first place, ran into the barn and returned two minutes later carrying a revolver that looked as though it might have been used by Billy the Kid. Mark was familiar with guns, had shot targets most of his life, but he never took them casually. Despite the gun's size, it was probably a long-barreled .22.

"Give it to me," Sarah said.

"I said I'd shoot her." Andrews stepped in front of her and took the gun.

The tall man turned on his heel, and from ten feet away shot at the cow's head. The report racketed around the small space. Mark could see the spurt of flame from the muzzle and smell the cordite in the smoke that eddied up from the barrel.

The cow stared at the man and continued to chew, completely unfazed by the shot.

"Hell, I know I hit her," the man said, and let fly another shot.

Sarah jumped. Mark jumped. For all he knew, the cow jumped. But there was no evidence that she was even aware of the man who was trying to assassinate her.

Sarah strode to the man and held out her hand. "Give me the gun, please." It was a command, not a request.

Sheepishly, the man offered her the butt of the pistol. She squared her shoulders, walked directly in front of the cow, held the barrel close to the cow's skull between its eyes, and pulled the trigger.

The cow sank instantly onto her haunches and rolled over. Sarah looked down at her, then took the gun to the man and handed it to him.

"While I'm here, shall I check the calf?" she asked calmly.

"Yes, ma'am, if you would."

Sarah nodded, and all four walked into the barn. Mark spared a glance at the carcass behind him. She'd done the job as she did everything else, with quiet professionalism.

The same way she checked the calf, gave it a couple of shots, pronounced it in excellent health and walked toward the front of the barn.

"We'll get that calf nursing on another cow," Andrews said. "Won't be no trouble. If not, we'll bottle-feed it. It's a finc heifer." He followed Sarah to her truck. She climbed into the passenger seat. Before she could shut the door, the man said, "Thanks, Doc. Wadn't none of this your fault. Earl shoulda kept her up 'til you got here."

"Outcome still might have been the same," Sarah said, turning to him.

"Might. Might not. Our fault, not yours. And Doc, thanks for—you know."

Sarah nodded.

As Mark backed out and turned around to start the trek down the road toward the highway, he glanced at Sarah. She sat stone-faced, her jaw set in a hard line.

"Can you tell me why you had to shoot her?" Mark asked.

She took a deep breath. "Sometimes when a cow calves, the entire uterus comes out with the calf. Doesn't bother her, and most of the time we can pop it back in if it's done soon enough. If those idiots had kept that cow inside in the stall where I could have worked on her, I could have saved her."

"Why couldn't you?"

She turned to him, and her voice had risen dangerously. "Didn't you see? She stepped on it, tore it out. She might have walked around for half an hour or longer, but she was as good as dead. All the veins and arteries that supply blood to the calf started pouring blood into her insides. Didn't matter that we couldn't see it, and that she couldn't feel it. She was bleeding to death. There wasn't a thing I, or anyone else, could do to save her.''

''So you put her out of her misery.''

''Somebody had to. And that idiot thought that because he was a big macho man with a big, big gun, he could do it and show off to the little lady what a tough guy he was. But there's only one spot between the eyes that's vulnerable. He could have shot her in the skull a dozen times, and still not gotten the job done. Meanwhile, she'd have bled to death slowly. I knew what I was doing and I did it. End of story. Happens all the time. Part of the job.''

Something in her tone alerted him. He pulled to the side of the road. She hunched against the passenger window with her arms locked around her body.

''I hate it! Damn death! Dammit, dammit, dammit!''

He reached for her, pulled her into his arms. She fought him, struggled against him, tried to get her arms up, but he held on hard, felt her thighs twist against his, her breasts strain against his chest.

Little by little her body began to relax. He could feel her muscles loosen. She wrapped her arms around his neck and clung to him as he stroked her back.

''It wasn't your fault,'' he whispered into her hair.

''She was a perfectly healthy cow. That's what I can't stand.''

''You helped her the only way you could.''

''It shouldn't be the only way, don't you see?'' She raised her tear-stained face for a moment, then hid it against his shoulder once more. ''I've done this sort of thing a hundred times, and anytime it's a healthy animal, it always gets to me. I know death is a part of life. God knows, I ought to, I've seen enough of it." She pulled away from him. This time he let her go. She stared out the window.

"The old ones, the sick ones, most of the time they let you know when they want to go. It's as if one morning they wake up and say, 'Hey, I don't want to do this any longer.' I help them let go, leave the pain and the arthritis and the congestive heart failure and the cancer behind. I'm fulfilling the contract we all sign when we take on the responsibility for any animal. We agree to love them and to care for them, and when at last they don't want to do it anymore, we make that easy and gentle for them, too, so they're not afraid, so they don't have to be tired or hurt any longer. It's more than we do for human beings."

"Tonight was different."

"Different because I might have saved her if I had gotten there sooner, or if that idiot hadn't let her run over him. She wasn't old or tired or in pain. She didn't even know she was dying. I couldn't save her, and so I killed her." She turned her face toward the glass and whispered, "I killed her."

"You said nobody could have saved her. You did the right thing, the only thing. Part of that contract."

"I know that intellectually, but it doesn't help make me feel good about it. Things ought to have worked out better." She sniffled.

He handed her his handkerchief. "I know."

"I'm sorry," she said, and blew her nose. "It's just that every time I fail like that, it's like I failed my mother all over again."

"You lost your mother?"

She nodded. "I have three brothers," she said bitterly, "but Lars Marsdon wanted a basketball team. So my mother tried to give him one.

"She got pregnant the last time when I was ten. That time, when she miscarried, they couldn't stop the bleeding—" Her voice broke.

Mark closed his eyes. Just like tonight, then. Watching the cow bleed to death that way, having to put it out of its misery, must have brought everything back.

"I never got to say goodbye," she whispered. "They wouldn't let me onto the OB-Gyn floor because I wasn't sixteen."

"I'm so sorry," Mark said, and touched her arm. She leaned against him, let him encircle her, press her against his side. She seemed drained, worn out.

"That's why I went to vet school," she said. "I didn't think I could ever deal with people, but I thought I could help animals."

"Your family must be proud."

She laughed and sat up. "My father hates what I do. As a matter of fact, he has always hated everything I did that took me away from home. He's furious at me for moving down here and depriving him of a rich son-in-law."

"You blame him for your mother's death?"

"Of course I do. He didn't give a damn whether she was risking her health to get his Scandinavian bruisers. Lars Marsdon gets what he wants, and when he doesn't, he roars. He was mad as hell at her for dying on him and leaving me to look after him and my three brothers."

"They have names, your brothers?"

"Sure. Nels, Lars Jr. and Peter. They're all at least as tall as you are, blond, blue-eyed, and with necks the size of a full-grown caribou's. They're all married to beautiful blondes who are well on the way to giving Daddy his basketball team. They're extremely nice guys and I love them all, but with the exception of Peter, my kid brother, they don't understand why I'd want to leave the place I was born in. Nels and Lars Jr. are totally content with their lives and their careers."

"What about Peter?"

"I think he's starting to get a little wanderlust. He's an industrial engineer, so he could get a job someplace else."

"What about his wife?"

"I think Mary Ellen would like to live where the rest of the wives didn't know every move she makes. Besides, she'd follow Peter to Mars. She's different—she paints wonderful watercolors and doesn't let a little dust bother her. The other two think that keeping a spotless house and cooking wonderful meals are a woman's greatest joy. When they thought I was finally going to marry Gerald, they were thrilled. Now..."

He saw that the talking had given her time to get herself back under control. Then she turned her face away from him. He laid a hand on her thigh. He had no idea whether she'd leave it there. When she covered his hand with hers and actually grasped his fingers, he was surprised and touched.

"Come on, I'll drive you home."

"That's okay. Let's go get your car at the restaurant. I can drive myself home."

"No, you can't. Forget my car."

"What about Nasdaq?"

He sighed. He'd forgotten he had other responsibilities now. "Then, I drive you to my house, we let Nasdaq out, and I drive you home. I am not letting you loose on the highway tonight. That's final.''

"Who made you the Supreme Ruler of the Western Hemisphere?''

"I did.''

For a moment, he thought she'd keep fighting, but the fight seemed to have gone out of her. She leaned her head back against the headrest. "I will never get used to these things if I live to be a million years old.''

"No wonder.''

By the time he drove into his garage, he realized she was asleep. Most women over the age of fifteen looked less than glamorous when they slept, but she slept neatly, her face composed, her hands folded in her lap. He hated to wake her. The moment the ignition cut off, however, she blinked and sat up.

"Sorry.''

"Come on.'' He walked around to the passenger side and opened the door. "I don't know how long it will take Nasdaq. You can at least be comfortable.''

"Could I have a soda? My mouth is so dry.''

"Sure.''

Nasdaq greeted them with joy. She danced around their feet, until Sarah went to her knees and cuddled her. When Mark came back from letting Nasdaq out and getting Sarah's soda, he saw that she had stretched out on the sofa and fallen asleep.

He pulled the comforter and sheets down on his bed, then went into the living room and slid his hands under her shoulders and knees. With her balanced against his chest, her head tucked under his chin, her hair falling over his shoulder, he felt as if he could have held her forever.

Instead, he walked to the bed and slid her down onto

it. She whimpered. He loosened her shoes and took them off, then pulled the comforter over her. She made a small sound when Nasdaq jumped up and snuggled against her back.

"Let her sleep," he admonished the dog. He slipped off his own shoes, jacket and tie, took off his belt and loosened his collar. He lay down beside her and rolled over on his side so that he could watch her.

Tough Dr. Marsdon. She looked like a little girl. Her tears had left streaks in her makeup. Her eyes would probably be swollen in the morning, but at the moment the long dark lashes swept her cheeks. He could see they were still wet.

He thought about what she'd told him about her family. Her father must be some piece of work, and her brothers didn't sound as though they were much help. Had she been landed at age ten with all the duties of a housewife? And how had she finally broken loose to go to school? He didn't think her father would have paid for an education he obviously didn't believe in. Still, she'd managed somehow. And finally, she'd walked away to make her own life.

He realized now why she'd been so angry with him about the rental house. She'd obviously been fighting all her life for control over her own destiny. He'd pushed her buttons without even realizing he was doing it.

And he also understood why she was so damn bull-headed about the equipment she wanted. Anything that would give her an edge in alleviating pain, in helping an animal heal, was worth fighting for.

Somehow he'd have to get it for her.

CHAPTER TEN

IN THE DARKNESS he felt her arm slide across his body. She curled against him with a sigh.

How in hell was he supposed to endure this? To lie here against her—feel her soft breasts against his chest, her sweet breath against his lips, her belly and hips fitted against him—and not respond?

He *was* responding. His body had developed a mind of its own. The closer she nestled, the more he responded. He kissed her forehead, then her eyebrows, and finally her eyelids, which still tasted of her tears.

She sighed softly and opened her eyes. He expected her to pull away now that she was conscious, but she didn't. She tilted her face up to him.

"If you don't kiss me, Mark Scott, I think I'll scream."

"We can't have that, Doctor," he whispered, and kissed her. Her lips felt bruised and swollen, and tasted of tears, too. She opened to him at once, joining him, touching the soft places in his mouth that sent shivers through him.

He could feel her fingertips along his spine, the movement of her hips against his, hear the soft sighs as she curved into him.

"Make love to me," she said softly.

"Are you sure?" She seemed so vulnerable, almost as though she were drunk.

"Yes."

Nasdaq whined, then barked. The next moment she was trying to wriggle between them.

"She's scared you're hurting me," Sarah murmured against his lips.

"More like she's jealous. What do I do?" he whispered back, also without breaking the kiss.

"Put her in her kennel."

"Now?" He rolled away, picked up Nasdaq and carried her to the kitchen, crooning to her as he went. "It's okay, girl. I'm not hurting her. You be good, all right?"

The instant he shut her into her kennel and put her coverlet over the top, she began to whine.

"Hush!" He shut his bedroom door on her and dove for the bed. "Now, where were we?"

Nasdaq howled again. It started soft, but grew to a keen so powerful that it was as though a tornado warning had gone off in the next room.

"Drat that dog!" Mark pulled Sarah into his arms and beneath him.

She looked into his eyes. And laughed. He could feel her body quivering with laughter, see the tears squeezed out from her closed lids.

He wanted to howl in sheer frustration.

But Sarah's laughter was infectious. He found himself chortling, then laughing out loud. He dropped his head against her shoulder.

She wrapped her fingers in his hair and whispered, "This is not going to work."

"It's got to work, dammit! I want you, and finally you want me."

"Not with the police breaking down the door and hauling us off for disturbing the whole street."

He raised himself on his elbows. She grinned at him.

A cheerful, friendly, *neighborly* grin. The spell was broken. At least one of them was thinking clearly again.

"Take me home, please," Sarah said, and kissed him lightly on the nose. A friendly, *neighborly* kiss.

"No. I swear I'll kill that dog."

"You don't mean that."

"At this moment, I do." He sat up and rolled away from her. "Okay, we pick up my car, then I follow you home and leave Nasdaq here. She'll quiet down once we're gone. And we can take up where we left off, when I get you home."

"Not tonight."

She stroked his back. He shivered under the touch of her fingers. He'd never wanted a woman this badly in his life. It was more than want, more than need. He ached for her, and not just physically. He'd seen a side of her tonight that he'd never seen before. He glanced at her. A glance was all he dared. This beautiful, gentle woman who seemed so strong and was really so vulnerable.

"She's still crying," Sarah said, and went to the kitchen. "It's all right, Nasdaq. See? We're fine."

He heard Nasdaq's toenails click on the floor as she capered around Sarah and barked joyfully, and a moment later she landed full throttle in the middle of his stomach and began to lick his face.

"All right, Nasdaq! Don't push your luck!"

Sarah leaned against the doorjamb. "Get your shoes back on, mister. Oh, and bring Nasdaq with us to pick up your car. She'd enjoy the ride."

"And I'm driving home alone?"

"Right."

"Hell."

"Life sure can be."

ON SUNDAY MORNING Mark had hoped to read the newspaper in bed with Sarah, and make leisurely love all day. Instead, he went for a run with Nasdaq, who could run neither very far nor very fast. He ended up carrying her part of the way back. For a small dog, she grew extremely weighty by the time he put her down on his kitchen floor.

She was a very nice pup, but she obviously was not going to work out in his life. He wanted to keep her, but he also wanted Sarah. The two weren't compatible.

He called Sarah, got her answering machine. He called her cell phone and got a ''This customer is out of range'' message. Since he knew she wouldn't leave her phone anywhere except when she was at the clinic, that's where she must be.

He dropped Nasdaq on the front seat of his car and drove to the clinic, stopping only long enough to pick up an order of sausage biscuits and coffee at a drive-through. One biscuit for Nasdaq, two apiece for him and Sarah.

As he drove around the corner of the clinic, his headlights picked up a figure in black standing in front of the flight cage, where Marvin, the eagle, still slept with his head tucked under his wing. The instant the figure saw him, it bolted.

Mark floored the Jag and cut off the trespasser's escape. He slammed on his brakes and was out of the car almost before it stopped rolling.

''Not this time, buddy,'' he said, and launched himself. He caught the back of the collar of a leather jacket as he knocked whoever it was down.

''Hey, man, leggo!'' The voice was high and very frightened.

''Settle down!''

The body was thin, the muscles ropy. Male. Young. No more than fifteen or sixteen.

The kid squirmed and grunted, but Mark had him facedown, with his weight keeping him there. "Stay still. I'm not going to hurt you."

"Lemme go! I'm not doing anything."

"I got here too soon for you, didn't I. What were you going to do? Finish the job on that eagle?"

"No! No, man! I wanted to see it close up, is all. Lemme up!"

Mark stood in one fluid movement and dragged the kid up with him by the scruff of his jacket—a very expensive leather, from the feel of it. He spun the boy to face him.

Instantly the kid launched a knee toward Mark's groin.

"No, you don't!"

Then the kid tried to worm out of his jacket, but Mark took hold of his belt and his arm. "Settle down, I tell you."

Suddenly the fight went out of the boy. He hung limp.

Mark wasn't fooled. The instant he loosened his grip, the kid would be off like a shot.

"Are you Kenny?"

"How do you know my name, man?" Now the kid was really scared.

"You're responsible for the gash on my head."

"I never meant to hurt anybody, man. My foot slipped, and everything started rolling." He spoke breathlessly. "You gonna call the cops?"

"Any reason I shouldn't?"

"I didn't *do* anything!"

"I don't know. Assault with a deadly weapon..."

"What deadly weapon?"

"A ten-foot fence post."

"I told you it was an accident, swear to God."

"Plus malicious mischief, criminal trespass, and probably attempting to kill an endangered species."

"No! Man, he's beautiful! I been watching him ever since you put him in that cage. I been coming over every morning before school and every night after everybody leaves. I'm just checking on him, man. I don't want nothing to happen to him."

"Anything," Mark corrected.

"Yeah." Kenny looked over at Mark's car. "That your Jag? Cool."

"And my dog—and probably the remains of my sausage biscuits, if I know Nasdaq. Come on, Kenny, you and I are going to have a serious talk."

"Nasdaq? Funny name for a dog."

"Funny dog. Come on. If I let go of you, can I trust you not to run away?"

Kenny thought for a minute.

"I know your first name, I've seen your face, and I'm guessing you live in the neighborhood. I can track you down if I have to."

"Yeah, man, okay. Just don't call the cops, okay? My old man would kill me if I got picked up by the cops."

"Behave yourself, and we'll see."

He opened the car door with a wary eye on Kenny, and waited while Nasdaq jumped out. The pup capered over to the boy, who instantly dropped to his knees and began to fondle her ears.

"Hey, boy," Kenny said.

"Girl, actually. Come on."

He followed Kenny into the clinic and down the hall to his office. He didn't see Sarah, but he knew she was here somewhere because he'd passed her truck on his way in.

"Sit down," he said to Kenny. "And take off your jacket. It's too hot for leather."

"It's the only black jacket I got."

"The better to hide out in." Mark passed a cup of coffee across the table along with one of the sausage biscuits. "Have some breakfast."

"Why you being so nice?"

"Why are you and your friends being such ass-holes?"

Kenny looked away, and Mark saw redness creep up his already-mottled skin. He had a spray of pimples across his forehead and his nose. He'd probably be a good-looking guy in a couple of years, but right at the moment he was like a yearling colt—all appendages, and totally uncoordinated.

"You've done some major damage, you know," Mark said quietly. "Caused some construction delays that have cost the clinic money."

"My dad said you didn't have any right to be here," Kenny said, and flushed even deeper. "I mean, he said you're going to screw up the property values."

"I see. Property values are important to you, are they?"

"My dad says—"

"And your friends' dads. They say the same thing."

"Yeah. Tommy's dad's real mad. Says you'll make more flies around his swimming pool."

"And where does he live?"

Kenny shut his mouth hard.

Mark tried another tack. "Okay. So Tommy's dad and your dad and the other dads don't want us here. What do you think?"

Kenny looked away. After a minute he said, "I don't know."

"The eagle. You think it's going to lower property values?"

"No, man, the eagle's cool. But pigs and goats and cows and crap..."

"Did your dad happen to mention that there's a sizable Black Angus farm about a mile-and-a-half down the road? With a great many more cows than we'll ever have here at one time?"

Now Kenny began to sulk. "It's not the same, my dad says. I mean, it's been here a long time."

"And your family has been here since..."

"We moved in a year ago."

"And Tommy's family?"

"In December."

"So your families moved in after the clinic was approved and already being built."

"Yeah. I guess."

"So, assuming we do lower property values—which isn't the case, by the way—your families knew we were going to be a part of the community before they bought their houses."

"Yeah, but my dad thought puppies and kittens, you know? Not pigs."

"Pigs?"

"Man, I've seen a pig come in here."

Mark laughed. "Egg Roll? He's a pet Vietnamese pot-bellied pig. He probably lives a more civilized life than you do. If we have pigs or goats, the chances are pretty good we'll go to them rather than the other way around. You like animals, Kenny?"

Suddenly the boy became animated. "Yeah, man. I really like wild animals. I was out with my dad once when he was hunting and we saw this little raccoon and I wanted to bring it home, keep it as a pet, but my dad said it was probably rabid and its momma was probably around somewhere, so we left it.''

"It probably wasn't rabid, not in this area, but your father was right that its momma was probably still around. Did you enjoy hunting with your dad?''

"I like being out in the woods, but I don't think I could ever, like, you know, *kill* something. He says you've got to cull the deer population or they die of starvation, and I know that's true, but the one time I tried to shoot I missed, like totally, you know? And I'm great on targets. It's just different when you shoot and things wind up dead, you know?''

"I do, indeed. Do you like horses and cows?''

"I don't know much about cows, but I like horses. I go riding out at Shelby Farms sometimes. I wish I had a horse, but my dad says we can't keep one.''

"Would you like to help me feed Marvin?'' Mark looked at Kenny's confused face and smiled. "The eagle. He likes mice.''

Kenny acted very casual. "I don't care, man. I guess so.''

"Okay. Let's do it.'' He picked up the telephone on his desk and dialed a number. "Bill? Mark. Sorry to wake you. I'm at the clinic and I thought I'd save you a trip to feed Marvin.'' He listened and made a couple of notes. "Sure. Five mice. Thawed.'' He hung up. "Come on, Kenny. And if you try to run away, I promise I will find you. And I will bring the police.''

They left Nasdaq happily chewing on the remains of a sausage biscuit, walked into the exotic-animal area and took a paper sack from the refrigerator.

Mark handed the sack to Kenny. "You want gloves?"

"Gross!" Kenny said, then he looked up. "You mean, you want me to do it?"

"Sure. Open the small trap door, toss in the mice one at a time, and wait until Marvin flies down and eats them. Simple."

"Yeah. Okay. Hey, man, but gimme a pair of gloves, okay?"

Mark stood back and watched Kenny toss the eagle his mice, then hunker down beside the cage while Marvin took his time getting around to eating them.

"Come on, boy, come on. Gourmet mice. Get your nice, fat, gourmet mice right here," Kenny crooned.

Eventually, Marvin flew down and fastidiously devoured the mice, then flew back to his perch with a single tail hanging out of his mouth like a limp toothpick.

Kenny stood and turned to Mark. His face betrayed his enthusiasm, though he tried hard to conceal it. "Hey, man, no big deal."

"Bring the bag in and wash your hands."

After they were once more sitting face-to-face in Mark's office, Mark said, "All right, Kenny, here's the deal. I want the names of your friends and their families—"

"Hell, no, man, I don't rat!"

"Then, you speak to them. I want to call on your families with Dr. Hazard and maybe do a better job of explaining what the clinic will mean to the community—that we're not a threat, we're an asset. Will you do that?"

"I can ask."

"Fine. And now, about you and your buddies. The

damage you have done has cost us time and money. So I think you have an obligation. You have an after-school job?''

"Uh-uh. I got soccer practice Tuesdays and Thursdays.''

"Then, I'm offering you a part-time job, one afternoon each a week and Saturday morning. You and your three buddies. We need kennel help—help cleaning up and scrubbing, looking after the animals. It's not easy and it's not clean, but it's honest.''

"How long would we have to work, to work off the money?''

"Probably forever, at the rates we're paying, but that's not what I'm offering. You get your buddies, and you come in here and talk to me. We'll pay you minimum wage and deduct a certain amount off what you've cost us. That's more than fair.''

"What's in it for you?''

"We get help, you get money and a clear conscience. And maybe you learn a little bit more about animals.''

"Tommy won't. He hates animals. He's scared. Stan might. He's younger than me, and he's got two dogs. He didn't much want to go along with us, anyway. Paulie'll just laugh and call me a wuss.''

"Then, talk to Stan. Talk to the others, too, if you can. And warn them that if there is any more vandalism, or if anyone so much as makes a move toward one of our animals, I'll come down on them and their dads with so many warrants and lawsuits, they'll wish they'd never left mid-town. Are we clear on that?''

"Yes, sir. So you're not going to call the police?''

"Not today. But I'll expect your answer tomorrow afternoon, and if Stan agrees, bring him along when you come back after school. I'll talk to your parents about the job offer, but I'll try to leave what you've done out of it. Okay?''

''Yeah, I guess.''

Mark stood and offered his hand. ''Then, you better get on home. It's only seven in the morning, and it's Sunday. I thought adolescents slept all the time.''

Kenny flushed. ''I wanted to see the—Marvin.''

''I'll tell Bill Chumney you're interested. He's our exotics man. You like lions and tigers?''

''Yeah.''

''Fine. Then, maybe you can do some work on them some time. Now, out the back door, and call me with your answer.''

Kenny scooted.

Mark sank into his chair. He had no idea whether he'd done the right thing, but he hadn't been able to think of anything better.

He'd barely started on his now lukewarm coffee, when Sarah came in.

''Who was that I saw leaving by the back door?''

''Kenny something-or-other. One of our marauders.''

''And you just let him go?''

''No, actually, I hired him—and I don't even know his last name.''

WHEN RICK DROPPED BY the clinic before church, he found Sarah with her feet propped on Mark's desk and a sausage biscuit firmly in hand. Mark told him about hiring Kenny.

''You did what?'' Rick yelped.

''Hired him. And we're going to spend some of our precious bucks having an open house for the neighbors to show them we're no threat. We should have done it before this, but I didn't think about it.''

"Most of the neighbors are already clients of ours. Hell, half of them own horses, and almost everybody owns dogs and cats."

"The small group that doesn't use our services apparently has more teenage sons than normal, and more blowhard fathers that those sons actually listen to— when it suits them."

"They won't come."

"They will if we send invitations to the wives, and if Margot calls those wives on the telephone to invite them personally. Margot wields a fair amount of social clout in this town. If anybody can do it, she can."

"God, another damn party!"

"I think you're wrong," Sarah said.

Mark turned to her with his eyebrows raised. "How so?"

"Aren't we due to have the grand opening party for all the clientele in the next two to three weeks?"

"Yeah, so?"

"Hold off until then. Invite all the neighborhood, along with the county and city bigwigs, to that party. A real fancy affair—not just the neighborhood. As much as I resent spending money on anything that doesn't have *laser* as part of its name, I think it is a good use of funds. Let them see who our clients are, listen to them talk about how wonderful we are. See how nice the clinic is, and that it doesn't smell like manure. That should impress them more than a tea party just for the neighbors, don't you think?"

"Can we make the deadline?" Rick asked.

Mark shrugged. "If we keep Kenny and his gang occupied here, if the weather cooperates, if nothing else goes wrong—then, yes, we can make it."

"That is," Sarah said sweetly, "the facility can make

it. We don't have nearly the equipment on hand we need to really show how up to date we are.''

"I'm working on it," Mark said.

"Sure you are." Sarah stood up. "I've got to go out and do a pre-purchase exam on a hunter prospect for a youngster. That's why I'm here."

"On Sunday?"

"Both parents work and the child is in school during the week. It's the only day they could set up with the prospective seller. If they had wanted X rays of the pony's legs, I'd have had to send them to another vet— but they don't. The pony is only four years old, so if it's sound and doesn't have any splints, it should be all right. I hope."

She never let a chance to dig at him go by, Mark thought. He didn't know when or how or from whom she'd gotten the idea that money was available and that he was just too stingy to use it on her equipment. He glanced at Rick. Rick was capable of putting the blame on him simply to avoid problems, and he knew Bill Chumney thought Mark was the reason the raptor cage was smaller than originally planned.

He caught up with Sarah in the hall. "Can we try for dinner again tonight?"

"Not tonight. I'm worn out, and I have to start getting my new place organized."

"I'll help."

"We wouldn't accomplish a thing, and you know it."

"But we could have fun."

She stroked her hand down his cheek. "Give me a rain check."

He watched her walk away and arch her back to ease her shoulders. No wonder she was worn out. She needed some tender, loving care—if only she'd let him give it to her.

He turned away, then stopped. She didn't need tender, loving care so much as she needed to feel she was being listened to, having her needs acknowledged. Maybe it was up to him to acknowledge them, even if it meant going against his own "prime directive"— never put your own money into an iffy investment just because you like the people.

"WHAT DO YOU MEAN you want to sell those stocks?" his stockbroker, Charlie Richardson, squawked down the telephone line. "They're still going up like a rocket. You are crazy to bail out now!"

"We've already made a bundle, Charlie. I need the money for another investment."

Instantly Charlie became serious. "Not all of it, no way. Mark, that's one hell of a chunk out of your net worth and just about all the liquid capital you have available."

"I realize that. I said I need the money for another purpose."

Charlie was silent for a moment. Then, he said, "Listen, Mark, I know you. You don't gamble, you don't take flyers, you don't make knee-jerk decisions. If you're dead set on doing this, then what you're going to be putting the money into must be good—hell, better than good. Great. So how about letting me in on it?"

"I'm investing in a blood chemistry analyzer and a portable fluoroscopy machine."

"New technology? What's their secret? Who's the company?"

"I have no idea. Sell, Charlie, and send me a check."

He put the telephone down, with Charlie's howls of outrage ringing in his ear.

He buzzed Beth. When she came in, he handed her Sarah's list. "Job for you, and you can refuse if you like. It's not Buchanan business."

"Uh-huh," she said, and took the list. "What is all this?"

"Find out if there's any way to buy top-of-the-line equipment at rock-bottom prices—reconditioned, maybe. Maybe people stuff and vet stuff is the same on some of this. I know there must be used–medical-supply houses. And quickly. Delivery time is of the essence."

"Right." Beth looked up. "Where are you getting the cash? You started embezzling company funds?"

"I wish. I just sold some stock."

Beth gaped at him. "Are you nuts? Mark Scott, the first thing you taught me was that you never, ever, under any circumstances, sell stock on the upswing to gamble on personal investments. It's that damn clinic, isn't it?"

"Who else uses portable fluoroscopes?" He smiled ruefully. "Look, Beth, if you're not comfortable…"

"Not comfortable? When my boss suddenly takes complete leave of his senses?"

"If the clinic succeeds, it's a good investment."

"Nonsense. If the clinic succeeds beyond everybody's wildest dreams, you're likely to make a profit sometime in the next century."

"I won't lose money."

"You won't make big dividends, either. You might as well put it into Krugerrands and stash them in a cardboard box under your bed."

"I won't starve. I'll still be able to pay my bills."

"So long as nothing that requires resources comes

out of the blue and bites you. Your mother, for instance. What happens if she needs help?''

"She won't. She doesn't. Are we through now?'' Mark said. His tone was becoming harsh.

"Sure. We're through." Beth stood. "I'll get your info for you before noon. And I'll have the men in the white suits standing by with the straightjacket." She shook her head. "I never thought I'd see the great Mark Scott, guardian of all things fiscal, go off his head over a woman. Even a nice woman." She stalked out, then a moment later stuck her head back inside his door. "How about long-term leases? That might cost less."

"I checked out the leasing possibilities initially, when Rick hit me with his own wish list of equipment back in November before the clinic opened in February. That's before Margot used up so much capital on fancy trimmings for the building. The few leasable items I found would have cost more in the long run. The leases would have counted as liabilities. When you own the equipment outright, the capital valuation shows up on your inventory as an asset."

"Only when you don't owe any money on them."

"Right, and if you and I work this right, we won't."

"I'll do what you want, but I am also going to check into leasing. I may find some better deals than you did."

"You think so, do you?" He grinned at her.

"Absolutely. I'm much better at this sort of thing than you are, and don't you forget it." She walked out and shut the door behind her.

Mark leaned back and closed his eyes. The worst thing about it was that there was no way he could ever let the "nice woman" know that he had bought her equipment with his own money. She wouldn't be happy or thankful. She'd probably explode. This was as bad as that house her fiancé had bought. She'd never speak to him again. She'd probably walk out and go back to St. Paul.

Hell, he couldn't let *anybody* know. Beth would keep her mouth shut, but if Coy or Rick got wind of it, they'd let something slip. He'd be a dead man. He had to continue to grump around and put Sarah off until he could present her with her new toys.

He didn't give a damn about the money. He had enough money for his needs, even after cashing in his stock. What he didn't have was Sarah. He reached for his mouse as his door opened.

Coy Buchanan stood in the doorway—no, loomed was more like it.

"Dammit! You're fired."

CHAPTER ELEVEN

MARK LOOKED UP in surprise. "I beg your pardon?".

Coy pointed a long, brown finger at him. "Any damn fool who sells good stocks to buy equipment for Margot's blasted clinic is too damn stupid to work for Buchanan Industries."

"I'll kill Beth." Mark could feel his jaw clench.

"No, you young idiot, Beth did not tell me. Charlie Richardson called me to ask how much money I was putting into that new medical equipment company you'd discovered."

"Then I'll kill *Charlie*. My trades are supposed to be confidential."

"Yeah, well, you know Charlie." Coy sank into the desk chair. "Boy, you gone plumb crazy? Margot told me you had a crush on that new lady vet. Never been a woman made worth that kind of investment on the front end." He glared at Mark. "It is on the front end, ain't it?"

Mark nodded. "Unfortunately."

"You think she's gonna go all gooey-eyed and fall into your arms when she finds out you've bought her equipment?"

Mark sat up and stabbed his finger at Coy's chest. "If she finds out—if anybody finds out—I will personally knock your block off, then I'll clear out my desk."

"Huh?"

"Sarah *cannot* find out about this. She'd blow up. She would see it as the worst kind of interfering."

"She got a screw loose?"

"About this sort of thing, definitely. So you keep your mouth shut if you want to keep your VP of Operations. Oh, I forgot, you just fired me."

Coy waved a hand. "Hell, you know I didn't mean that. I'm worried about you, boy, is all. First that rag mop you been carrying around like it's a grand champion, and now this. You going soft in the head?"

"Probably. I promise it will not adversely impact my ability to make heads roll around here when you need them to. And I can afford the money."

"Nobody can afford that kind of a gesture—not without letting the woman know about it. You give her diamonds, you want her to know who they're from, don't you? Same thing with a what-you-call-it fluoroscope."

"She might accept the diamonds. She would not accept the fluoroscope—not as a gift from me. I mean this, Coy. You keep your mouth shut. And make sure Beth keeps hers shut, as well."

"Hell, she'd no more betray your confidence than mine. Woman's a clam. Great legs, though."

"Tell her that, why don't you?"

"And get hit for a multi-million-dollar sexual harassment lawsuit?" Coy shook his head. "Sometimes I wish I was about twenty years younger."

Mark leaned forward. "I don't think Beth gives a damn how old you are, you old coot."

"You think maybe she'd have dinner with me sometime?" Coy sounded wistful. "I mean, we've had plenty of meals together when we're working—but just me and her? No business?"

"I'd be very surprised if she said no. Try it, why don't you."

"Yeah, maybe I will." Coy stood up. "Women. Sure do make us men do crazy things, don't they?"

"Absolutely. Oh, and Coy, don't mention Beth to Margot."

"Huh? Why?"

"Just don't."

"Yeah, sure." He walked out shaking his head.

Mark leaned back and templed his fingers. Beth might think he was blind, but he knew how she felt about Coy. Maybe he'd just brought a bit of happiness into *somebody's* life. Maybe some would spill over into his own.

TUESDAY MORNING, Mark called Sarah before she'd gotten out of bed.

"Look, sorry it's so early. I've got to fly to Texas this morning. I'll probably be gone all week."

Sarah felt a stab of misery at the prospect of not seeing him all week.

"I hope that groan I heard is anguish at not seeing me for three or four days."

"In your dreams," Sarah said. "The groan came from the fact that I am on four-to-midnight again and it's only five a.m."

"I said I was sorry. The thing is, would you take Nasdaq while I'm gone?"

Sarah thought a moment. "Sure. I'm working at home days, trying to get my few household goods unpacked, and she can stay in her kennel when I'm at the clinic. Why not?"

"Fine. I'll drop her by in a few minutes." He hung up without waiting for Sarah's goodbye.

"Oh Lord," she said, "look at this place. Look at *me!*"

By the time Mark swept in with Nasdaq on a leash and a bag full of food and toys, the coffee was ready to pour and there were two glasses of orange juice on the kitchen counter.

"You look gorgeous," Mark said, and reached for her.

"So do you," she said, neatly avoiding him. He did. His suit was beautifully tailored, his shirt was blindingly white, and his tie radiated power. "Is that the way you normally travel?"

"I'm flying commercial. No time to change before I meet the clients. But I'll happily endure looking like a derelict if you'd like to mess me up a little."

"I'll spare you."

"The hell you will."

This time his grab was more successful. Sarah resisted only a moment before she gave in to the passion of his kiss. She had to stand on her tiptoes to reach his mouth. He tasted of hot latte and toothpaste, and smelled just slightly of lemons. When she encircled the back of his head, the hair at the nape of his neck was still damp. His shirt was slick and cool against her chest, but his arms felt anything but cool.

She could feel the power in his arms and shoulders, the thrust of his hips as he slid his hands down to cup her against his groin. She wanted to kiss him and keep kissing him until she'd tasted every inch of his mouth, nibbled his tongue, let herself float in the warmth of being held tight and safe against him.

She broke the kiss and gasped, "You'll miss your plane."

"There'll be others." He began to kiss her again.

"But the clients will be waiting for you."

He sighed. "Damn, I would have to get myself involved with a practical woman."

"Involved? Is that what we are?"

"Not nearly as involved as I wish we were."

She shoved him back a step. "Get thee to Texas. I'll watch Nasdaq."

"I wish…"

"So do I. Now go."

She stood at the door with Nasdaq beside her on her leash. "And don't forget, you owe me a fluoroscope!"

"And you owe me a home for Nasdaq."

She watched him drive away, then patted her chest. Nasdaq jumped into her arms. "Nasdaq, I have always considered myself a very strong woman."

Nasdaq wriggled joyfully.

"I make all these resolutions about not getting involved with Mark until I get my equipment, but every time he touches me, all my willpower goes right out the window." She nuzzled Nasdaq's neck. The pup responded by licking Sarah's cheek. "Don't you start too." She held Nasdaq out in front of her. "Okay. That is absolutely, positively the last time I am going to let my libido override my good sense. You got that?"

Nasdaq barked and Sarah cuddled her close once more. "I cannot believe he's not giving up on getting rid of you. How could anybody let you go?" She thought a moment, then nodded. "Right. Let's just see how he handles the real possibility of losing you."

"MARK IS STILL TALKING about finding Nasdaq a home," Sarah said to Mabel that evening. She sat with her rear propped against Mabel's reception desk, arms crossed, ankles crossed. "I thought the minute he took

her home with him that he'd never mention giving her
to anybody else, but he keeps harping on the time he
spends away from home and in the office—the Buchanan office, which apparently isn't as dog-friendly as
we are. Think he could be right?''

''Of course not. He needs that dog as much as she
needs him.''

Sarah continued as though Mabel hadn't spoken.
''I'm stretching Rick's rules about our own pets, just
by letting Mark keep her here when he's away for the
day. How would you feel about running a scam on him?
Telling him you've found her a good home with children?''

''It could backfire. He could say yes.''

''I know. If that happens, we'll know he can live
without her. If worse comes to worst, I'll take her myself. I don't have all that much time, either, but I won't
let her go to strangers.''

''If you're sure, I'll work out a story that he'll believe.''

Sarah nodded. ''He'll be back on Friday afternoon.
Until then, I have Nasdaq and I'm going to train her to
stay in her house at night without sleeping on the bed
or yelling her head off. It's something she's got to
learn.''

Mabel looked narrowly at Sarah. ''She been causing
you problems at night, Doctor?''

Sarah knew she was blushing. ''It's just good dog
manners, that's all.''

FRIDAY AFTERNOON, Sarah was finishing the sutures to
close up an incision in the belly of a golden python that
had eaten a bright orange tennis ball, when Mabel stuck
her head in the door.

"He's baaaack."

Sarah felt a warm flow rush through her veins. She hadn't realized how much she'd missed him. "Okay, you got your story straight?"

"I still don't think it's a great idea, but yes."

After Jack, and Kenny—whose last name was Nichols—carried the python to recovery, Sarah went looking for Mark. He wasn't in his office, but his immaculate suit jacket hung beside the door. Nasdaq was not in her kennel.

He must be taking her for a walk behind the clinic. Sarah walked out the door and stopped on the stoop when she saw them. Mark had rolled up his sleeves and loosened his tie. He threw a soft ball underhand. The minute it left his hands, Nasdaq began to chase it on short little legs, barking merrily until she grabbed it in midair. Then she raced back to him, stood on her hind legs and dropped it ceremoniously into his outstretched palm. And the process was repeated.

"Mark?" she called quietly.

He dropped the ball at his feet and turned to smile at her. He trotted over, Nasdaq at his heels carrying a ball nearly as big as her head. He reached out to take Sarah in his arms, but she stopped him.

"I've done as you asked," Sarah said.

He looked puzzled.

"Nasdaq. You told me to find her a good home."

His frown was instantaneous. "What the hell are you talking about?"

"Mabel's granddaughter recently lost her dog. She's eight. They're willing to take him. You said acreage and children. They have both."

Nasdaq put her paws on Mark's knee and bopped him with the ball. "Not now," he snapped. She dropped onto her belly. He closed his eyes and fell to his knees to pet her. "Sorry, Nasdaq, old girl. I didn't mean it."

"They can come get her tonight. I can pack up her toys."

"Yeah, sure." He ruffled the dog's ears. "Great. Just what she needs."

Sarah's heart plummeted; she felt on the verge of tears. "So you want me to tell them?"

He stood. "Why not? She's been taking up too much of my time, anyway." He turned and strode away. Nasdaq hurried after him, but he ignored her.

Sarah watched him. He was too hardheaded to admit that he needed the little dog as much as she needed him.

She sighed and turned to go find Mabel, to tell her she'd been right. Mark was willing and able to let Nasdaq go with no fight at all. She heard the soft *shush* of the outside door as it closed behind her.

Mabel was in the break room with her feet propped up and a mystery novel in her hands.

"Well?"

"I'll take her."

"Oh, Sarah. Are you sure? Is he?"

"I think he's miserable, but he's too stubborn to admit it." She sank into the chair opposite Mabel. "I was so sure. I ought to learn by now not to try to organize people's lives. I've done to him just what I accused him of doing to me with the house. Oh, heck!"

Mabel touched her shoulder. "You tried, Sarah."

"Why couldn't I just leave it alone? Let him find out over time that he needed her? Why do I always push—?"

The door to the break room banged against the wall. Both women jumped.

Mark stood in the doorway looking like an avenging

angel. Nasdaq cowered in his arms. "Have you called those people yet?" he asked Mabel.

"No, sir."

"But the kid knows she's getting a new dog, right?"

Mabel shook her head. "It's a surprise."

"At least you've got *some* sense." He glared at Sarah. "Tell the parents to buy the kid a puppy. I'll pay for it." He turned and started out the door, then turned back. "And you, Doctor—I would suggest that in future you refrain from giving away people's dogs without even discussing it with them." The door slammed behind him.

Sarah gulped. "Of all the... I mean..."

Mabel laughed so hard that her potato chips flew out of the bag. "Oh, Sarah. I hope you never take up fishing because you don't have a clue when you have a big one on the line."

"Mark, Mark!" She ran after him. He turned to her with Nasdaq hugged against him.

"Well?"

"I'm so sorry. I don't—I mean—I'm an idiot."

"You sure are." His shoulders slumped. "I know I kept saying, 'Find her a home,' but dammit, it should have been obvious to you—"

"The person it wasn't obvious to was you, you muttonhead! You wouldn't admit you wanted to keep her, so Mabel and I—Mark I'm sorry. We scammed you."

"You what?"

"We scammed you."

"There was never any granddaughter who needed a puppy?"

Sarah dropped her eyes and shook her head. "It's not Mabel's fault. It's mine." She raised her eyes. "It worked, didn't it?"

For a moment she had no way of gauging his reaction. He set Nasdaq down at his feet. He sighed deeply. "It worked."

Sarah smiled tentatively. "Forgive me? Please?"

He grinned. "I forgive you. But promise me you'll never do anything like that again."

"I promise. Not unless I have to."

"Not good enough."

"It's the best you'll get. And, by the way, Nasdaq and I have been having a few lessons in ladylike manners while you've been gone. She's a very smart little dog. Smart and manipulative."

"I realize that."

"Every night she slept in her kennel in my kitchen. Alone. And quiet."

"How'd you manage that?"

"A hard heart and a few treats. Anyway, please reinforce that training tonight, even if it kills you. She will quiet down eventually. Tell her to 'kennel up,' give her a treat and a couple of her favorite toys, then shut the door on her and go to bed. Alone."

He looked at her and a slow grin spread across his face.

Sarah shifted uncomfortably, avoided his eyes. She could feel the flush mount up her cheeks. "What?"

"You know darn well, what. When do we get to test her out?"

"I have no idea what you're talking about."

"Oh, yes, you do. I'm flattered that you took the trouble."

"To teach your ratty little dog some manners? Puhleeze."

"Sarah Marsdon, you're a fraud."

"If you're going to insult me, I have work to do."

She went to the door. ''It was worth a try.'' She winked at him and ran out the door before he could react.

MARK WENT into his office and clicked on to the Internet. Amazing the bargains in medical equipment you could find if you really dug deep enough. And if you could pay cash for them.

He should have tried harder sooner. He'd been so busy saying no to everyone's requests that he'd neglected to figure out ways to say yes.

Sarah was right. He hadn't done his homework. He'd lost sight of the fact that part of his job was to make the right things happen—not only to keep disasters at bay.

One laser was on its way to the clinic via overnight express. He'd ordered it while he'd been away. It should be waiting for Sarah when she came in tomorrow afternoon. He longed to see her face when she saw it, but was afraid his own would betray his part in it. He'd arrange to be at Buchanan rather than the clinic.

If everything checked out, the portable fluoroscope and X-ray machine would arrive by the beginning of the week.

Now, where on earth could he find that blood chemistry thing or the anesthesia machine?

CHAPTER TWELVE

"HE DID IT!" Sarah grabbed Jack's tough little hands and began to dance around the room. "I can't believe it! He actually found the money!"

"Settle down, Doctor," Jack said. "It's a bloody laser, girl, not the crown jewels."

"As good as." She leaned her head back and closed her eyes. "It's a start. Now that he's managed to come up with the cash for this, maybe he'll cut the purse strings on the portable fluoroscope, at least." She began to stroke the tall pedestal on which the laser perched like a knight's lance.

"Bill swore there was plenty of money in the cash reserves for a bigger flight cage," Sarah continued. "He swears Mark's been hoarding cash in case we needed it to tide us over the tight times."

"Can't fault the man for that. It's what he's paid for, isn't it? We're not to know how close to the edge we're skating. Worry about my salary, then, I would."

"You'll get your salary if I have to pay it out of my own pocket." She laughed. "Rejoice with me, Jack Renfro!"

He grumbled. "Hope the lad knows what he's doing, is what I say." He shook his head. "So how does the bloody thing work, then?" He regarded it with deep suspicion.

"You don't have to work it, I do. But here's the manual that came with it. Now, the next time we get a roarer in we can laser the inside of the throat and take a little tuck here and there, and *bingo,* no more roaring horse. Of course, we'll need the endoscope so we can confirm the diagnosis.''

''What else's it good for, then?''

''Wounds, tumors, delicate carving where blood interferes with the surgeon's ability to perform.''

''We'll have to share with Dr. Thorn once he finds out we've got it.''

''No problem, so long as he knows it's mine, mine, mine, and that it lives here in this section and not in a corner of his.''

''I'll leave you to gloat, then, shall I? Time I checked the dressing on that bull's abscess, anyway.''

''Thanks, Jack. I'll sit here and pore over the manual. I haven't used one for a couple of years. Do you know where Mark is? I'm dying to thank him.''

''Not here, or at least his car's not in the lot. Working at his real job, probably, if you get my meaning.''

''Go away,'' she said again. ''You grumpy old thing, I refuse to allow you to spoil my happiness.''

She sat down in her chair and opened the manual. So Bill had been right all along. She'd never believed what he said, or what Rick had intimated—that it was all Mark's fault she didn't have the equipment she'd been promised. Obviously once she'd made a good enough case, he'd come through like a champion.

Next step, the fluoroscope. Then the anesthesia machine, and then the blood chemistry analyzer and the endoscope. Maybe a long way down the line, a consortium to get an MRI and train someone to operate it.

Once her equipment was in place, she could safely allow her emotions full rein.

What were they, exactly? What did she want from Mark?

More.

How could any woman taste his lips, feel the caress of his fingertips on her breast, the strength of his arms, and not want more? But her longing went far beyond the physical, beyond that pleasurable ache whenever he came into a room, smiled at her, touched her.

She wanted to know him—not merely his body. They'd sparred, they'd kissed, they'd nearly made love, and yet she felt that she knew only a tiny bit of how he had come to be the man he was.

How had he become so blasted responsible? Something had turned him cautious. He was stingy in his relationships as well as in his finances. He even had to be goaded to admit his fondness for Nasdaq.

He wanted her and she wanted him, but she'd never be satisfied with a casual affair, even a torrid one. She longed to reach deep inside him to understand and care for the whole man.

And allow him to know her in return?

She'd already revealed more than she'd planned about herself. He had an inkling about the problems with Gerald, with her job, *her family.* But he had no idea of the depths of the problems or the duration or how close she'd come to knuckling under to everybody else's goals for her. Would she feel comfortable talking to him?

More important, would he be comfortable listening?

At least she could call him at Buchanan to thank him.

But she reached Beth instead of Mark.

"Sorry, Sarah, he's gone. Said he wouldn't be back until sometime tomorrow."

"Oh." Sarah felt amazingly deflated. She had been primed to hear his voice, excited at the prospect of telling him he was wonderful. "Is he at home?"

"No idea. You can try him there."

"Thanks."

But all she got at Mark's house was his answering machine. She left a message for him to call her back at his convenience, and went back to work. Did he have a date? No reason he shouldn't, although five o'clock in the afternoon seemed a bit early. She'd simply assumed there wasn't a woman in his life, but there well could be. All that stuff at Rick's party about coming home with him, all his attempts at seduction—that didn't have to mean that he was pursuing her exclusively.

Dadgummit, she *wanted* to be exclusive. *She* certainly didn't have any interest in anyone else. Gerald was over and done with, and even Mac Thorn—who, heaven knows, was gorgeous—didn't make her temperature rise.

Somehow, without even realizing it, she'd allowed herself to fall for Mark, the kind of man she'd sworn never to get involved with again.

Her door opened and Liz Carlyle burst in. "I had to see the laser!"

"I thought this was your day off."

"I had to come by and pick up my check, and Jack told me about it. When can we start training on it?"

"I'm taking the manual home with me tonight. Ever used one of these things?"

"I worked with them a lot in school. The things they can do for eyes, you wouldn't believe." Liz caressed the laser. "This looks like the model I used."

"Then, you've worked more closely with them than I have, and definitely more recently. If anybody's going to do the training, it's you. You can train us all. I'm sure everybody will be interested."

"Really? Now I can finally feel as though I'm of some use around here."

WHEN SHE GOT HOME after her shift ended at midnight, Sarah found a message from Mark on her answering machine. It had been left at two-twenty in the afternoon, when she'd been grocery shopping and before she went to the clinic.

"Hope you liked your present. Call me when you get home. I'll be awake."

But all she got when she called was his answering machine again.

She tried not to worry, not to drive herself crazy thinking that he'd had a date with somebody else and decided to sleep over. What he did was his business. They'd never even had a complete date. Shooting a cow wasn't likely to endear her to any man.

She rolled over on her air mattress and pulled the thick down comforter around her shoulders.

Her last thoughts were of Mark. Mark holding the laser out to her. It had a bright red ribbon tied around it.

WHEN THE TELEPHONE RANG at six, Sarah was sleeping so deeply that it took her a moment to identify the sound.

"Hello?"

"Sarah? It's Mark. I'm sorry to keep calling so early."

"Where were you last night? You asked me to call."

"I had a minor emergency, and now I've got a real one. I need you."

"At this hour?"

"My mother and stepfather own a cabin down at Pickwick Lake. It's about an hour-and-a-half from the clinic. While they're cruising the Greek Isles, the neighbors have my number if anything happens that I should know about."

"Don't tell me it burned down."

"Nothing so drastic. The neighbors noticed the ground at the side of the cabin was muddy. They have a key, and they found the water heater had sprung a leak and had been draining itself onto the ground for about a week. It's a quagmire. They called me to come deal with it."

"So that's where you are?"

"I turned off the water, and went into Iuka to get another heater. But by the time it had been delivered and set up, it was dark, so I stayed over."

"If it's sprung another leak, I'm afraid that's outside my domain."

"I wish it were that simple. I've got kittens."

"I beg your pardon?"

"When I let Nasdaq out for her late-night stroll, she didn't come back, and I could hear her barking. I followed her with a flashlight. She'd found a litter of kittens—very, very small kittens."

"I hope you left them alone. The mother will find them and move them someplace where they'll be safe."

"Not this mother. She won't be coming back."

"How do you know?"

"I know, and you don't want to hear about it. I knew if I left the kittens, the raccoons would get them, so I scooped them up and took them back to the house. At the moment, they're on a quilt in front of the fire. I tried to get some warm milk down them with one of my mother's eyedroppers, but I don't know how successful I was. What the hell am I supposed to do with them?"

She leaned her head into her hands. "Give them kitten formula milk every three to four hours around the clock."

"What kitten milk? Help me out here. I've never been around cats, and certainly not kittens this small."

Sarah didn't want to tell him that if they really were so small, their chances of survival were slim. "I can make it in an hour-and-a-half?"

She heard his sigh of either satisfaction or relief, she wasn't certain which.

"Yeah. I'll give you directions."

"I'll have to be back before my shift starts."

"Call Eleanor. She'll cover for you tonight."

She wrote down the directions he gave and called Eleanor. It was a number she'd memorized her first day on the job.

When Sarah had explained the situation, Eleanor said, "Take an overnight bag."

"I'm not planning to stay."

"Then, you're an idiot. I'll handle the clinic tonight and tomorrow night, too, for that matter. Go. Grab a couple of pairs of jeans, your birth control pills, and go."

"You'd be working double shifts."

"Big deal. What else do I have to do?"

"I promised I wouldn't get that involved. He may not want me to stay."

"Oh, for pity's sake, of course he does. He may even have made up the kittens. If so, he's smarter than I gave him credit for. You listen to me, Sarah Marsdon, if you don't seize this day, I will come over there and spank you."

"You think I should?"

"What have I just said?" Eleanor's voice became serious. "You do not know how long you will have together. Every day, every moment is precious. Don't waste a one. You're alive. Be alive with *him*."

ONCE SARAH LEFT the main highway to Pickwick Lake, the road became a narrow lane stretching between trees newly leafed in pale green. Sarah saw wild dogwoods dancing through the trees like fairies. Pale lavender wild iris nodded on the banks beside the road. To her left she caught glimpses of sunshine glittering on water. It might still be chilly in Minnesota, but that business about "nothing like a day in May" definitely held true down here.

A fragile breeze chased mare's-tail clouds across a sky so blue that it was nearly indigo.

At one point, she had to jam on her brakes as a doe and two yearling fawns ran across the road in front of her.

She hadn't had a chance to see any of the countryside in the two weeks since she'd arrived. She'd been working too hard. It wasn't Minnesota with its pines and loons calling, but it had a gentle beauty of its own. She felt the tension draining out of her neck and shoulders as she drove.

She missed the gravel driveway that Mark had indicated and had to turn around on the shoulder of the road to drive back. Before she made the turn, she pulled to a stop beside the mailbox.

Whether the kittens were real or made up, once she turned into that driveway she was committed. But to what?

Her body felt more alive than it ever had. Anticipatory warmth spread over her. Mark was everything she said she did not want, and yet she wanted him as she'd never wanted anyone. One look into those deep-set eyes of his, and she knew she'd be lost.

Would he?

Suddenly that didn't matter. What mattered was the vista that opened before her, the log house set among the trees, the hill dropping beyond to the glittering surface of the lake. And there was Mark. He raised his head from a flower bed beside the porch, and stood.

She parked the car and got out, but stopped with her hand on the door handle as though she were ready to jump in and drive off again. He waited, made no move to come toward her.

The only time she'd ever seen him out of business clothes before had been at Rick's party, and even then, once he'd changed from his swim trunks, he'd worn "business casual."

Today he wore a pair of threadbare jeans and a plaid shirt that looked as though it had been washed many times. The breeze lifted his short hair, and the corners of his eyes crinkled as he squinted against the sunlight. He'd rolled his sleeves up to his elbows. She thought of how strong his arms had felt around her, the breadth of his shoulders. Her pulse thrummed in her throat. She took one step toward him, then another. He peeled off his gardening gloves, tossed them aside, and came to her. She couldn't look away from him, couldn't breathe.

He lifted his strong hands to her face. Gently he bent to kiss her lips. A moment later she melted against him, her mouth open, her tongue seeking his, her body fitting itself against him like lock seeking key. She moaned as she felt heat flood upward and outward, so that even her fingertips tingled.

As he broke the kiss, she whispered, "Are there really kittens?"

He held her folded in his arms. "Oh, yes, there are kittens. I wasn't certain you'd come."

"For kittens? Of course I'd come."

He looked down at her. "Would you have come for me?"

She closed her eyes for a moment, then whispered, "For you, too."

He kissed her again, with more demand, more urgency. This time she was the one to pull back. "Kittens."

"Damn. Come on. Kittens first, then..."

"Where's Nasdaq?" she asked. Her arm felt good around his waist. She seemed to slip under his arm as though she'd always been there.

He smiled down at her. "Come and see. Nasdaq found them."

He'd kindled a small fire in the big stone fireplace. It might be early May, but the inside of the log house was cool and shadowy. A big cardboard box sat in front of the fire, and as Sarah walked toward it she heard the thump of Nasdaq's stump of a tail. A moment later the dog's little nose peeked over the edge of the box.

"Oh, my goodness," Sarah said as she dropped to her knees and stroked Nasdaq's head. The pup lay on her side on a folded blanket inside the box. Curled against her tummy lay two kittens—a black and a tabby.

"Yin and Yang," Sarah said.

"Good names for them."

She reached in, careful to tell Nasdaq what she was going to do. Nasdaq seemed to accept that she was there to help, and let her have the black kitten. The moment it was lifted it opened its tiny mouth in a distressed mew.

"They're not as young as I thought," Sarah said. "Their eyes are open. They're still at the swimming stage when they can't move very well, but they're at least two weeks old. That's good. If they'd been newborns, they wouldn't have lasted a day without milk."

"I've been trying to feed them milk with an eyedropper."

"Cow's milk can really upset their tummies, but it's

better than starvation or dehydration. I collected some stuff from the clinic before I came. Would you get it?''

"Sure."

She set down one kitten and picked up the other. The tabby was a female, and complained the instant she left Nasdaq's warm, furry side. "We'll get some kitten formula down you, young lady, and then you can go back to sleep." She stroked Nasdaq. "You're a very remarkable little dog."

Nasdaq wriggled.

"I brought your overnight bag in, too," Mark said from behind her.

"I...uh...didn't know how long you'd need me."

"You know the answer to that."

"Come over here, we've got kittens to feed."

Mark did very well, considering his big hands and his lack of experience, and in a few minutes the two kittens, bellies bulging, snuggled against Nasdaq again.

"We'll need to feed them every four hours," Sarah said.

He reached out and pulled her up. "Good, that means we have a whole four hours to ourselves."

"It's nearly noon."

"So it is. I'm starving. For you."

THIS TIME Sarah held nothing back. There was no quibbling, no wavering. He'd always known she'd have to come to him. He'd tried to influence her decision, but whatever had kept her from his arms, from his love, she'd had to work through alone.

And now she was ready. One moment she was his gentle, vulnerable girl. The next she held him fiercely, her mouth demanding, her skin hot where he touched her. He encircled her waist and half led, half carried her to his bedroom.

All the pent-up longing, the passion held in check, seemed to explode in them both at the same time. He heard the buttons on his shirt pop as he tore them loose with one hand, while he helped her remove her thin sweater with the other.

He didn't want to lose her mouth, the soft places his tongue sought, tasted, the sweetness of her kiss. He unhooked her bra, and she pulled it down and dropped it on the floor so that he could brush his palms across her swollen nipples, hear her sighs of pleasure, feel his own body responding when she slid her hand over his waist and below to find him hard against her. He felt clumsy trying to unbutton her jeans, but she helped him, and as he slid her zipper down he felt her hands, so much more sensitive than his, open his jeans.

It seemed only an instant before they held one another naked, body to body, hot skin against hot skin. This time his lips and tongue found her breast, and she gasped, sunk her nails into his shoulders.

His questing fingers sought her as hers encircled him, caressing, stroking, until he was nearly mad with wanting her. He had no more rational mind, only this terrible longing to find her with his body, to reach deep inside her to the secret places of her heart he had never seen, could not touch. Some instinct told him that he needed to love her with passion so strong she couldn't fight, couldn't resist. Only then would she truly be his.

When at last his body joined with hers, he felt an elation he'd never known before, as though he'd never been whole until now. When she arched against him and cried out, he knew he would never let her out of his life. A moment later he reached his own crest.

Afterward, she lay drowsily in his arms. He stroked her hair and felt her curling her fingers in the hair on his chest.

"Why did we wait so long?" she whispered, and kissed his shoulder.

"Not my fault. I tried to convince you to come home with me at Rick's party. And then there was the Nasdaq incident."

She muffled a laugh against his chest. "Nasdaq has other fish to fry right now. I guess we can be thankful for that." She glanced down at her watch. "We still have a little time before we feed the kittens again."

"Oh, we do, do we?" He nibbled her ear. "Do you have any special way you'd like to spend that time?"

"Indeed I do."

"And that would be?" He kissed the top of her head.

She lifted herself on her forearms and kissed the corner of his mouth. "Since you got me up at six in the morning, and since we've had all this exercise, I ought to be hungry, but actually, I can barely keep my eyes open."

"Good." He rolled her over so that she lay with her back to him, and spooned his body against hers. "One of the comedians—I don't remember which one—said that if you make love and your lady doesn't feel sleepy afterward, you have some more work to do."

"You did fine," she whispered sleepily. "Just fine."

Minutes later he raised his head to look down at her. Her lips, still swollen from his kisses, were slightly parted, her breathing slow and even. He laid his head back down on the pillow. "So did you, my love, so did you."

CHAPTER THIRTEEN

HE WOKE and reached for Sarah, only to find the other side of the bed vacant but still warm. He checked his watch. Almost four in the afternoon. Time to feed the brood. He swung out of bed and reached for his shirt, but it wasn't where he'd dropped it. He dug an old sweater out of his chest of drawers and dragged it over his head, then pulled on his jeans and walked barefoot into the living room.

Sarah knelt beside Nasdaq's box with two bottles of kitten formula. She wore his shirt held together by a single button halfway down.

Just then, Nasdaq began to bark outside the front door. Sarah must have let her out. She turned at the sound, saw Mark and smiled. He was dazzled by the warmth in her eyes.

"Even foster mommas need a break," she said.

He let Nasdaq in. She trotted over to the box, hopped in and began nuzzling her brood.

"They're fine," Sarah assured her. "Time for a little afternoon snack." She handed the black kitten to Mark and began to feed the tabby. Mark's kitten didn't seem to get it this time. His small legs scrabbled in Mark's hand and he mewed plaintively.

"He needs something to hold on to, the way he'd hold on to his momma," Sarah told him. "Unless you want those little needle claws in your sweater, I'd suggest you try a sofa cushion.'' Her kitten was busy slurping milk and kneading Nasdaq's side.

He arranged his kitten, but he kept his eye on Sarah. She knelt beside the box with his shirt barely covering her bottom. It kept falling open in front. She didn't seem to notice, but he definitely did. The flashes of Sarah's fair skin were much more arousing than if she'd been completely naked—although, as he thought about it, that wouldn't be such a bad thing, either.

He set his kitten into the box beside Sarah's, then sat cross-legged beside her and pulled her back against him. She lifted her hands behind her and encircled his neck, while he undid the single button, spread her shirt and began to caress her breasts gently. Her nipples were already erect, her bosom swollen. His hands moved down across her stomach and below. She arched back against him, turned in one fluid motion and straddled his lap. This time her kisses were deep and gentle, teasing, tasting him as he tasted her. He pulled her against him, then lifted his hips only enough to slide his jeans down.

SARAH WANTED to taste all of him, to run her tongue over him, to find the ridges of muscle that ran down his stomach and across his hips, the hollow of his belly and then the sweet swelling below. She ached to have this closeness last forever, as though they could drift in sensation untouched by the world outside, safe within themselves.

She longed to become as familiar with the feel of his body as she was with his scent, the way he moved his shoulders and the deep timbre of his voice. When had her universe narrowed so that he was the only one in focus?

He groaned with pleasure when she took him, and when she slid herself up to hold him warm inside her and began to move slowly to the rhythm of their breathing, she watched his face, felt his fingers slide along her spine and below.

When at last she collapsed against his chest, he wrapped her in his arms. "I had no idea this rug was so thin. But then, I wasn't lying on it," she said.

"I must admit, I didn't notice until now," he said, and sat up. "Kiss me."

"And then what?"

"It's five o'clock in the afternoon and we both missed lunch. I don't know about you, but after all this exertion I'm hungry." As if to punctuate his words, his stomach growled.

Sarah laughed. "Me, too. Is there anything to eat or drink in this place besides cat formula and dog food?"

"I think we can find something. Mom usually keeps a freezer stocked full for when they come down." He stood, pulled up his jeans and zipped them, then reached down to Sarah.

"You said this is your parents' place?" Sarah asked. "It's really nice."

"Actually, it belonged to my stepfather before he married my mother," Mark said. He opened the big chest freezer. "How about lasagna? It's homemade, not store-bought, and it won't take long to microwave. My mother makes great lasagna. I bought some salad stuff when I picked up the water heater, and there's wine and soda."

"Is there enough for two monumental appetites? I'm so hungry I could eat a bear." She wrapped her arms around herself. "I'm also cold."

"No wonder." He ran his gaze down her body. "The

nights are still chilly. I'll put another log on the fire to keep us and the kittens warm. There are some old sweatshirts in the bureau in my room. You're welcome to one of them.''

"Thanks. It's your room, then?"

"Mine. Theirs is across the hall. I use the place when Mom and Bob are traveling, which is a great deal of the time these days. And I take care of things like the water heater."

"You're certain it's fixed?"

"Absolutely. You can have a hot shower, I promise. Although, the ground on the north side of the house will take a couple of weeks to dry out completely." While Mark slid the lasagna into the microwave and began to punch buttons, Sarah went into his room and opened the top drawer of his bureau. She felt like an intruder pawing through his clothes. He was, as she'd expected, very neat—or his mother was. She pulled a worn gray sweatshirt over her head. As she started to shut the drawer, she saw a five-by-seven framed photograph lying on top of the sweatshirt underneath, and picked it up.

She recognized Mark immediately, though he was much younger—probably high-school age. He already had the height and a hint of the muscles that he would develop fully as he matured, but there was a coltish quality about him that was incredibly appealing. His brown hair fell in an unruly shock over his forehead instead of in the neat trim he now wore. How the girls must have adored him!

In the picture, he had his arm around the shoulders of a man who was not quite as tall, but much broader, and whose features marked him as someone closely related to Mark. They were both smiling at the camera.

She'd never seen Mark smile like that—unguarded, happy and open. She looked at the back of the frame but there was no inscription.

It had to be Mark's father. No doubt, he kept the photo in his drawer so as not to upset his mother and stepfather. She carefully put it back. She didn't think he'd want to know she'd found it.

"That's my father."

Sarah jumped. "I didn't mean to pry."

He lounged against the door frame. "I told you to look there. You're not prying." Still, he came over and shut the drawer.

"I'm sorry. You must have loved him very much."

He turned his back on her. "Yeah. Sure, I loved him. What I knew about him I loved. Want a glass of wine?"

She followed him into the kitchen. He handed her a goblet of red wine. "Toast? To us?"

"Why not?" She smiled and took a sip, although she was still far from certain there was any "us" to toast. "You want me to fix the salad?"

"You're company. Sit at the counter and talk to me. I'm a very good cook."

"Good, because except for a couple of hot dishes, I'm not. Lutefisk and lefsa are only considered gourmet fare in Minnesota."

"What is it? Or are they?"

"Lutefisk is a white fish that is soaked in lye until it nearly falls apart, and it's eaten with lefsa, a flat bread that has the taste and consistency of a desk blotter."

He made a face. "I don't *think* so."

He kept up pleasant social chatter throughout dinner and the cleanup afterward, but Sarah felt he'd drawn away from her after she'd found that picture. Instinct told her that his relationship with his dad might well be the key to why he had become the man he was. While she didn't want to push, she did want to know more about him.

Later, as they sat side-by-side on the worn leather sofa, feet stretched toward the fire, his arm around her shoulders, she asked softly, "Can you talk about your father?"

He drew away instantly. "Sure. Why not? Everybody knows. Why not you? It's no big secret." His voice was cold and flat.

Instantly she regretted her question, but he went on.

"Big Tom Scott. Finest friend a man could ever have. Nobody ever picked up a check when Big Tom was in the party. Anything you needed done, Big Tom could manage it somehow. If you had money problems, or needed financing for a project, or if there was a little finagling to be done on a contract, Big Tom could find a way to make it come out right. Never say no to a friend—that was Big Tom's slogan."

Sarah stared at him. His voice was dry, matter-of-fact, yet she could hear the pain ringing through.

"He gave Mom and me what he thought we wanted. Big house, best schools. I was headed to Princeton to become a lawyer. Big Tom was a lawyer, too, though not from any fancy school. My grandparents were second-generation Irish, and struggled for everything they had. Big Tom inherited the blarney and the need to be loved by everybody. The problem was, he wasn't as good a businessman as everybody thought he was."

"He got into financial trouble?"

"You could say that. He did a lot of big real estate closings, handled a lot of escrow money. I don't know when he first got into trouble, and I suppose, like so many white-collar criminals, he didn't think there was anything wrong with what he did—just borrow some-one's escrow money to pay off a few stock debts. He could always put it back in a few days or weeks, right? Only, he never seemed to be able to, I guess. Then, whenever anybody questioned the escrow, he'd pay them off with the escrow from the next guy's closing. I'm sure he intended to get even. But he never did.''

''And then he died?''

''Yeah. He died.'' Mark took a deep draft of his wine.

Sarah had never seen him drink like this, not even at Rick's party. She watched him pour another glass. ''I shouldn't have asked.''

''Sure you should. Big Tom Scott died, all right. He ran his Lincoln into a bridge abutment at eighty miles an hour on a rainy highway.''

''Oh, Mark!''

''The IRS, SEC and the real estate board had all ap-parently started investigating him. It was about to hit the fan.''

''Suicide?''

''The insurance company tried to claim it was suicide because he had a half-million dollar, double-indemnity life insurance policy. They tried, but they could never prove he knew about the investigation. Then they said there weren't any skid marks, but it had been raining hard all day. They finally paid off.'' He drank the rest of his wine, reached for the bottle, then set the glass down empty.

''Mom and I used the money to pay his debts. We sold the house and moved into an apartment. She got a job selling cosmetics at Bettman's, and I went to the University of Memphis in finance rather than to Prince-ton to be a lawyer. Coy picked me up as a kind of gopher while I was in college. He's been my mentor. Took Big Tom's place in a way. I owe him everything.''

"You give him a great deal back.''

"In a lot of ways he's like my father, only smarter. He loves to be loved, and he can skate pretty close to the wind. It's my job to stop him. And when he wants somebody's head lopped off, I'm the one who gets to handle the ax, so he can still be the beloved boss.''

"That's what you've been doing at the clinic.''

"It's my job to be a hardnose. And I believe in what I do. Nobody is going to lose money because I screwed up and said yes when I should have said no— Isn't it time to feed those cats?'' He got up and started for the kitchen, but Sarah caught his hand, stood and put her arms around him.

"I haven't even thanked you for finding the money for my laser. Now I know how hard it was. I'm sorry I was such a whiner.''

He held her hard, his face buried against her shoulder. After a moment he said, "One thing about my father, he was a stickler for seat belts. He always buckled up the minute he got into a car. When he hit that bridge, he wasn't wearing one.''

"Oh, Mark.'' She held him.

"I'll never know.'' He broke away, went into the kitchen to find the kitten bottles, and came back.

"The insurance company was satisfied,'' she prompted.

"Oh, sure.'' He handed Sarah a bottle. "The crazy thing is that my stepfather, Bob, is the guy who investigated the claim. He and Mother met again four or five years after Big Tom died, and they hit it off, though they'd certainly been adversaries before. He'd gotten divorced by then and his daughters were grown and married. He's as different from Dad as he can be. An easygoing, kind man who adores my mother. She's happier than she ever was with Dad.''

''You like him?''

''I like him a lot. You'll have to meet them, if they ever come back from the Greek Isles. At least, I think that's where they are at the moment. Shall we feed some kittens?''

Later Mark made powerful love to her. It was as if he had to fight the demons of his memories. Afterward, she held him until he fell asleep.

She wondered how many people knew the story of his father's death. Coy, certainly. His parents, maybe Beth, possibly even Rick, although she doubted it. She was among a privileged few who'd been allowed access to his secret. He must never regret having confided in her.

CHAPTER FOURTEEN

At four a.m. Sarah slipped out of bed, fed the kittens, let Nasdaq out for a few minutes, and then slid back into bed.

"Woman, your feet are like ice," Mark said muzzily.

Sarah worked her toes between his ankles. "I, unlike you, have been doing my duty to those kittens."

He groaned, then said, "You're the vet, it's your job."

She slapped him gently on the shoulder.

He opened his eyes long enough to kiss her, then, when she turned over, he pulled her against him. "I'll warm you up."

"You're too kind."

He sounded drowsy. "I promise I'll take the two o'clock feeding on all our babies."

Sarah's eyes flew open. Babies? *All our* babies? As in more than one? When had they gone from making love to making babies? Surely he was just kidding. Did people kid like that when they were more than half asleep?

She came wide awake. His soft breath caressed the nape of her neck, and his body began to feel like an electric blanket.

Once she was certain he slept deeply again, she slipped out of his arms. She needed a glass of water badly. That remark about babies had made her mouth go dry.

She used the light from the dying fire to find her way to the kitchen, drank deeply, then checked Nasdaq, who woke long enough to wag her rear.

Sarah carefully laid another small log on the embers of the fire. Then she pulled the afghan off the couch, wrapped her naked body in it and stretched her feet toward the fire so they'd warm up enough to not wake Mark when she went back to bed.

Was it possible to fall in love, real love, so quickly? Mark didn't seem like a rebound. What she felt for him was something she hadn't believed existed. Was this love? If so, it was a whole lot harder to handle than she'd ever considered. She'd never truly cared about much except the animals, their welfare, what they needed.

Now suddenly the man who had started out as her adversary had become more important to her than anyone else she'd ever known.

For the first time in a long time, she was scared. Her relationship with Mark and her feelings for him had grown so deep so fast. He might not feel the same way about her. In her limited experience, men often said things at the start of relationships that they regretted the minute their heads cleared.

She didn't even know that much about Mark.

He could have been married half a dozen times, and even have a child or two. He'd never mentioned them, but then why should he? Until he'd told her the story about his father he'd never revealed anything about himself, and she'd never asked. Beth said he wasn't involved at the moment, but what did that mean? That he was between girlfriends? Getting over a bad relationship or even a bad marriage?

She dropped the afghan on the couch on her way to bed, and kept her feet on her own side when she climbed in next to Mark.

WHEN SARAH WOKE AGAIN she heard birds chirping. She was alone in the big warm bed. She checked the clock: eight-fifteen. She didn't want to get up. She felt warm and relaxed and pleasurably achy. But the kittens needed feeding. She rolled out of bed and found that Mark had laid a terry-cloth robe over the foot of the bed. Even as she slipped it on, she wondered how many women he'd brought here.

She stumbled into the bathroom and saw that her cheeks were rosy from Mark's beard, her lips still swollen from his kisses, not to mention the warmth that spread over the rest of her body.

She washed her face, brushed her teeth and went to find him.

He was in the kitchen whistling. *Whistling?* Mark? He handed her a cup of coffee across the counter. "Morning, sleepyhead. The babies are fed. Least I could do."

"Morning." She stretched, took the cup and cradled it in her hands. "They made it through the night, then?"

"They're swimming all over their box. Nasdaq keeps trying to herd them back to her, but they want to go exploring."

Sarah knelt beside the box and scratched Nasdaq's ears. "I wasn't sure they'd survive."

"Why?"

She sat on the floor. "They were so young."

"But now you are?"

"Yes."

"So what do we do with them? And don't you look at me that way. One dog is all I can handle."

"I'll take them back to the clinic and hand them over to one of the techs. There are always homes for kittens, once they're eating solid food."

"Won't Nasdaq be upset?"

"Probably. She'll get over it," Sarah said.

"Damn."

Sarah heard the resignation in his voice and laughed. "You're going to keep them, aren't you?"

"At least until they're weaned, I guess I'll have to. My office at the clinic is starting to look like a zoo. What do you want for breakfast?"

"Just coffee. You know I have to get back to town."

He said nothing for a moment. "You need more than that. How about some toast and a couple of sunny-side-up eggs?"

"I certainly won't turn them down. Right now, I'm going to take a shower."

She turned on the shower head in the bathtub and waited for the water to heat. Mark hadn't even kissed her good morning. It was all so casual, as though last night had never happened. She felt hot tears sting her eyes. She dropped her robe, climbed into the tub and turned her back so that the hot shower struck her shoulder blades. She scrubbed herself raw, washed her hair, then let the water course over her until it started to go cold. Her tears mingled with the water. The last feeling she should have after last night was frustration. They'd made wonderful love. Mark was so tender, yet so passionately male. Now this morning he acted as though they were old college roommates.

At least she knew where she stood.

She turned off the water and reached for the shower curtain.

As her hand touched it, it was jerked back.

Mark stood there naked. He wrapped his arms around her and lifted her over the rim of the tub. She was dripping and slippery as a salamander. He kissed her mouth, her eyes, her throat and buried his face between her breasts. Then he swung her up in his arms, carried her to the bed and lay beside her. His hands swept across her stomach; his lips followed the curve of her breasts, the hollow of her navel, and deeper, his kisses and his tongue teasing, exploring between her thighs.

Her fingers dug into his shoulders as she cried out with pleasure. "Now!" she pleaded. "Please, please."

He took her strong and fast, and she met him thrust for thrust, her breath sobbing in her throat. They reached the crest together this time. It was like sailing off a cliff with the winds swirling them higher and higher.

When he sank into her arms, she held him and heard his heart beating. He slid over and pulled her against his chest.

"Last night was real, Sarah. I couldn't just let you go back as if nothing had happened."

She stroked his cheek and felt the stubble rough under her fingertips. "You seemed so...casual. So I tried to be, as well."

He kissed the top of her head. "There's nothing casual about the way I feel. Don't go. Stay with me."

"Oh, Mark, I can't." She sat up. "It'll always be this way with me. Cows calve on Thanksgiving, and sheep drop lambs on New Year's Day, and horses get cut up with barbed wire on the Fourth of July. They seem to know the worst possible time to have major crises that require the services of a vet. No matter how much I want to stay here with you, I can't.''

He stroked her arm. "Eleanor can handle another night.''

"It's not fair to ask her.'' She slid back down beside him. "She was so sweet. She told me to go, seize the day.''

"She knows how important that is.''

"I know about her husband. So sad.''

"According to Rick, it nearly broke her—that and losing the practice. He and Margot knew her and Jerry from conventions. Even at Jerry's funeral she never let anyone know how tough things were. Thought she could handle everything herself. When Rick found out about the bankruptcy and that she'd basically disappeared, he tracked her down and put her back to work.''

"That's obviously what she needed. She credits Rick and Creature Comfort with bringing her back from the brink, but I worry about putting too much pressure on her.''

"She'd tell you if she felt you were taking advantage.''

"You know, I believe she would.''

"So stay.'' He cupped her breast gently, and with each stroke of his palm she felt the embers begin to glow again.

She caught her breath and curled her fingers into the dark hair on his chest. "Are you trying to keep me a prisoner?''

He smiled sleepily. "I love the feel of your skin, and, yes, if I had enough rope I would.''

"I wish I could stay.''

He stopped what he was doing and rested his arm across her, instead. "Okay. You win. This time. Anyway, you're not the only one with an inconvenient job. I have to fly off to Alaska or Albuquerque at a moment's notice to pull Coy's chestnuts out of whatever fire he's dropped them into. I never know when and I never know for how long. Everybody has lives, my love. The trick is to make the most of the time we spend together.''

My love? Did he mean that? Sarah felt a wave of tenderness sweep over her, so powerful that she lost her breath.

"Now, I suggest you come share my shower, and then I'll finish breakfast and we can take Nasdaq for a run. If you're determined to be at work by four, you can stay until after lunch, at least. I'd like you to see the lake.''

After breakfast they walked down the hill behind the house to the lake and sat on the small dock.

"It's a funny color,'' Sarah said.

"Green and brown. Not like Minnesota lakes, I guess.''

"Not a bit. But pretty.''

"I have a sailboat in storage down at the main dock. I usually get it out about now, but this year there hasn't been time. This is the first time I've had a couple of days free in months, ever since Coy landed me with the clinic on top of my other duties. Ever been sailing?''

"Actually, I'm pretty good.''

"Good. We'll do it.'' He put his arm around her. She leaned against him and slipped her hand along his thigh.

"Your father teach you to sail?'' he asked.

"He spent all his time playing catch with my brothers. I learned to sail in college, then I had a friend in vet school who had a Hobie Cat.''

"From what you've told me about your family, I'm

surprised your father sprung for tuition to vet school,''
Mark said.

"He didn't. I got a good scholarship to college and
worked on the side. I could never have gone on to become a veterinarian if my aunt Louise, my mother's
sister, hadn't helped with the tuition and the fees.''

"Nice of her.''

"She doesn't have any children of her own, but the
important thing is that she really doesn't like my father.
Anything he disapproves of, she's all for.'' She
shrugged. "Of course, everything comes with a price.''

"And her price was…?''

"I should have seen it coming. She breeds show
dogs—Dandie Dinmont terriers. Know what they are?''

"Haven't a clue.''

"They look like animated, white, fuzzy cigars with
pom-poms on their heads. Nice dogs, but pretty silly to
look at. I didn't know at the time I accepted her help,
but she expected me to become her full-time vet the
minute I graduated from vet school.''

"How'd you get out of it?''

"I'm paying her back. She was pretty upset at first,
but we've made up. She believes women should have
careers so that they don't need men. She's never married, wears elderly corduroy jeans and Wellington
boots. I love her dearly, but I sure don't want to live in
a kennel in the middle of the Minnesota woods with
her. I'm just about out of debt to her. That means I can
begin to save some money to buy a partnership of my
own.''

"How did you hope to buy into the one in Minnesota?''

"You mean if my boss had agreed to sell the partnership to me instead of his nephew? I would have bor-

rowed every cent I could, and worked out an installment plan for the rest. It's a small practice. I couldn't hope to buy a partnership in a group this large for years, and even then, only if I scrimp for every last dollar.'' She reached up and kissed his chin. ''Now that I've got my laser, I'm glad I moved. Any chance I can have some of the other equipment I need?''

''You're insatiable. I'm working on it.''

''Thank you. Oh, look at the time. I've got to start back.''

He held her. ''Don't go.''

''We've been all over this. Don't you have to get back to work, too?''

''Of course, but I'd lie like a rug to Beth if you'd stay another night.''

''No can do. Shall I take the kittens?''

He sighed. ''I'll bring them with me. No sense in upsetting Nasdaq.''

After she had stowed her gear in her truck, Mark put his arms around her and kissed her gently at first, then deeper.

When at last she broke the kiss, she asked, ''I'd love to come back sometime.''

''How about tomorrow?''

She laughed. ''I didn't have quite so soon in mind.''

''The first weekend we have off.''

''What if your mother and stepfather come home?''

''I'll tell them to stay in town because I have a taw-dry assignation with a working girl and that they'd better stay away if they don't want to be shocked.''

''You would, too.''

''Sure I would. Kiss me.''

She did. Then she climbed into her truck and drove away.

He watched her until she was out of sight, then went back into the cabin to collect his gear and his new family. At the rate he was going, he'd probably have a full-grown buffalo in his living room in a couple of weeks.

Would the fluoroscope and the other items have been delivered by the time she went into the clinic?

Now that he and Sarah had finally made love, he was more worried than ever about the way she'd react if she found out he was the one who'd paid for her equipment.

Could he trust Coy to keep his mouth shut about the source of the funds?

CHAPTER FIFTEEN

"You CAN'T JUST hightail it out of here when I need you." Coy Buchanan sounded petulant. He'd stormed into Mark's office as soon as he'd come in and had plopped himself down in the chair across from Mark's desk, even though it wasn't really big enough for him.

Mark was used to Coy's moods, but today all he wanted to do was to finish up in the Buchanan offices and go to the clinic to find Sarah. Still, he composed himself to endure a minor tirade.

"Then you turned off the damn phone down at that cabin and switched off your cell phone. I almost sent Beth down to get you personally."

That would have been interesting. "You knew where I was and what I was doing. I haven't had two days off at one time for the past four months, Coy. I needed to get my parents' water heater replaced. I told Beth that."

"You took almost *three* days. It's damn near five o'clock in the afternoon, and you've finally deigned to appear. I've been sweating bullets over that blasted high-rise in Dallas. The whole deal's about to blow up in our faces. Some stupid stipulation about a water catchment basin they're acting like horses' asses over."

"I know about it, Coy. I'm working with the planning commission on the changes. It's going to be fine."

"How the hell am I supposed to know that?"

"I'm sorry. I should have kept you better informed."

"Damn tough to inform me when you're never here. If you're not at the lake, you're out at the damn clinic."

Mark felt his temper start to fray. Too little sleep, missing Sarah in his arms, and a feeling that he'd been pushed over the limit by the man in front of him made his gut churn. "You're the one who gave me the assignment, Coy. You're the one who said I should take all the time I needed—just ride herd on that clinic and keep Margot from spending the national debt. Am I quoting you accurately?"

"Yeah, but I thought you could do it after work on your own time."

"That's the problem, I *have* been doing it on my own time. And that means I don't have *any* time of my own. I can't even manage to pick up my cleaning."

"Get Beth to do it."

"That's not her job. She's a beautiful, intelligent and highly paid employee, and Buchanan Enterprises is lucky to have her. She does not need to be picking up anybody's cleaning, least of all mine."

Coy drew himself up. "You got something going there?"

"No, I have not. There's only one man around this place that Beth is interested in, and he's too big a darn fool to notice."

Coy's eyes narrowed. "Who is it? I won't have anybody harassing my employees."

Mark laughed and shook his head. "It's you, you idiot."

"Me? I'm old enough to be her father."

"There's no accounting for tastes."

Coy's face took on a look of wonder. "Me? We went out to dinner but I thought she was just being nice to a lonely old man."

"She doesn't see you as a lonely old man, and if she ever finds out I told you, she'll kill me and then she'll quit, and I can't manage without her."

"Uh-huh." Coy turned toward the door. "I came in here to fire you. Guess I won't, after all." He opened the door, walked through, and shut it quietly after him. Since he generally slammed doors as a matter of course, Mark realized how completely thrown the man had been by Mark's revelation.

Had Mark done the right thing? Coy certainly never would have clued in to Beth's interest on his own. Suddenly Mark wanted everyone he knew to find the same kind of love he'd discovered.

Love?

Yes, he was in love with Sarah—the most opinionated, difficult, career-driven over-achieving female he'd ever met.

"SARAH, this is Steve."

Sarah sat down in her desk chair too hard and too fast. "Steve? Still in the office this late? How nice to hear from you."

"Yeah, yeah. You ready to come back to Minnesota to work yet?"

"Boy, that sure makes me pine for home. You think I'm on vacation down here?"

"You know me. I don't stand on ceremony. The thing is, Sarah, I want you back. I'll give you a raise."

Sarah sat back in her chair. "Back, as in back in your practice? Giving shots to puppies and kitties?"

"What's wrong with puppies and kitties? They're the backbone of the practice. That's where the money is."

"We've had this conversation a million times, Steve.

No, I am not ready to come back to Minnesota to work in your clinic.''

"Not even for a partnership?''

"I beg your pardon?''

"Listen, Sarah, it's hard for an old man like me to admit he was wrong, but I was. You're the best damn vet I've ever had working here. A lot better than my wife's nephew.''

"What's been happening, Steve? Something sure changed your mind.''

She could hear him clearing his throat. That meant he was going to waffle about what he told her.

"Nothing. I miss you.''

"Bull.''

"Well, okay, so we've lost a few clients. Apparently some of them didn't like him. They wanted you.''

"Wonder of wonders. But the partnership wasn't the only reason I left.''

"Yeah. Okay. If you want to increase the large-animal side of the practice, you can try it.''

"Thanks a bunch.''

"You know I'm planning to retire in two years. I'll sell you the practice.''

Now, this was new. He'd always refused in the past. Sarah leaned forward, propped her elbows on the table and her fist against her chin. "I can't afford to buy the practice, Steve. You know that. I could barely afford to become a partner, and even then I'd have to mortgage my soul to get the money.''

"I'll make you a good deal. Time payments. Start out with a partnership. You know the practice makes good money. I don't want to see it go down the tubes. With you, I know I'll have a source of income for a few years after I retire. We'll work something out when you get back.''

"Oh, no. How many times have you told me you'd consider taking me in as a partner? Suddenly your memory becomes all foggy when it comes to the details.''

"Not this time, Sarah, I promise." He sounded desperate. "I got to get rid of my wife's nephew somehow. He's incompetent and rude to the clients. But my wife'll kill me if I just fire him. If you come back, I can.''

"I see. Tell you what, Steve, I'm not really interested. Thanks, anyway.''

"But Sarah...''

"Thanks for calling, Steve. Bye.''

She leaned back and swung her feet up on the desk. She had no intention of returning to Minnesota. Maybe it was wrong to slam doors. But even if something awful happened—Creature Comfort went bankrupt—she wouldn't go back to Minnesota.

Please, God, she prayed, I can stand losing the clinic. Just don't let me lose Mark.

She had just finished shooting steroids into the swollen knee of a Thoroughbred jumper, when her telephone rang again. She picked up the one on the wall beside the stocks.

"Dr. Marsdon.''

"Sarah, it's long distance.''

Sarah sighed. "Thanks, Mabel. Put it through." She started to motion to Jack to get the horse out of the stocks and lead it into a stall for the night. He was already doing it.

She answered the call.

"Are you determined to destroy your life?''

She leaned against the wall. "Hello to you, too, Dad. So Steve's already been on the phone to you.''

"He called me before he called you, and then after you as good as hung up on him. What has gotten into you? This is what you said you wanted."

"That was then, this is now."

"What's that supposed to mean?"

"Dad, I have moved to Tennessee. I have accepted another job. I have a house, friends. This is the sort of clinic I've always dreamed of working in. I'm doing some good work here. And it's not snowing."

"It's not snowing here, either."

Sarah shook her head as though her father could see it. "No, but it'll start again in September. I just spent a couple of hours walking in the woods. The leaves on the trees are already completely out, Dad, and there are wild dogwoods and iris everywhere you look. And azaleas."

Lars harrumphed. "You don't give a damn about flowers."

"I like it here, Dad. I am not coming back."

"Then, you're a fool."

"Answer me one question. Honestly."

"Ask. I'll see."

"Why is it so important to you that I come back to Minnesota? I'm happy here. I'm making a life. If you care about me, why aren't you happy for me?"

Dead silence, then he said, "Down there we can't protect you."

"Why do you think I need protection?"

"I already lost the only other woman in my life that meant a damn to me. I don't plan to lose you, too."

Sarah simply gaped at the telephone.

"Sarah?" Her father sounded even gruffer.

"Daddy, why on earth haven't you ever said that before?"

"Thought it was obvious. Hell and damnation, girl, you think it's easy to worry about you going head-to-head with some Brahma bull, or driving back roads in a blizzard and forty-below windchill? Why can't you marry Gerald, look after dogs and cats in the daytime, and give me a granddaughter?"

"Daddy, I'm sorry. I just can't. You can't protect me. Nobody can. All you do is try not to worry so much. If you'll stop driving me nuts about coming home, I promise I'll keep in better touch. Deal?"

"Humph. I'll consider it."

The line clicked. Her hand was shaking as she put the phone back into its cradle.

It seemed as though she'd fought her father all her life, even before her mother died. He'd forbidden her to play hockey with her brothers, and punished her when she did—although she skated better than any of them. She'd never broken *her* nose like Nels. After her mother died, she'd begged to go to summer camp. Her brothers went, but she only went when she was in college and old enough to work as a counselor without his permission.

She'd had to work two jobs in college to afford to live in the dorm. Her father wanted her living at home and refused to pay the room fees. Without her aunt's help she'd never have made it to vet school.

She'd blamed him for her mother's death. Now she realized for the first time how deeply it had affected him. That had been the real start of his anger whenever she'd gone against his wishes. She'd thought he simply wanted a live-in housekeeper. It had never occurred to her that he worried about losing her, that he might actually love her. The idea would take some getting used to.

As she went to find Jack and their next patient—a cow with bloat—she wondered how long it would be before one of her brothers or their wives phoned to re-inforce her dad's call. He wouldn't stop trying to get her home—of that she was certain. Now she could sym-pathize a bit. But she couldn't do as he asked.

She worked nonstop until early evening on horses, cows, and even a goat that had ripped a horn halfway off and was bleeding badly. It was the first time she'd actually had enough large-animal cases to keep her busy. Things were picking up.

At six in the evening, as she was getting ready to eat a couple of packages of peanut butter crackers from the machine, Mabel buzzed her.

"Okay, Mabel," she said. "Which one of my sib-lings is on the line?"

"Would you tell Jack to raise the back door? There's a delivery for you."

"A delivery? I'm not expecting any more drugs."

"This is big."

"Oh."

It *was* big. Three large boxes, all labelled This Side Up and Fragile.

Jack opened each one carefully. It was like Christ-mas, only better. First came the portable fluoroscope—not a new one, but top-of-the-line nonetheless. Next, the laptop computer, printer and centrifuge for the blood chemistry analyzer. Then, the portable X ray. And at the very bottom of the box, an endoscope.

"That bloody man pulled it off!" Jack said. "Wouldn't have believed it if I hadn't seen it with my own eyes."

"He knew! Mark knew these were already on the way! I don't know whether to kill him or kiss him!"

"I wouldn't kill him, girl. Where'd he find the money, is what I want to know."

"I don't know and I don't care! Come on, Jack, we've got some work to do. We have to set all this stuff up so we can test it tomorrow."

"And teach me to use it? I'm an old dog, girl."

"You're about to learn some new tricks."

In her excitement Sarah had forgotten the family calls that were sure to come. Now the ringing telephone reminded her. "Please, God, let it be Mark."

Unfortunately, it was Gretchen, Nels's wife. The bossy one. "Daddy Lars told me Steve is going to sell you a partnership. Isn't that wonderful news? You can come home to your family where you belong."

"When did you talk to my father?"

"Just before lunchtime. Why?"

"I think he already knows I won't be coming back."

"You can't be serious. This is your home." Her voice dropped, became conspiratorial. "I saw Gerald last week. He had a woman with him."

"Glad to hear it."

"She wasn't nearly as pretty as you. Very crass. Overdressed. It's no wonder. I betcha he's picked up some floozy on the rebound."

"That's his problem."

"For goodness' sake, Sarah Marsdon, you are throwing away a man any woman would kill for."

"Not me. Sorry, Gretchen. Listen, I don't know who else Dad lined up to call me, but you should save them the long-distance charges."

"What about your nieces and nephews? They miss their auntie Sarah. And Daddy Lars—he's turned into an old man since you left. He won't admit it, but he misses you, too. I'm worried about him."

Sarah closed her eyes. Guilt was Gretchen's thing. It always got to Sarah. This time it would not work. "I'm sorry to hear that, Gretchen. I'm so glad that he has you and the others to look after him."

"But…"

"Sorry, Gretchen, gotta go. Nice talking to you." She hung up firmly.

She'd forgotten Jack.

He raised his head from behind the box. "Families, right?"

"How did your family take it when you moved over here from England?"

"Me mum 'n dad was dead already, so t'wasn't much to leave. I came to ride the American race courses. I met my lady wife during the racing season at Hot Springs my first year, and never looked back. She stuck with me even when my riding days were over."

"I've never asked. Do you have children?"

"Two girls. Both grown. Elspeth married a trainer. Maggie never liked horses. Works for a computer company in California. Making pots of money, she says."

"You sound proud of them."

"I am. Good kids, the both of them. Listen, girl, I never wanted Elspeth to marry the man she did. It's a hard life, moving from racetrack to racetrack, and not much money in it unless you're one of the top lads— but it seems to agree with her. What I'm saying is that parents often want something for their children that the children don't want."

"But you accepted her decision?"

"Real dustup we had. Threatened to disown her, I did. Ashamed of it now, but then it seemed the right thing to do."

"My family drives me crazy."

"You do what you want. They'll get used to it. I did." He grinned. "Now, about this blood chemistry thing. How do you work it?"

MARK WORKED until nearly eight in his office at Buchanan, catching up, then he drove to the clinic. Although he tried to keep a straight face, he knew he was smiling. He parked in back and came in the employees' door. He could see light spilling into the aisle from Sarah's office and hear both her voice and Jack's. He sauntered over to the door as casually as he could.

Surrounded by boxes, Sarah sat cross-legged on the floor in a sea of foam popcorn that the equipment had been boxed in. Jack saw him first and nodded to Sarah. She turned toward him. The light caught her hair as it swung, but the real light came from her eyes and her smile.

"You devil!" She rose smoothly and took the two steps into his arms. "You knew, and you didn't tell me!"

He hugged her back, while Jack raised his eyebrows. "I didn't know it would be delivered today."

"But you knew it was all ordered. How did you do it?"

"Trade secret."

"Bill Chumney's going to have a fit when he sees all this. He swears you've been hoarding money that was budgeted for his flight cage."

"He's wrong, but I'll never convince him of that."

She grabbed his hand and dragged him to the boxes like a child showing her new Christmas doll. "It's all marvelous! Of course, there are still some big-ticket items we'll have to have, but at least with this I can actually tell clients I can treat their horses and cows as they should be treated. Most of the time, at any rate.''

"You don't give up, do you?"

"Never. I'm insatiable." She caught his eye, and blushed.

"Well, I think I'll pack it in for the evening," Jack said. "This can wait until tomorrow. G'night, all." He strode out and shut the door behind him.

"He's being discreet." Mark sank into Sarah's desk chair and pulled her down into his lap, where he kissed her soundly.

When she broke the kiss, she said, "We're not. And we must be. At least here in the office."

"Don't see why." He nuzzled her neck.

"You do, too. What do you think Bill and Mac are going to say when they see all this bounty? I know Bill has some things he wants badly, and I can't imagine Mac accepting anybody else's goodies gracefully, can you? There's bound to be talk, as in, 'You found the money for her, why not for us?'"

"You made a better case. And Mac got most of his on the front end."

"Nobody will believe that. Certainly not if we're acting like a couple of over-sexed adolescents."

Mark laughed and ran his hand over her hip. "I'm no adolescent, but I'll buy the over-sexed part." His face turned serious. "You're right. It's going to be hard for you to deal with this. I don't need to make it harder." He moved her gently off his lap. "But I did enjoy seeing your face."

"Tell me the truth. How much of this is because you know we need it, and how much is because we're...you know?"

"Don't ask me that, Sarah. I don't make business

decisions based on 'you know.' You convinced me that the equipment was needed, that you'd never be able to grow the practice if you couldn't provide all the services you should. You were right. Between Beth and me, we managed to get some very good deals. You don't have the most expensive, newest, or fanciest, but it will have to do for now. We'll upgrade and add more as soon as finances permit.''

"An MRI?"

"Not for a long time, and not without a consortium of vet practices to share the cost plus the cost of hiring and training a technician. We might get the anesthetic equipment sometime in the near future.''

"Okay. Deal." She slipped back onto his lap and nibbled his ear. "Tomorrow I promise I'll be very businesslike, but tonight, I just want to eat you alive.''

"Sounds like a plan." He began to kiss her face and throat.

Sarah broke away. "That wasn't exactly what I meant. Somebody could walk in on us.''

"Lock the door,'' he said into the hollow between her breasts.

"Mark, Mark darling…'' She sank back into his embrace.

The telephone rang. Without breaking his hold on Sarah, Mark reached up a foot and kicked the thing off the other side of the desk onto the floor.

Sarah pushed him away and stretched across the desk to pick it up.

"Dr. Marsdon. How may I help you? Oh, Mabel, no you're not disturbing me. I was just unpacking some things. What kind of a monkey? Uh-huh. Brown. It's named Algernon?" She rolled her eyes at Mark. "Does it have a tail? Okay, I'll be right there. And for pity's sake, don't let it out of its carrier until I get there."

She reeled in the telephone by its cord, turned and sat on the desk. "Why do people wait until night for these things? I've got a pet monkey named Algernon with what his owner says is an abscessed tooth. He is not a happy camper."

"God, Sarah, monkeys have fearsome teeth."

"And nasty tempers. Mabel says monkey and not ape, so it shouldn't be a chimp, but I'll still have to sedate it before I can treat it."

"Shall I wait?"

She shook her head. "This could take a while, and I'm not officially off until midnight, though I can probably leave earlier if there's no business." She stroked his cheek. "Go home. Feed your brood. How're the kittens doing?"

"Fine. But it's been over four hours since they were fed."

"I think you can safely bump it to six now. Bring them with you when you drop off Nasdaq tomorrow morning. I'll leave instructions with Alva Jean on how to feed them. We'll have them weaned to a bowl with kitten food mushed up in it in a couple of days. Then we can start to find them homes." She narrowed her eyes at him. "Before I start giving away people's kittens, Mr. Scott, you do want me to find homes for them?"

"Yeah, this time I do."

"Not a problem." He kissed her, but when his hands began to move, she broke away. "Are you trying to seduce me away from my duty?"

"Just trying to show you there are better things to do at night than simian dentistry."

"I agree a hundred per cent." She smiled at him. "Now, I really want to watch you explain that to the monkey."

Despite her four-to-midnight shift, Sarah had to get going early the following day to do a pre-purchase exam on a horse. Then she had an entire barn of quarter horses to vaccinate. When she swung by the clinic afterward, Rick called her into his office.

"Got your equipment, I see." He grinned at her and waved her to a chair.

"Don't know how he did it, but I'm grateful to you both."

"I'd love to take credit, but it's not my doing. I just wanted to let you know that I've had nothing but great feedback on you since you got here."

"Thanks."

"I didn't expect it to happen in only a couple of weeks, but I think we can rearrange your schedule so that you work days. Eleanor will take the four-to-midnight full time, and Liz will take over midnight to eight. We'll cut back on the casual labor. It's time we ran full-time with our own people."

"Can Liz do that, with a husband and children?"

"It was her idea. She can go home, get the kids and her husband off to school, then crash and be awake in time to pick them up after school. It's usually so quiet after midnight that she can study. She's still planning to go back to school in the fall to specialize in opthalmology. I'm interviewing a couple of vet techs today. If they work out, they'll be able to do Liz's shift, plus work with Nancy and Jack. So, you interested in having your nights and weekends back?"

"You have no idea how much."

"One more thing. Margot's working on the guest list

for the grand opening. We've put it off for a few more weeks so things will be totally finished. She's going to invite all the clients we've got now, plus all the horse-and-cow people from the area. She wants to invite all the other vets in the region, too, but I'm not certain that's a good idea.''

"I don't think you can avoid inviting them.''

"You're probably right, but there are still some big holes in our permanent staffing. Margot wants to gloat over the clinic, but other vets are likely to pick out the places where we're still weak.''

"A good many of them have opened practices themselves. They know how hard the shakedown phase is. Besides, you've got two weeks to fill the vacancies.''

"Shoot, I haven't been able to do it in four months—and now I'm expected to come up with trained personnel in two weeks?''

"Not trained. What we need is warm and willing bodies. Cleanup personnel, people we can really count on to take up the slack. At this point, if Nancy or Jack comes down with the flu or, God forbid, quits, we're really up the creek.''

"I'm trying.'' Rick sounded depressed. "At least Mark understands we've got to hire a few more people, although I don't think he likes it.''

"He does listen to reason.''

"Sometimes.'' Rick brightened. "Anyway, Margo wants to go all out for the party. Black tie optional, fancy dresses for the ladies. She's in her element at this sort of thing. That's why they make her chairman of the symphony ball every year. Mention it to your clients, will you?''

"Sure. That everything?''

"For the moment. Keep up the good work.''

She shut the door quietly behind her, barely able to contain herself. Weekends, actual weekends. And nights when she could have a decent dinner and sleep in her own bed.

Well, somebody's bed.

OVER THE NEXT WEEKS Sarah and Mark slipped into a routine. Sometimes Mark would cook at his house. Sometimes Sarah bought takeout, or tried to fix a decent meal when he finally came by her duplex. She now had furniture. Since the items were rented on a monthly basis, they weren't precisely what she would have chosen, but they were serviceable and comfortable. The bed was definitely better than the air mattress.

One or the other usually slept over, unless Sarah got called out to an emergency that Eleanor or Liz couldn't handle alone.

One afternoon Mark called her from Buchanan. "Hi. My mother and stepfather are finally back from their cruise. How about we get together someplace for dinner tonight? I'd like you to meet them."

Sarah gulped. "Oh, Mark, I don't know."

"My mother is not a gargoyle. She won't bite."

"All right. What do I wear?"

VIRGINIA SCOTT OGLESBY was as far from being a gargoyle as was possible. As tall as Sarah, slim, with short, silver hair cut in layers around her elegant head, a simple blue silk shift that slid over her body and a coral necklace that set off her golden skin, Mark's mother belonged in *Town and Country Magazine*.

Bob Oglesby was five inches shorter and forty pounds heavier than his wife. He was almost bald, with twinkly gray eyes and a quirky mouth that always seemed to be smiling.

Looking at Virginia's superbly manicured hands, Sarah wanted to hide her own work-roughened paws with their short unvarnished nails inside the sleeves of her cotton sweater.

"I'm so delighted finally to meet you," Virginia said with a smile. "Mark's told me all about you and how you helped him with the water heater down at the lake."

Sarah turned to Mark with her eyebrows raised all the way to her hairline. "Uh, yes."

"You must come down the next weekend that both of you are free, so Mark can take you sailing. Bob and I are home for the summer, unless we get wanderlust again and take off for Canada or Alaska or someplace cool. And, of course, Mark can always use the cabin when we're not here."

Bob slipped his arm around his wife's waist and twinkled at Sarah. "Don't take the heat as well as I used to. It was really too hot for me in the Isles. I was glad to come home before my bald spot got permanently roasted."

The dinner went surprisingly well. Mark and his mother seemed in complete rapport. He relaxed in a way he didn't even manage with Sarah. She liked Bob enormously and could see why Virginia had fallen for him.

As they were leaving the restaurant, Virginia leaned over. "Can you take time off for lunch on Tuesday?"

"I don't usually eat lunch, and I'll be in my working clothes."

"Doesn't matter. I know a great barbecue place. Mark can give you directions. If you get an emergency, don't worry about it. Mark's explained that you can't really call your time your own.''

That night, while Mark snored softly beside her, she wondered what on earth she would say to Virginia Oglesby? She'd learned that mothers were sometimes peculiar about the women their sons dated. Although Virginia had been perfectly charming to Sarah, maybe she felt that Sarah didn't fit the corporate image for an up-and-comer like Mark.

Was Momma about to explain that to her in terms even she could understand?

CHAPTER SIXTEEN

"I LOVE GOOD BARBECUE; the browner the better," Virginia said as she picked up a fried onion ring and began to nibble around its edges. "It's a southern thing."

"It's very good," Sarah said after her first bite.

"And greasy onion rings. I have to watch Bob's cholesterol, so I enjoy escaping to wallow in pure lard—Mark's crazy about you, you know."

"Is he?" Sarah asked, surprised by the sudden intimacy.

"Come on, Sarah, you don't have to play games with me." Virginia put down her sandwich and leaned her elbows on the table. "You know he is. I suspect you're rather fond of him, as well."

"You could say that, Mrs. Oglesby."

"Oh, for heaven's sake, call me Ginnie. Everybody does. Even Big Tom did." She picked up her sandwich but didn't bite into it. She avoided Sarah's eyes and said casually, "Has Mark mentioned Big Tom to you?"

"A time or two."

"His father's death changed him. Mark grew up wild as a hare. A good student, but a real hell-raiser, just like Tom. I was afraid he'd end up with a DUI or something equally tawdry before I could get him off to Princeton. Never anything really serious—no drugs, no pregnant girlfriends. He wanted to be just like Tom—a party animal. What happened after Tom died changed all that. Made him bitter.''

"He doesn't seem bitter now.''

"That's partly your doing, I think, Sarah, and I'm grateful to you. I think he hated what Tom's death did to me more than anything else. I never really cared about the big house and the servants and the constant parties. I hate big parties, actually. I'd rather work in my flower beds. But Tom always said we had to be part of the money-making crowd or we wouldn't make money. And what Tom wanted, Tom got. Eat up while it's hot.''

"Of course." Sarah picked up an onion ring and took a bite, then gulped some iced tea to keep from burning the roof of her mouth.

"Anyway, the insurance company didn't want to pay up, and I desperately needed the money from that policy to settle all the closing costs and escrows that Tom had been kiting from place to place. Bob is the one who tried to convince everyone that Tom committed suicide. Needless to say, I wasn't too happy to see him, at first, when we ran into each other five years later. Funny the way things work out, isn't it?''

"But the insurance company finally paid, didn't they?''

"They did. I've never known whether Tom drove into that post on purpose. If he did, it was a spur-of-the-moment thing. He'd never plan to do something like that to his family. At any rate, the insurance paid off his debts, but we had to scale down our lifestyle drastically. I regretted that Mark couldn't go to Princeton.''

"You think *he* regrets it?''

"I don't think so, but then Coy Buchanan has been like a second father to him. He's brought Mark along fast, and Mark deserves it. But he hasn't been happy, not for a long time. Until now. I think that's your doing.''

"Oh, I'm sure there are a lot of reasons."

"He hasn't had many women friends. No time, or maybe it was just that nobody could hold his interest for long. You're very different from the women he's dated through the years."

- *Meaning I've got calluses on my hands and horse manure on most of my shoes.*

"I'm his mother, so I won't ask you your intentions. God, how Victorian that sounds! But please, try not to hurt him. He's been hurt so deeply."

"I wouldn't hurt him for the world," Sarah said.

"Good. Now let's eat."

On her way back to the clinic, Sarah thought back over what was probably the strangest lunch she'd ever had. All families interfered, apparently, most with the best intentions. Amazing that they screwed up so often.

AT LAST SARAH'S PRACTICE was keeping her busy. Half of each day she spent in the field, going from farm to farm, barn to barn, vaccinating, palpating and ultra-sounding for pregnancies, pulling blood samples for Coggins tests—the standard things that all vets did on a daily basis. The work would never become routine, because each animal reacted differently.

She narrowly avoided having her foot stepped on by an annoyed Limousin bull who needed a boil lanced, and having her head kicked by an Arabian stallion who didn't like having a needle stuck in his neck. Most of the large pig farms in the area had their own vets on staff, as did the chicken farms, so she found herself working mostly with cattle and horses, with the occa-sional herd of goats or sheep thrown in for fun.

Except for a couple of rainy days, on which she wound up flat on her back in the mud at least three times, the early-June weather stayed perfect. Everyone warned her about the heat that was still to come, but at this point she would take mud over sleet any day.

Most afternoons she worked on animals that had been brought to the clinic for surgery or supportive care that they couldn't get in their own facilities.

"I can't do it all alone," Jack complained one after-noon while he held a billy goat down long enough for Sarah to de-billy him.

"Be grateful we're busy. You've got Kenny after school, and Rick keeps interviewing. There— You can let him up. And get out of the way fast."

Sarah and Jack both vaulted the enclosure fence, as the infuriated goat charged at them.

"Kenny's got a crush on you," Jack said.

"I think he regards me as a big sister. He's a good worker, and he loves animals. I wish he'd get his friends to come in, too. We could use the help."

"Leastways they've stopped vandalizing the place. Looks like the only area that won't be finished for the party is Dr. Weincroft's research building."

"He says he can keep working where he is for a few more months, but I gather his present facility is on ex-tremely valuable land. He'd like to sell it and move in here."

"Uh-oh, here comes trouble." Jack jerked his head toward the door to the hall. Bill pattered in.

"Sarah, we have to talk."

"Sure, Bill, what's up?"

Bill glanced at Jack. "In your office."

Sarah rolled her eyes at Jack, but followed Bill. She took her desk chair. He stood with his hands clasped behind his back, and rocked back and forth on his small feet.

"I have kept my mouth shut as long as I can."

"Sit down, Bill."

"I prefer to stand, thank you. I would hate to think you brought undue pressure to bear on Mark Scott to get all this equipment."

"So would I."

"However, it has been brought to my attention that the two of you are carrying on. I do not think that is professional, and I intend to speak to Rick about it."

"I don't think what we do outside the office is any of your concern."

"It is if it results in your getting a bunch of expensive equipment, when I can't even have a decent flight cage." Bill's face was growing alarmingly red. "I think you're an excellent vet, Sarah, and I like you personally, but I refuse to countenance your using the influence of your sex to get what you want."

Sarah took a deep breath. Losing her temper wouldn't help. "Bill, please believe me when I tell you that I did not use the influence of my sex to get this equipment. I used reason. We could not advertise ourselves as a state-of-the-art clinic without it. Neither horsemen nor cattlemen could trust us to be able to give them full service, and without them, this place would go under before the end of the year. Mark found the money for that equipment because it made solid economic sense, period."

"Nonsense."

"I beg your pardon."

Now Bill was close to tears. "You tell your Mr.

Wonderful that he'd better come up with the money for my flight cage the way he did for your equipment—hell, we can do it for under ten thousand dollars—or I swear I'll go to Rick and Margot about it.''

Sarah asked incredulously, ''Are you trying to black-mail me?''

''No! But my birds are every bit as important as your damn horses. I want my flight cage!''

''Bill, there is not one thing I can do to get your flight cage. I have already explained that I don't control Mark, and I certainly don't have any influence over his financial decisions. You'll have to plead your own case.''

''Hah. Apparently pleading only works when you're beautiful and female and make *house* calls.''

He stomped out of her office.

She stared after him with her mouth open. Her face felt as hot as though he'd slapped her. She told herself she had no reason to feel embarrassed, and definitely none to feel guilty.

But she did. This was the thing she'd worried about from the start, the reason she'd tried so hard—and so unsuccessfully—to keep her relationship with Mark strictly professional.

From the start, she'd never given Mark any reason to think her feelings for him had anything to do with her equipment. She knew now that he'd already bought her equipment before that weekend at Pickwick Lake.

How could anybody who knew him believe he'd let *his* feelings for her or anyone else influence his financial decisions? He'd bought the equipment because she'd made her case for it, period.

Bill would never believe that. There was no point in trying to explain that to him until he'd calmed down. Maybe not even then. She and Mark had never tried to conceal their relationship from the members of the staff. They hadn't done anything wrong.

No matter what Bill Chumney thought.

THE CLINIC was closed—except for emergencies—on the day of the grand opening party. Margot demanded the time to decorate and set up the food, bars and music.

Mark mentioned the music to Sarah as they were lazing over their second cup of morning coffee in Sarah's king-size bed.

"Music?" Sarah asked Mark. "As in live music?"

He nodded. "Coy approved it. What could I do? He's footing the bill for this shindig personally. I think it's partly to pacify Margot. She's found out he's dating Beth Marelli."

"Oh, good. I'm glad."

"Margot isn't happy about it. For one thing, Beth is still young enough to have babies if she and Coy were to get married. And Margot doesn't intend to share her inheritance with anyone—wife or child. So far, she's been highly successful in torpedoing Coy's relationships with women. But I don't think Beth is going to slink away like the others."

"Good for her."

"Coy is doing enough slinking for both of them, but he's still taking Beth out to dinner and such."

"And such?"

"Your guess is as good as mine, but he's still a relatively young man, and Beth is a very beautiful and very determined young woman. I hope for both their sakes that there's plenty of 'and such.'"

"Me, too. I wish everybody plenty of 'and such.'" She cuddled against him.

"Bill Chumney tell you about our meeting?" he asked as he stroked her hair.

"Nope. He's been very quiet."

"I promised him we'd enlarge his flight cage as soon as Sol Weincroft's research wing is finished."

"Good."

"The clinic is more than living up to its business plan, largely due to your efforts. In another couple of months, we should be able to afford ten thousand dollars easily."

"Boy, have you gotten profligate in your old age."

"Not that old. Come here."

THE PARTY was supposed to start at seven and go on until midnight, with champagne, heavy hors d'oeuvres and dancing. Margot had collected RSVPs from almost a hundred clients and would-be clients. Sarah noted on the guest list that a quarter of them, at least, were her horse people, with a few big cattlemen sprinkled in. With their wives in tow, that made nearly two hundred in all, plus the staff of the clinic, and the neighborhood group that Margot had invited personally by telephone and by written invitation.

Even Kenny's father and mother had reluctantly agreed to show up.

"I'll pick you up about six-thirty," Mark said.

"I'll bring my truck. I may want to sneak out before it's over. I wish I had the nerve to stay away like Eleanor."

"Eleanor's not coming?"

"She says she's going to stay home with a good book and go to bed early for a change. I don't think she's comfortable around all those people at one time."

"I agree with her," Mark said. "I can't wait for this thing to be over with."

"You may not be able to sneak out, even if I can," she teased.

Sarah pulled into the back parking lot at a quarter-to-seven and found the area was already full—everything from fancy sedans to rusty pickups. However, fancy diesel trucks that could haul big trailers behind them predominated. Sarah slid out of her vehicle and adjusted her spaghetti straps. She'd put her hair up in a French twist and given herself a manicure, but in her full-length, maroon, satin shift with its knee-high slit, she felt almost naked.

As she opened the back door she nearly ran into Bill, who had a glass of champagne in his hand.

"Woo-ee, sugar," he said. The "sugar" came out slightly slurred. Not his first glass of champagne, then, or even his second. "Hell, if I looked like that, I'd have a dozen flight cages."

"Thanks, Bill, what a sweet thing to say." Sarah tried to brush past him, but he put his hand on her arm—not roughly, but insistently.

"Listen, I mean it. I got to hand it to you. Don't know what you've got, but it must be something else to get Scott to sell his stocks to buy your equipment."

"I beg your pardon."

"Hell, he keeps saying how he never puts a dime of his own money into something like this, and then he puts a couple of hundred thousand smackeroos right in that little office of yours."

Sarah felt goose bumps rise on her arms, and not from the breeze that whispered outside the door. She tried to keep her face composed. Bill was probably too snockered to notice how stunned she was.

"Hey, you got it, you flaunt it, is what I say. And boy, are you flaunting it tonight."

"What a compliment." This time she managed to get away from him. As she slipped past, he lifted his glass to her.

"Here's to our Sarah, the best little...veterinarian... in the business."

She maneuvered through the crowd, unlocked her office and slipped in. She didn't turn on the lights, just stood with her back to the door as she tried to catch her breath.

Bill was mistaken. He had to be. Mark had never actually told her he'd found money from the clinic budget but he'd intimated that he had. He wouldn't lie. He swore he never put his own money into this kind of thing. Why should he do it now? But my God, if it was true, she couldn't stay in this practice—not with everyone thinking the same thing Bill did. She laughed bitterly. She just might be the first woman in history to have sold her body for a fluoroscope—however unwittingly.

But it hadn't happened that way. Mark hadn't enticed her into his bed with promises of anesthesia machines. He'd ordered the things before she'd gone to him at Pickwick and had never even mentioned them to her. Then again, he'd never told where the money had come from. Instead, he'd tried to hide it from her....

How had Bill found out?

Maybe Mark had told Coy and Coy had said something to Rick. What Rick knew, Margot knew. What Margot knew, Bill could easily find out.

Maybe, just maybe, Bill had his facts wrong. She couldn't ask Mark. She didn't want to ask Rick. Beth would plead employer–employee confidentiality.

There was only one person who might tell her.

CHAPTER SEVENTEEN

SARAH WENT LOOKING for Margot Hazard.

She found her talking earnestly to the leader of the small combo that had been set up in the large-animal area.

"No hard rock. Swing. Easy listening. Most of these people consider the Beatles to be New Wave. We want them to dance. And not too loud. People should be able to converse with one another without shouting."

"Yes, ma'am."

Margot turned away, and the band leader snapped a military salute to her back.

"Sarah, you do look marvelous. You don't think we clash, do you?"

Margot wore a long slip dress of fire-engine red sequins and a necklace with a ruby-and-diamond pendant. If the pendant was real, Sarah thought, it could probably buy the clinic's way out of debt.

"No," Sarah said, looking down at her column of dark maroon silk. She hitched one of the spaghetti straps higher on her shoulder. "We blend."

"Good." Margot moved off at a fast clip.

"Margot, wait a minute," Sarah said, following her.

Margot heaved a mighty sigh. "Sarah, this isn't the best time."

"I'm sorry. This won't take but a moment. Do you happen to know how much Mark is out-of-pocket for the new equipment? I'm interested in what kind of deals he got.''

Margot blinked. "I didn't realize you knew. Rick said it was a secret, but I told him that was stupid. No man would liquidate two hundred thousand dollars worth of stocks to spend on his mistress without letting her know about it. Now, I really must check on the shrimp.'' She strode away.

Sarah was too stunned to move.

Two hundred thousand dollars for his *mistress*.

SHE WALKED SLOWLY back to her office, locked the door behind her and sat in the dark.

How could Mark have spent his own money—the one thing he said he'd never do—without consulting her? Didn't he realize how it would look? What her colleagues would think? Margot's words rang in her ears. *His mistress.*

She had to find Mark now. She owed him a chance to explain. She stepped out of her office into a crush of party-goers. She worked her way through the crowd, fighting tears of frustration.

"Hello, gorgeous,'' Mark said from behind her. His hands slid around her waist. "You clean up pretty well.''

"We have to talk. Now. In private.'' She led the way to her office, and after Mark followed her, she shut the door and turned to him.

"One question.''

"Anything,'' he said.

"You bought my equipment with your own money, didn't you?''

"Who told you that?''

"Bill. Is it true?''

"How did he know?"

"So it *is* true. I hoped…" She closed her eyes for a moment, then took a deep breath. "Apparently everyone knows except me. Margot confirmed it. She assumed you'd told me because no man would spend two hundred thousand dollars on his *mistress* without letting her know."

"God, Sarah. I'll kill her."

"Why? That's what I am, isn't it? Would it have been better if she'd called me your lover?"

"She shouldn't have called you anything."

"I'm not ashamed of our relationship. Or I wasn't. At this moment I'm not so sure."

CHAPTER EIGHTEEN

MARK SANK into the chair across from her desk. "I sure didn't plan for you to find out this way."

"Why didn't you just tell me you'd paid for everything yourself?" Sarah asked.

"Because I didn't think you'd want me to do it."

"So you didn't ask. You just went bulling ahead, then covered it up."

"I was right, apparently." He was trying to sound cool, instead he sounded cold and flat.

She laughed, but there was no warmth in it. "I swore to Bill I had absolutely no influence in your financial decisions."

"You didn't have. Not the way you mean."

"How do I convince Bill or everybody in the clinic of that? How do I convince myself?" She hugged her arms across her breasts. "No wonder Bill was so angry."

"I wanted to give you diamonds, but you wanted a laser instead. What's wrong with that?"

"The difference is that you made a commitment in my name without giving me a chance to say yes or no. You put me under an obligation I'll never be able to fulfill." She turned to him with tears in her eyes. "How can you ever be certain when I come into your arms, into your bed, that I'm not just paying my debts? It's what everyone else will think." She turned away. "I can't face those people. God, I can't even stay in this practice."

"You don't mean that."

"My old boss Steve has asked me to come back. I told him no, but maybe I should think about it."

He took her arms and held her away from him. The tears were now threatening to roll down her cheeks. "I never thought... Let me deal with Bill. With all of them. I'll find some way to fix this. I only wanted—"

The door opened and Mabel stuck her head in. "Mark, Sarah, we need you. The toasts are about to start."

"In a minute," Mark said.

"Now," Sarah said. As she brushed by him, she said, "I've got to have some time to process all this. I might be better off back in St. Paul. At least there I *know* the rules."

THE PARTY was in full swing. Even Kenny's parents seemed to be enjoying themselves. Some people simply wore their best dress jeans, but most had taken the opportunity to dress up. Margot, resplendent in her red sequins, greeted her guests graciously with a touch of royal noblesse oblige thrown in for good luck. Rick fluttered around slapping backs and shaking hands. Several couples had moved into the aisle between the ICU and operating theater to dance to Margot's band.

Sarah made her way through the crowd, always keeping a few people between her and Mark. He suspected his jaw looked like granite. He couldn't even paste a smile on his face—not until he'd had a chance to convince Sarah of his motives.

He felt an insistent hand on his arm, and turned to find Mabel, her face drained, her eyes wild.

"Mark, where's Rick?"

"What is it? What's happened?"

"You need me?" Rick turned and joined them. He carried a full champagne glass, but Mark doubted he'd been drinking much. This party was, after all, business.

"Rick, it's horrible!" Mabel said.

"What's horrible? I can't hear you over the music."

Mark opened the door to Sarah's office and shoved both Rick and Mabel inside. "Now, Mabel, what's all this about?"

"Oh God, Rick. There's been a terrible wreck on the interstate just this side of the Arlington exit. An eighteen-wheeler on its way from Lexington to Louisiana. It lost its brakes, went out of control, flipped over on its side. It's full of racehorses." Mabel began to cry. "The fire department called us because we're closest and they know we treat horses. They don't know what to do. They've wet down the area, so there's no fire, but there still could be. The highway patrol wants to shoot the horses."

"Get on the phone. Tell them we'll be there in twenty minutes. In the meantime, tell the fire department to try to pry the top off the trailer. And nobody shoots anything until we get there."

Rick left the office, jumped up on the impromptu stage and grabbed the microphone. "Listen, everybody. I'm sorry to say this, but we've got an emergency." He explained the situation. "We're going to need help transporting the wounded to the clinic."

"I've got my truck outside," somebody said. "Vickie, come on, honey, we'll pick up our four-horse trailer and meet these guys at the wreck."

"I've got a two-horse," somebody else volunteered.

"Will a stock trailer help...?"

"My four-horse is just down the road..." someone else called.

"You're going to need extra hands to hold animals and help load. We'll come..."

"Hell, we'll all come...!"

Mark saw that Sarah, Nancy, Jack, Bill, and even Kenny were already collecting equipment and medications and tossing them into feed buckets and cardboard boxes.

"I'll bring the surgical packs," Mac said as he disappeared down the hall.

Kenny, his arms full of bandages, ran past his father.

"Kenny, where you going, son?"

"With them!"

The neighborhood group and some of the small-animal owners stood watching, as everyone scattered to trucks and cars at a dead run. The band members stopped playing and simply gaped.

Mark ran to Sarah's truck, saw her keys in the ignition, jumped into the driver's side and started it. She opened the rear door, tossed a box of supplies inside and climbed in beside him.

"Let's go."

As they started out, Kenny yelled, "Wait for me!" and threw himself into the back seat.

"What do we do when we get there?" Kenny asked excitedly.

"No idea until we see how bad it is. Could be pretty bloody, Kenny. You up for that?" Sarah asked.

"You need me, you got me, Doc," he said, although his voice quavered.

"Drat, I took my gym bag out of the truck this morning. I thought today would be the one day I'd be safe to wash everything," Sarah said, and looked down at her cocktail dress. "Kenny, dig around on the floor and see if you can find my old running shoes, will you? I'll have to work the way I am."

Mark broke every speed record getting to the interstate. He could see the flashing lights and hear the sirens from three or four miles away. Once a police car tried to stop him, but he leaned out and said, "We're the vets, and there'll be a bunch of people in trucks with empty horse trailers coming. Get them through, will you, even if you have to use the median?"

"We'll do what we can."

Somehow Rick and Margot had beaten them to the scene. Margot had hiked up her dress and tied a knot in the tail so that it hung halfway down her thighs.

The van and its cab now lay on its left side in the center of the westbound lane of the interstate.

Rick pulled himself up onto the cab and then onto the van.

"The only doors are facedown on the side that's lying against the roadway. We can't get to them unless we right this van, and I don't think that's going to happen soon enough," Rick said. "Bring that bar thing up here. We'll have to pry the original roof off. It's the only way to reach the horses."

"There's a set of doors in back," said one of the firemen. "They're on their side, too, but we may be able to get them open."

"Won't help the rest of the horses," Rick shouted. "There's usually a strong set of bars between the back stalls and the rest of the van. Anybody know how many horses we got here? Where's the driver?"

"On his way to the hospital with a concussion and a broken arm."

"Margot?" Rick called. "Look in the cab and find the registration, then call the van owner from my cell phone. Tell him to get in touch with the owners of these horses and their insurance companies, and inform them we're treating on an emergency basis. Get us permission to keep treating at the clinic. All right?''

''Done,'' Margot said.

''Mabel?'' Rick shouted. When she answered, he said, ''Call Eleanor Grayson at home and get her to the clinic. Tell her to get ready for anything. Then go back and run the show at the clinic. Can I count on you?''

''Need you ask? Let's go, Mrs. Hazard.''

The kicking and whinnies from inside the truck sounded horrendous. ''Okay. Let's get those doors off the back,'' Rick shouted. ''And bring that pry bar thing up here. We've got to shoot some sedatives into those horses before they tear themselves up.''

''Kenny, Mark, grab the Ringer's,'' Sarah said, running toward the trailer.

''Out of the way,'' Jack said to Mark. He yanked open the cover of Sarah's medicine chest and began to pull out syringes, vet wrap, and bottles of what Mark assumed were sedatives.

''Here, carry these—'' Jack thrust the bandages at Mark.

''Get some lights up here.''

Mark passed his bandages to a nearby highway patrol officer, grabbed one of the floodlights and rolled it to the edge of the trailer.

''Boost me,'' Sarah said at his elbow. She put a foot into his hand. He tossed her up, then Rick caught her hands and pulled her to the rim of the trailer beside him.

''Mark,'' Rick said, ''get them to pry those doors off the back. We're going to have to slide some of these horses out sideways. Watch it, Sarah!''

Mark's heart gave a lurch. He wanted to be up there with her to protect her from the danger of those flailing hooves or the possibility of falling off the trailer into the midst of the injured animals.

As if she knew what he felt, she leaned over and smiled down at him. "I'll be fine. This is what I do, Mark."

Her face glowed. She was in her element. So was Rick. Mark glanced around him. The adrenaline was nearly palpable.

She was right. He couldn't protect her. In fact, he'd be more of a liability than an asset. He went to help the firefighters at the back of the trailer. Out of the corner of his eye, he saw Mac haul himself up beside Sarah.

The world became a blur of lights, sirens, people milling, yelling at one another. Metal ripped, horns blared, lights blazed. When they finally managed to break open the rear doors of the van, Mark expected to see carnage.

Instead, he found himself looking into the frightened liquid eyes of a foal probably no more than three months old. It stood with its back braced against what had been the floor of the van, its legs carefully positioned between those of a big bay mare who must be its mother.

"Get that colt out of there," one of the firefighters shouted.

"Wait!" Mark said. "Kenny, did we remember to bring extra lead lines?"

"Right here," Kenny said, and slapped the brass end of a cotton rope into Mark's hand.

"The last thing we need is any of these animals running loose on the highway," Mark said to the firefighter. "I've got to snap the lead onto that little fellow's halter, then we can lift him out and hang on to him until we can get his mother out."

"I'll do it," Kenny said.

"You'll get kicked by the mare."

"No, I won't." Kenny jumped up on the end of the trailer and began talking to the frightened foal. The mare raised her head and began to struggle.

"Watch her!" Mark shouted.

"It's okay," Kenny said. He jumped down with the end of the lead line in his hand. "I hooked it onto the little guy's halter. He wasn't tied in front the way the mare is."

"Look, if we put a line around that mare's back legs, we can ease the foal out and then slide her out after him," one of the firefighters suggested.

"I'll do it," Kenny said.

"No, I'll do it," Mark said. He tossed his jacket so that it landed on top of the mare's head. Once her eyes were covered, she settled down.

At that moment the foal vaulted straight into one of the firefighters and knocked him sprawling. If Kenny hadn't been holding the lead rope, the foal would have been off and running down the highway. As it was, the young horse fought and bucked.

"I'll take him," said a voice from the darkness. Mark turned to see a tall man, his tux shirtsleeves rolled up. "Once we get a line around his butt, he'll settle down and lead fine, won't you, son," the man said. He took the line from Kenny, slipped it around behind the foal and held the terrified youngster, who stopped straining and instead stood spraddled and nickering softly to his mother.

With the foal out of the way, there was room for Mark to slide in alongside the mare's back. He untied the lead line that held her head hard up against the loop at the front of her stall and carefully backed out of the trailer. "Once we haul her hind legs out, she should be able to scramble the rest of the way by herself."

The moment her hind hooves touched the roadway, she came up with a great thrust and groan, leaving Mark's jacket in a pile of manure on the floor of the van. The mare whickered and fought until she saw her foal.

"Give me a hand, son," the man with the foal said to Kenny. "Mare looks like she can walk. Some blood, but no bad cuts I can see. We'll get them both in my trailer and take her back to the clinic to check her out."

"Yes, sir," Kenny said.

With mare and foal safely out of the way, Mark looked for Sarah. Her dress glittered in the lights as she bent over thrashing horses and inserted needles into their necks. Beyond her, Mac and Rick were working, as well.

"Full load," Rick shouted from the darkness somewhere deep inside the trailer. "Damn. Twelve Thoroughbreds, some stallions. Can't tell how many—"

"Mr. Scott, where do we park our trailers?"

Mark turned to see one of the guests, her diamonds still encircling her throat, her perfectly coiffed hair still in place, but her silver shoes caked with mud. "Turn around and park so that you're headed back west to the clinic," Mark said. "Open your trailer doors. Then, if you don't mind, get the others positioned the same way. Leave room to load."

Without another word, the woman nodded and moved off.

Traffic on the other side going east backed up, as trucks with empty horse trailers drove down the median and began to turn and pull in, ready to take freed injured back to the clinic.

"Bring one of those back doors we broke off around the side of the trailer where we pried the roof off," Mac told the firefighter beside him. "We can't get to the ramp on the trailer, but I think we can slide at least one of these doors into the opening where the roof used to be. It should be easier to get the horses from the bottom tier of stalls out first.''

It took a dozen burly firefighters and Mark to shift one of the heavy rear doors into position. Mark jumped on it. It gave slightly under his weight but stayed in place.

The horses had been tied into four stalls on either side of a center aisle. The front four horses rode facing backward, the back four faced forward. The horses lay tied in their stalls stacked like cordwood, four on either side of the center aisle.

Sarah knelt at Mark's feet, inserting a needle into the jugular vein of a big gray Thoroughbred whose eyes rolled with fear. Even in the shadows, Mark could see the horse's sides heave.

''That's the last one to tranquilize,'' Sarah said.

Mark gave her a hand up.

''So far, the bars dividing the stalls from each other are holding.'' Sarah shoved her hair out of her eyes. ''That means the horses in the center and bottom tiers still have just enough room to breathe, but horses don't do well lying on their sides for long. Their lungs are in that little area between the shoulders. Not much room to expand. And they're terrified. Horses can die of fear. I'm really worried about the two up in the nose of the van. I can't get to them to sedate them. They've been too quiet for the past five minutes.''

''How do we get them out?''

''I don't know.'' She raked her hands through her hair in frustration. ''The ones on the top tier are now lying damn near eight feet in the air with nothing between them and the floor except three other horses underneath them. If we just drag them out, they'll fall down on their heads. They could break their necks. They're too heavy to pick up, even if we could reach their entire bodies to do it.''

"If we get them down to the floor of the trailer, can they jump down from the trailer to the ground outside?''

"Sure, with the trailer lying on its side, it's barely two feet to the ground.''

"Okay, then, I think I can help.'' He checked the bars on the stalls. He had to hope they'd hold under pressure. "If we can get the horses on the bottom tier out first, we can bring in the door we sprung off the back and brace it against the bottom stalls on the back side like a ramp. The horses will slide down, but they won't fall. Once they're free, they should be able to scramble up on their own.''

Sarah looked at him in silence, then nodded. "There are a couple of horse blankets over there in the corner. We can fold one and use it to keep the horse's head from bashing into the stall below. And we can use the other to pad the ramp so we can slide the horses down easier.''

"Do it," Rick said, from the front of the trailer. "I've popped these two with some Ace, but I don't know how long they'll last up here. Their noses are right up against the stalls in front of them and their necks are really wrenched. We have to do something fast.''

Several firefighters at the front door had been listening, and began to lift the metal door to the floor of the trailer even before Rick finished speaking.

"Not yet," Mark told them. "First give us a hand with the horses lying on the bottom row of stalls.''

"Sure. We got ropes.''

Sarah supervised as the firefighters ran heavy ropes under the bodies of the two bottom horses. Then she untied the lines that held their halters to the stall bars. "Okay. Heave."

The first horse, a bay filly, popped out of her prison like a cork out of a bottle. The firefighters dove for the door, as she began to thrash. The rope slipped off her belly, and Mark grabbed the lead line to her halter.

"Steady," he soothed her.

Miraculously, she stood still, and a moment later walked to the improvised door and hopped down. Someone in a tuxedo took the line from Mark's hands and led her away.

The second horse on the bottom tier didn't fight, but he didn't help, either. In the end, it took Mark and three firefighters to get him onto his feet. Blood poured from a long gash on his shoulder, but he limped to the door, jumped down, and was led off to a trailer.

Then the same firefighters and Mark picked up the heavy metal door and braced it against the bottom stall. The angle of descent was steep, but it was no longer a sheer drop into space from eight feet in the air.

Sarah folded one horse blanket and propped it against the bottom end of the makeshift ramp, spread the other over the metal. Then she climbed up, cut the lead line that was holding the top horse, fastened another lead line to its halter and scrambled down again.

"Okay, pull, but easy. We have to slide him forward. We don't know for certain whether he can stand on his own, much less walk. Try to keep him from crashing into the lower end of the ramp headfirst."

"Out of the way," Mark shouted to the firefighters as the horse began to slide, first quietly, then in a welter of flailing hooves.

Once free, the horse kicked his way off the ramp, and fell the few feet to the floor with a *thump* that rocked the van. A moment later, he clambered to his feet and stood upright, quivering with terror.

Sarah handed Mark the lead line. "Get him out of here. Then let's get the horse on the right side, top tier, down."

As soon as the horses on top were out of the way, sliding the middle horses out was relatively simple, and those next to the bottom only required a few good hauls on a rope before they kicked themselves free and stood up.

"Hey, guys, I'm still up here," Rick called. "I got two scared horses and no damn room to get them out."

"Break out the forward stalls," Mark said to a nearby firefighter."

"Whatever you do, do it fast." Rick sounded worried.

The first horse from the nose of the trailer came out fighting. One of the firefighters narrowly avoided having his head split open by a flashing front hoof. The second horse slid down and lay there, eyes open, lungs heaving, sweat pouring off. Rick slid down after him and began to kick at him.

"Hey, man, don't do that!" one of the firefighters said. "It's not his fault."

"I'm trying to make him respond," Rick snapped. "Grab that line and heave. We've got to get him up right now."

"Maybe he's hurt."

"All the more reason. Sarah, Mark, give me a hand."

Sarah started shouting and hauling at the lead line attached to the horse's halter. "Get up! Don't you dare die on us, you stupid horse. Right this minute, dammit, I mean it!"

Finally, the horse snorted, heaved a mighty sigh and began to kick. A minute later, it fought its way off the ramp, shivered from head to tail and jumped out of the trailer, dragging Sarah behind it.

"Grab him!" Mark shouted, but Sarah already had the animal under control. She was stroking its face, crooning to it sweetly.

"Is that it?" the firefighter asked.

"Yeah," Rick replied. "Now we get to see how bad it is."

Jack took the last horse from Sarah. He turned to Rick. "Seemed to me we're better off treating 'em at the clinic, if we can get them there."

"Good thinking."

"Not this one—" Rick said, pointing at the last horse to come out.

"Oh Lord," Sarah breathed. "Lights! Get me some lights. And where's Mac with those surgery packs?"

"We need help loading," someone said over Mark's shoulder. "Got a crazy gray stallion who's trying to kill us."

"Coming," Mark said.

"Coming," Jack said. "Nancy, you take this lead."

Mark heard the stallion before he saw him. The animal was big—close to seventeen hands. A heavyset gray-haired man hung doggedly to the horse's lead shank.

Jack grabbed the lead line, yanked on it. The instant the startled horse stood still, Jack clipped another line on him and ran the shank over his nose. "That's it, my lad. No more fancy tricks from you."

"He badly hurt?" Mark asked.

"Just pissed off. I've ridden worse a hundred times. Sarah's tranquilizer should have settled him down enough to load, but now we'll do it the old-fashioned way."

Jack turned toward the big trailer in front of him. "Now, me old lad, stop playing up and get on in there."

For a moment the stallion hesitated, then bolted into the trailer, nearly dragging Jack off his feet.

"Shut him in!" Jack shouted.

"Stupid bugger," Jack said, as the trailer pulled away. "Come on. Sarah may need help. Done one hell of a job, has our Sarah. It's a fine line between giving 'em so much junk they'll fall down in the trailers on the way to the clinic, and having them kick the bejesus out of you."

They found her on the side of the road with a pair of floodlights aimed down at her. She knelt on the grass with her head and hands under the horse. Its drowsy head hung low.

Mac held a heavy flashlight over her shoulder, aimed up at the horse's belly. He glanced at Mark. "This is a bad one. We can't wait until we get back to the clinic to stitch the cut. Gut's starting to fall out. Must have ripped it open on a piece of metal when the van went over. Could strangulate if it's not sutured right now."

Sarah's gloved hands were covered in blood. She blew her hair out of her face and stood. "Not pretty, but it'll do for the moment. Let's get him on a trailer."

She saw Mark and grinned. "Better than we deserved. Lucky the van didn't slide off down the ravine, and, thank God, the firefighters kept it from catching fire. I'll know more when we get X rays and fluoroscopes back at the clinic."

"Then, let's go."

"Rick's a remarkable organizer. He handled all this like a field marshal."

"Damn if he didn't." Coy Buchanan walked up with his arm around Beth. "Banged my trick knee on the car door," he said seriously. Then he winked at Mark.

"That boy has hidden depths. Maybe Margot wasn't such a fool to marry him, after all."

"Thanks, Pops," Rick said. His hair was tousled, his shirt was bloody and there was a six-inch rip in the trousers of his tux. He was grinning from ear to ear.

"Hey, I didn't mean—"

"Sure you did, but who cares? I know I'm good and so does Margot."

"Got to admit it. You're right."

"Damn right." Rick turned, cupped his hands around his mouth and shouted, "Hey, people, we got work to do back at the clinic. Let's clean up this mess and get out of here." He turned to the nearest firefighter. "Hell of a job, buddy."

"You, too. All of you. How do we find out how they are?"

"Come on by the clinic when you get off. We'll be there." Rick clapped the firefighter on the back and trotted back toward his truck. It was obvious from the set of Rick's shoulders that he was feeling good about a job well done.

Mark saw him throw an arm around Margot's shoulders. Under the fierce glow of the lights, Margot looked transported. She wrapped her arms around Rick and kissed him passionately, then hiked up her ruined dress even higher and climbed into his truck beside him.

Sarah rode in a four-horse trailer with the wounded stallion. Mark followed in her truck, with Kenny beside him bubbling with stories.

The parking lot was full of trucks and horse trailers the clinic ablaze with lights. The rear doors were wide open.

"Where are we going to put them all?" Eleano called from the doorway.

"We'll move the worst cases into the ICU stalls, pu

the others into the bovine stalls, and the mare and foal into the cattle pen,'' Rick said. "If we still have some horses left over, we'll have to leave them in the trailers until we can check them over. Okay, Bill, you and I can triage. Sarah, Eleanor and Mac can do the work. Jack, you handle the horses. Nancy can assist with any surgery.''

"Let's get some pictures here,'' Sarah shouted. "Kenny, wheel over the X ray.''

"I'll go handle the party,'' Margot said. "People are going to be hungry after this, and they don't need to drink champagne and drive. Mark, mind giving me a hand in case we have to placate some people?''

The party had moved lock, stock and finger foods to the registration area. Someone had set up the bar behind the registration desk and hauled the conference table out of Rick's office for the food.

The band had packed up and left, but several of the neighbors had gone home and returned with ice chests full of soft drinks and platters of sandwiches to add to the hors d'oeuvres. Someone had brought an industrial-size coffee urn that gurgled on the registration desk, stacks of plastic cups beside it.

As the trailer crowd unloaded and came in to relax and to clean up, they fell on the food and drink like starving sailors. Nobody wanted to go home. Everybody was energized.

The police and highway patrol cars dropped by; then came two fire chiefs and a half-dozen firefighters at the end of their shifts. Finally, two paramedic units stopped by on the way to their stations.

And then the media descended. A helicopter hovered overhead, and camera crews from all three local networks set up in the parking lot to try to invade the clinic.

Mark stopped them and sent them up front to Margot. She'd have them interviewing clients before they knew what hit them.

Mabel whispered to Mark, "Talk about your free publicity! Couldn't have planned it better."

The neighbors had changed to jeans and comfortable clothes, but none of the rescue squad had changed. The men's tuxes were muddy, their shirts were creased, most of their neat black bow ties had disappeared. The women's hair was falling loose from fancy coiffures and their dresses looked bedraggled. Nobody seemed to mind.

The door behind Mark opened. "Been looking for you."

Kenny's father, Mr. Nichols. Mark groaned. The man carried a beer, and from the way he walked, it wasn't his first of the evening.

"Best party of the year!" Kenny's father slapped Mark on the back.

Mark could not have been more surprised if the man had slugged him.

"Got to admit, I may have been wrong about this place. You've done one hell of a job turning my boy around."

"Kenny was great tonight. Couldn't have managed without him," Mark said honestly. "Thanks for bringing the food and drinks."

"Shoot, it's our neighborhood, too." Mr. Nichols laughed his rich laugh and wandered off down the driveway. Mark assumed he was walking home. Probably a good thing.

Mark turned to go back into the reception area, and saw Rick come out of the back. Rick jumped up on the reception counter and held up his hands. After a moment everyone settled down to listen. Television lights flashed on his face and cameras began to hum. Rick seemed to enjoy the attention.

"Status report, people. The van driver is being held for observation overnight. Concussion and a broken arm. At this point, all the horses are breathing on their own. We've got cuts and gashes, and some pulled suspensories, maybe some concussions, but a horse can't tell you he's got a headache, right? We have one major abdominal injury, but we think it's going to heal well. We had to pull one small bone chip out of a hock—or, at least, Dr. Marsdon did. Several of the horses had the backs of their heels cut off—probably stepped on them themselves. Should grow back in time. The cuts we stitched likely won't even leave scars once the hair grows back. We had to drain some hematomas, and may have to drain them again tomorrow. Dr. Grayson had to stitch up one ear that was torn loose, but it should knit all right. All told, we were damn lucky."

"Do we know what caused it?" asked a reporter, shoving a microphone at Rick.

"He told the highway patrol that another driver pulled too tight in front of him going down the hill. He slammed on his brakes and lost control."

"People!" a woman snapped. "They have absolutely no sense about horses and vans. Ought to be a law."

"There is," Mark said. "But nobody pays any attention to it."

"How's the foal?" someone else asked.

"Doing fine. Nursed, hunkered down and went to sleep. Thanks to all of you, this disaster has turned into a triumph."

Everybody began to cheer. The media types demanded to see the mare and foal. Rick seemed to be holding his own.

Mark went looking for Sarah. He found her sitting

on the edge of the pre-surgery platform with her knees together and her hands drooping between her knees. Her hair had worked its way loose from its upswept do, and one of her shoulder straps was broken. She had apparently, either by accident or intention, ripped the side seam of her dress up to her hip. Her panty hose were in shreds, but she hadn't bothered to remove them.

She looked up at him. Her nose was shiny and there were dark circles under her eyes, but she glowed.

"I feel like I've been through a war."

He sat beside her, put his arm around her shoulders and leaned her against him. Recalling how angry she'd been earlier, he expected her to resist, but she relaxed at once.

"You still mad?" he whispered, almost afraid to remind her.

She laid a hand on his knee and began to stroke his thigh. His blood pressure rose about fifty points.

"Tonight we had all the equipment we needed because of you. How can I be angry? Nobody's ever done anything like that for me before. It scared me, but I've finally realized it's not like you bought the house *you* wanted and then presented it to me. I thought it was like that, but I was wrong. You found out what I *really* wanted, what I needed, and then you did something crazy to make certain I got it—and you didn't even try to take the credit. Who cares what people think? That's, that's…"

"That's a man in love."

She looked up at him. "In love? Really?"

"Really."

"Is this what it feels like? I never knew."

"What does it feel like, Sarah?"

She closed her eyes but her voice sounded strong. "I look for your face in every crowd, I listen for your voice, I watch for the size and shape of you. I even look for your shadow on the wall before I see you, and then my skin comes alive when I do. I cherish the sound of your voice, the way you walk, and the way you prop your telephone on your neck, and that pocket thing you write your notes on. When I'm away from you I long to see you, to touch you, just to have you in the same room. You make me so mad I want to scream. I don't care enough about anybody else to get mad at them that way. You punch every button I have and you drive me crazy. I'd be happy to sit in front of a fire and read a book so long as you were in the same room and I could touch you once in a while. I can't imagine being without you. And then there's...passion." She reached up to touch his face. "That's a whole new ball game, too. At least for me."

"At your service."

"I sincerely hope so."

"So you forgive me?"

"Only if you forgive me for being an ungrateful idiot. I was afraid of obligation—that you'd demand something in return, that you'd hold what you'd done for me over my head. That's the way it's always worked in my family. But you did what needed to be done, and then didn't even want the credit for it."

"Don't get used to it. I'm still the guy who says no, remember?"

"Oh, really?" She kissed his jaw. "I can think of a few things I'll bet you won't say no to." She slid her hand up his thigh and into his lap.

He caught his breath. "*Yes,* Sarah. And if you don't watch it, it's going to be yes right here and right this minute."

EPILOGUE

"YOU'RE GOING TO HAVE a pig at your wedding?" Beth asked.

She stood behind Sarah, who sat at her desk in the clinic. It had been turned into a makeshift dressing table so that Beth could fix Sarah's hair and makeup.

"Egg Roll wanted to come—at least, according to his owner—and what Egg Roll wants, Egg Roll gets. Actually, his owner Judy gave me the idea of inviting my patients, the animals, along with their humans. I did draw the line at the parrot who keeps calling me a fat slut."

"Oh, I *am* glad. Sit still while I brush on this blush."

"I never use that stuff."

"Today you will. I know what I'm doing, Sarah. You will not look like a high-class hooker, I promise. What else am I likely to run into out there?"

"We did have a lot of acceptances. George and Marian, the bull terriers, are coming, and Mrs. Morrison's Siamese cat Ping Ping, and Sweetums, the Maine coon cat, and Joan Morgan's rottweiler, and Nasdaq's kittens who now belong to Mabel's granddaughter. I think there's at least one Albino Ball's python whose stomach I took a tennis ball out of, and maybe an iguana or two. I don't know. I lost count."

"Mark agreed to this?"

"Mark thought it would be a great idea. I think Rick only agreed to have the wedding here at the clinic because it would be good publicity. The guys I treat are all my friends, Beth. I wanted them to share our happiness."

"Did you invite whole herds of cattle and horses?"

"Nope. Not enough space. But most of the horsemen and cattlemen are coming."

"Well, I think the whole thing is loony, and so does Coy."

"The two of you can have a stuffy old ceremony with 'Here Comes the Bride.' It's your choice."

Beth blushed. "We're a long way from any ceremony. Never, if Margot has her way. She thinks it's horrible that 'Daddy' is dating a woman younger than she is."

"Do you care?"

"Only because it upsets Coy. I thought he'd cave. But he's hanging tough. Says he deserves some happiness after all those years without a woman in his life. Sarah, if you don't stop turning your head, I'm going to stick this rose in your ear instead of in your hair."

"Sorry. I'm nervous. You're not the only ones who think Mark and I are crazy to have the ceremony here and invite the animals. My father threw up his hands, but he agreed to give me away. Two of my sisters-in-law are glad we're five hundred miles from St. Paul so they don't have to let anybody know what's happening."

"And your brothers?"

"Two of them don't really understand, but they're being good about it. But Peter—he's my youngest brother—think it's great, and his wife, Mary Ellen, is the only sister-in-law who thinks the whole thing is a hoot. Of course, my nieces and nephews love the whole idea. Let's face it, Beth, I am not the white-lace-and-frothy-veil type. All I want is a simple ceremony with a pretty dress, lots of flowers and lots of fun—and afterwards, Mark all to myself.''

''For two weeks in Antigua, lucky dog.''

''How do you know where we're spending our honeymoon? Oh, I forgot. You probably picked the spot and made the arrangements.''

''Mark picked the spot, but I did make the arrangements. Your own private pool, your own private sailboat, horseback riding, swimming, parasailing...''

''No way am I parasailing. And Mark isn't, either, if I have to hog-tie him to the bed.''

''Sounds good to me.''

The door opened and Mabel came in. ''Oh, Sarah, you look lovely! I adore the roses in your hair.''

''Not too cute?''

''Not at all. Very sophisticated.''

''Thanks for looking after Nasdaq while we're gone.''

''Of course, dear. She'll be fine here with me. We're about ready to start the ceremony, if you're all set.''

''How's the air-conditioning holding up? We *would* have to get married on the hottest day of August.''

''We warned you about August in Memphis, dear. The air-conditioning is fine. I snuck in at five-thirty this morning and turned it down as low as it would go. Rick will probably have a fit when he gets the electric bill this month, but I refuse to let anybody sweat.'' She opened the door, peeked out and shut it again. ''I hope the trumpets play loud. It's starting to sound like a petting zoo out there.''

Beth raised her eyebrows. ''You asked for it, Sarah.''

"I may regret it. No, I won't. Let's do it."

Folding chairs had been set up in the wide aisle of the large-animal area of the clinic. Ribbons and roses divided the groups of chairs into two sides, with a center aisle for the bride. At the end was a bower of flowers for the ceremony. The rest of the long hall had been set up to accommodate the reception. There was, after all, plenty of room. At the moment, only one horse was in residence—a big walking horse with a bad case of founder. Sarah hoped he'd keep his mouth shut when the trumpets started.

The bride's side of the aisle was packed with Sarah's brothers and their families. The animals and their owners had spread out without regard for whose side was whose.

What mattered was avoiding combat. Egg Roll had pride of place down front in the row right behind Mark's mother and stepfather, and beside Mabel, who kept Nasdaq on a short lead. Nasdaq's kittens slept peacefully in a carrier. Egg Roll's owner kept feeding him a steady supply of candy to keep him quiet.

Ping Ping sat regally on Mrs. Morrison's lap, a rhinestone collar around her silky throat, her milky eyes surveying the crowd as though she could see them.

George, still wearing his cast, and Marian, completely recovered, slept peacefully at Mrs. Jepson's feet.

Sarah noted that the chairs on either side of the python, whose name was Miss Pretty, were empty, and that both the iguanas were safely caged.

Algernon, the rhesus monkey, was securely leashed to his owner. He sat on her shoulder and chittered at the python.

As the music started, however, the chorus of yips and barks grew.

Sarah met her father at the head of the makeshift aisle. He was trying to look stern, but making a lousy job of it. He leaned down and whispered, "This is insanity. I can't believe your man let you do it."

"He didn't *let* me, Dad. We agreed on it together. He's a very nice man."

"He seems to be."

"And bigger than you, remember." She smiled up at her father. "He can protect me very well, Dad, so you can stop worrying. You look very handsome, by the way. Now give me your arm and smile."

Lars was indeed a handsome man. He also obviously enjoyed her compliment, although he tried to conceal his pleasure. "I never thought I'd see you married."

"Well, you're seeing it now."

Mark and Rick came out of the exotic-animal door at the far end of the hall and walked up to stand under the bower of roses. The priest who was to perform the ceremony looked down the aisle at Sarah and smiled.

Sarah caught Mark's eye. He mouthed, *I love you, beautiful.* Then he winked.

They had both come a very long way from that first prickly meeting. All the way to love.

She slipped her hand under her father's arm, took a deep breath, and as the trumpets began to celebrate the occasion with a Purcell trumpet voluntary, she started down the aisle.

The trumpets could only partially drown out the enthusiastic contributions from the animals. But as Sarah took her place beside Mark, both instruments and animals fell silent. Miraculously, all the animals except

Algernon stayed quiet while Mark and Sarah repeated their vows.

When Mark leaned over to kiss Sarah, he said, "You are completely crazy and I love you."

"Back at ya, buster."

The reception featured people food, plus treats for all the animals, and everyone was having a splendid time. The telephone rang. Mabel answered it, cupping her hand to her ear. "Uh-huh." She handed the phone to Sarah. "Colic."

Mark took the telephone from her hand and handed it to Eleanor Grayson.

"But…" Sarah began.

"Go!" Eleanor said. "Get her out of here while you still can. Sarah, I'll deal with the colic."

"Are you sure you can handle it alone?"

"I am *not* alone. Mark! Grab her. Go! Get out of here!"

"Right." Mark put his arm firmly around Sarah and began to walk toward the door.

Everyone cheered.

"Wait a minute, I have to—"

"Not on your life. We're on our way to Antigua and two weeks basking in the sun. Peter, Nels, go unlock the Jag. If anybody wants to toss birdseed, let them do it now or forever hold their peace!"

As they pulled out of the parking lot to the clatter of old shoes trailing behind them, Sarah leaned her head against Mark's shoulder. "You think Eleanor can handle things while we're gone?"

"Yes, and so do you. What's the matter?"

"I'm scared. Scared that you'll discover what a fraud I really am and that I'm not going to be able to keep you happy and that my career will get in the way and that it's all happened so fast and—"

Mark pulled over to the side of the road and turned around. "Want to call it off? We can always get an annulment."

Sarah's eyes grew huge. "No! Never!"

Mark pulled her across the bucket seat and into his lap. "Good. Listen, love, we both have careers we like, and we're both opinionated. With you, I'm alive. I'd rather have you driving me crazy than any other woman in the world feeding me pomegranates."

Sarah laughed. "I don't even know what a pomegranate looks like."

"Neither do I. That's not the point. The point is I love you. That's what that ceremony we just went through was about. Forever. Good, bad, rich, poor, colics at three a.m., flights to Houston at five in the morning, dogs and cats and babies disrupting the order of our days. But through it all, we'll keep finding each other"

Sarah leaned her head so that she nestled under his chin. "I love you, Mark."

"And I love you. Now that that's settled, you think we have time for a little afternoon delight before we have to catch our plane?"

"Oh, sure," Sarah said. "*That's* why you carried me off in such a hurry. I hardly got a bite of my own wedding cake."

"Mabel will freeze it for us," Mark said. "We're supposed to have wedding cake to toast our first anniversary."

"Most people at least get a taste on their wedding day." Sarah thought a minute. "That means we'll *have* a first wedding anniversary, right?"

"I was thinking more in terms of sixty or seventy. Since your engagement present was a laser, do I at least get to give you diamonds on our seventieth wedding anniversary?"

She snuggled against him. "Seventy years from now the clinic may be on a space ship. As soon as I find out what kind of equipment I'm going to need to treat four-legged creatures from Mars, I promise, darling, you'll be the first to know."

* * * * *

*Watch for the next book
in this heartwarming series,
THE PAYBACK MAN
(Harlequin Superromance #1011,)
coming to your favorite retail outlet
in September 2001.
You won't want to miss
Dr. Eleanor Grayson's story.*

AN INTERVIEW WITH
CAROLYN McSPARREN

Carolyn McSparren—creator of CREATURE COM-FORT, a series set in a state-of-the-art veterinary clinic in Tennessee—talks about what inspired her to write these touching, poignant, often humorous stories about animals and their owners...and the men and women who love and care for all creatures—great and small.

This vet series is obviously going to feature lots of animals. Do you yourself have pets? Can you tell us a bit about them?

Boy, do I have pets!

Two cats: a huge tabby named Calvin-Hobbes (he looks like Hobbes and acts like Calvin) and a small monkey-faced Burmese named Monty. They adore one another. We actually got Monty because our last cat died at eighteen. He had no tail and three legs—the result of encounters with a horse's hoof and a possum. Poor Calvin-Hobbes was grieving until the little guy arrived, so Monty is actually his cat.

I have two outside dogs, both foundlings. Since we live in the country, dreadful people toss dogs out and expect them to survive. Precious, the female, is very shy. Falco, who is mostly yellow Labrador, is named after Marcus

Didius Falco, Lindsay Davis's Roman detective. Our Falco talks a great deal, but almost never barks.

My first foundling, a big black part Lab, died last year at sixteen. Everybody is entitled to one truly remarkable dog. Bruin was mine. My daughter picked him up on the highway in a driving rainstorm on Christmas night many years ago and brought him to me. He was huddled beside his dead sister. He couldn't have been more than two weeks old. If indeed dogs do wait in heaven for their masters to show up, I hope he'll be waiting for me.

At the moment I'm down to three very large horses. My Canadian hunter mare is thirty-one years old, retired and queen of the pasture. Her daughter Fudge (real name is Chocolate Fox—what else would her stable name be?) is thirteen. She's my dressage horse, and knows much more than I do, which can cause problems. She's tossed me into the dirt more times than I can remember. The newest member of the entourage is a crossbreed shire-Thoroughbred filly known as Zoe the Tank. Zoe prefers driving to riding, and believes that all pockets must contain carrots.

Do you have a favorite vet real-life story?

There are so many! My vets are wonderful. One Sunday afternoon in hundred-degree temperature I was helping my vet tube my mare because she'd choked on her feed. It was a really dirty job, and we were both filthy and drenched with perspiration. He looked up at me and said, "You know, I got into vet school as an alternate when the guy ahead of me dropped out to go to med school to become a dermatologist. What do you think *he's* doing this afternoon?"

It seems every time I'm sitting around the lunch table with an animal person I am regaled with stories—usually funny stories. I suppose vets are like soldiers—they never like to talk about the bad times.

Why do you think people who love romance also love animals?

Because our hearts are open to love, and animals have so much of it to give. They love us without reservation, without assessing our worthiness, how pretty or thin or smart we are. And we love them because we know we can count on them. They are never petty or spiteful, and constantly remind us of the truly important things in life.

In *The Money Man*, Sarah Marsdon tells the hero that animals can and do promote emotional and physical health in people. Can you give some examples?

Absolutely. It's been proven that stroking a dog or cat will lower blood pressure. Mine frequently needs that kind of help.

If you've ever seen a Special Cargo class where kids with disabilities learn to ride horses, there's no way you could ever forget the joy on their faces. Not only that, but with time they improve balance and coordination. I have seen a young lady in a wheelchair, paralyzed from the waist down, whose big Friesian gelding follows her around like a puppy. He has learned to lie down so that she can be helped to mount and ride him. That's a pretty miraculous sight. People who say horses aren't capable of love ought to see her and her gelding.

I have a friend who has a rescue dog. She's lost count

of the number of Alzheimer's patients she and her dog have found huddled in the woods after they wandered away from home. Not only that, but visitation dogs in nursing homes frequently help Alzheimer's patients connect with life again, if only for a little while. I could go on and on.

And of course there are several prison programs that use animals. In fact, my idea for my next Superromance novel, *The Payback Man* (September 2001), came from my research into several actual prison programs in which inmates are trained to work with cattle and horses. One of the greatest problems prisoners face when they are released is finding a good job. As we become more of an urban society, horse and cattle operations are having increasing difficulty finding capable help, so these men are in great demand. Angola Prison even has an annual rodeo showcasing inmates' skills to the local population. Tickets are in great demand.

As well, several women's facilities have introduced dog rehabilitation programs. The women learn responsibility, but they also learn to love again. The recidivism rate has gone down significantly.

What gave you the idea of doing a series about vets?

My life revolves around animals, and so do many of the lives of my friends. We all value our vets and love listening to their stories. A great many of the incidents in my books come from their experiences.

So often we take our vets for granted until we have an emergency, then we realize how much we need them. They don't make a bunch of money, and their patients often get them up at 3:00 a.m. on Christmas morning.

They get stepped on, bitten, scratched, kicked or stomped by the patients they are trying to help, yet I've never seen a vet lose his or her temper. I know it happens, but they keep their cool when I would have lost mine a long time earlier.

I have never met a vet I didn't like. And they have that thing that is most attractive in either a hero or heroine. They're *competent*.

Can you really have a hero who doesn't like animals?

So far I haven't been able to come up with a hero who doesn't like animals and remains a hero. I suppose he could have had a terrible experience with wild dogs as a child, or be horribly allergic—but that's why we have antihistamines. Maybe a hero doesn't truly understand the value of animals. If he learns, then he's a hero, but if he can't see the value of preserving the rhino, or would even consider buying a leopard coat, he'll never be a hero in my book. Or even a nodding acquaintance, for that matter.

How did you do your research about vets?

I talked to all my vet friends and their staff. I visited the vet school at Mississippi State University with Melissa Poole, one of their large-animal vets. They have a large-animal section, one for small animals and another for exotics. The setup of CREATURE COMFORT is based on that clinic—the finest I've ever seen.

My own vet, Bruce Bowling, a surgical genius, lets me watch procedures on both large and small animals.

I also read tons of vet textbooks, used the Internet extensively and dragged Mark Akins's wife out to his equine clinic on a hot Sunday afternoon to show me every bit of fancy equipment they use. I subscribe to a number of animal magazines, and read them voraciously from cover to cover, usually on the day they arrive.

Finally, unfortunately, I've had to assist at several necropsies on horses—my own. I know much more about what the inside of a horse looks like than I should. I've buried twin foals who died at birth, and put down my Thoroughbred stallion at sixteen. I understand death is a part of life, but I keep thinking things ought to be organized better.

I've birthed foals, both normal and breech (and nearly had my arm broken in the process), and treated wounds and wrapped legs and given shots and walked out colics and on and on and on. It's amazing what you can do when a beloved animal's well-being is at stake. I just wish they'd sometimes pick a day when it wasn't raining or snowing to have their crises.

Finally, I'd just like to add that we're enriched by the creatures who share their lives with us—I won't say the creatures we own, because we don't own them. In many ways they own us. They bring us joy, and sometimes they break our hearts.

The vets who spend their lives maximizing the joy and keeping the heartbreak at bay for as long as possible deserve praise. I hope you enjoy reading their stories as much as I enjoyed writing them.

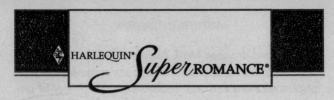

Harlequin truly does
make any time special....
This year we are celebrating
weddings in style!

To help us celebrate, we want you to tell us how wearing the Harlequin wedding gown will make your wedding day special. As the grand prize, Harlequin will offer one lucky bride the chance to **"Walk Down the Aisle"** in the Harlequin wedding gown!

There's more...

For her honeymoon, she and her groom will spend five nights at the **Hyatt Regency Maui.** As part of this five-night honeymoon at the hotel renowned for its romantic attractions, the couple will enjoy a candlelit dinner for two in Swan Court, a sunset sail on the hotel's catamaran, and duet spa treatments.

Maui • Molokai • Lanai

To enter, please write, in, 250 words or less, how wearing the Harlequin wedding gown will make your wedding day special. The entry will be judged based on its emotionally compelling nature, its originality and creativity, and its sincerity. This contest is open to Canadian and U.S. residents only and to those who are 18 years of age and older. There is no purchase necessary to enter. Void where prohibited. See further contest rules attached. Please send your entry to:

Walk Down the Aisle Contest

In Canada	In U.S.A.
P.O. Box 637	P.O. Box 9076
Fort Erie, Ontario	3010 Walden Ave.
L2A 5X3	Buffalo, NY 14269-9076

You can also enter by visiting www.eHarlequin.com
Win the Harlequin wedding gown and the vacation of a lifetime!
The deadline for entries is October 1, 2001.

PHWDACONT1

HARLEQUIN WALK DOWN THE AISLE TO MAUI CONTEST 1197
OFFICIAL RULES
NO PURCHASE NECESSARY TO ENTER

1. To enter, follow directions published in the offer to which you are responding. Contest begins April 2, 2001, and ends on October 1, 2001. Method of entry may vary. Mailed entries must be postmarked by October 1, 2001, and received by October 8, 2001.

2. Contest entry may be, at times, presented via the Internet, but will be restricted solely to residents of certain geographic areas that are disclosed on the Web site. To enter via the Internet, if permissible, access the Harlequin Web site (www.eHarlequin.com) and follow the directions displayed online. Online entries must be received by 11:59 p.m. E.S.T. on October 1, 2001.

   In lieu of submitting an entry online, enter by mail by hand-printing (or typing) on an 8½" x 11" plain piece of paper, your name, address (including zip code), Contest number/name and in 250 words or fewer, why winning a Harlequin wedding dress would make your wedding day special. Mail via first-class mail to: Harlequin Walk Down the Aisle Contest 1197, (in the U.S.) P.O. Box 9076, 3010 Walden Avenue, Buffalo, NY 14269-9076, (in Canada) P.O. Box 637, Fort Erie, Ontario L2A 5X3, Canada.

   Limit one entry per person, household address and e-mail address. Online and/or mailed entries received from persons residing in geographic areas in which Internet entry is not permissible will be disqualified.

3. Contests will be judged by a panel of members of the Harlequin editorial, marketing and public relations staff based on the following criteria:

   - Originality and Creativity—50%
   - Emotionally Compelling—25%
   - Sincerity—25%

   In the event of a tie, duplicate prizes will be awarded. Decisions of the judges are final.

4. All entries become the property of Torstar Corp. and will not be returned. No responsibility is assumed for lost, late, illegible, incomplete, inaccurate, nondelivered or misdirected mail or misdirected e-mail, for technical, hardware or software failures of any kind, lost or unavailable network connections, or failed, incomplete, garbled or delayed computer transmission or any human error which may occur in the receipt or processing of the entries in this Contest.

5. Contest open only to residents of the U.S. (except Puerto Rico) and Canada, who are 18 years of age or older, and is void wherever prohibited by law; all applicable laws and regulations apply. Any litigation within the Province of Quebec respecting the conduct or organization of a publicity contest may be submitted to the Régie des alcools, des courses et des jeux for a ruling. Any litigation respecting the awarding of a prize may be submitted to the Régie des alcools, des courses et des jeux only for the purpose of helping the parties reach a settlement. Employees and immediate family members of Torstar Corp. and D. L. Blair, Inc., their affiliates, subsidiaries and all other agencies, entities and persons connected with the use, marketing or conduct of this Contest are not eligible to enter. Taxes on prizes are the sole responsibility of winners. Acceptance of any prize offered constitutes permission to use winner's name, photograph or other likeness for the purposes of advertising, trade and promotion on behalf of Torstar Corp., its affiliates and subsidiaries without further compensation to the winner, unless prohibited by law.

6. Winners will be determined no later than November 15, 2001, and will be notified by mail. Winners will be required to sign and return an Affidavit of Eligibility form within 15 days after winner notification. Noncompliance within that time period may result in disqualification and an alternative winner may be selected. Winners of trip must execute a Release of Liability prior to ticketing and must possess required travel documents (e.g. passport, photo ID) where applicable. Trip must be completed by November 2002. No substitution of prize permitted by winner. Torstar Corp. and D. L. Blair, Inc., their parents, affiliates, and subsidiaries are not responsible for errors in printing or electronic presentation of Contest, entries and/or game pieces. In the event of printing or other errors which may result in unintended prize values or duplication of prizes, all affected game pieces or entries shall be null and void. If for any reason the Internet portion of the Contest is not capable of running as planned, including infection by computer virus, bugs, tampering, unauthorized intervention, fraud, technical failures, or any other causes beyond the control of Torstar Corp. which corrupt or affect the administration, secrecy, fairness, integrity or proper conduct of the Contest, Torstar Corp. reserves the right, at its sole discretion, to disqualify any individual who tampers with the entry process and to cancel, terminate, modify or suspend the Contest or the Internet portion thereof. In the event of a dispute regarding an online entry, the entry will be deemed submitted by the authorized holder of the e-mail account submitted at the time of entry. Authorized account holder is defined as the natural person who is assigned to an e-mail address by an Internet access provider, online service provider or other organization that is responsible for arranging e-mail address for the domain associated with the submitted e-mail address. **Purchase or acceptance of a product offer does not improve your chances of winning.**

7. Prizes: (1) Grand Prize—A Harlequin wedding dress (approximate retail value: $3,500) and a 5-night/6-day honeymoon trip to Maui, HI, including round-trip air transportation provided by Maui Visitors Bureau from Los Angeles International Airport (winner is responsible for transportation to and from Los Angeles International Airport) and a Harlequin Romance Package, including hotel accomodations (double occupancy) at the Hyatt Regency Maui Resort and Spa, dinner for (2) two at Swan Court, a sunset sail on Kiele V and a spa treatment for the winner (approximate retail value: $4,000); (5) Five runner-up prizes of a $1000 gift certificate to selected retail outlets to be determined by Sponsor (retail value $1000 ea.). Prizes consist of only those items listed as part of the prize. Limit one prize per person. All prizes are valued in U.S. currency.

8. For a list of winners (available after December 17, 2001) send a self-addressed, stamped envelope to: Harlequin Walk Down the Aisle Contest 1197 Winners, P.O. Box 4200 Blair, NE 68009-4200 or you may access the www.eHarlequin.com Web site through January 15, 2002.

Contest sponsored by Torstar Corp., P.O. Box 9042, Buffalo, NY 14269-9042, U.S.A.

PHWDACONT2

If you enjoyed what you just read,
then we've got an offer you can't resist!

Take 2 bestselling love stories FREE!

Plus get a FREE surprise gift!

Clip this page and mail it to Harlequin Reader Service®

IN U.S.A.
3010 Walden Ave.
P.O. Box 1867
Buffalo, N.Y. 14240-1867

IN CANADA
P.O. Box 609
Fort Erie, Ontario
L2A 5X3

YES! Please send me 2 free Harlequin Superromance® novels and my free surprise gift. After receiving them, if I don't wish to receive anymore, I can return the shipping statement marked cancel. If I don't cancel, I will receive 6 brand-new novels every month, before they're available in stores. In the U.S.A., bill me at the bargain price of $4.05 plus 25¢ shipping and handling per book and applicable sales tax, if any*. In Canada, bill me at the bargain price of $4.46 plus 25¢ shipping and handling per book and applicable taxes**. That's the complete price, and a saving of at least 10% off the cover prices—what a great deal! I understand that accepting the 2 free books and gift places me under no obligation ever to buy any books. I can always return a shipment and cancel at any time. Even if I never buy another book from Harlequin, the 2 free books and gift are mine to keep forever.

135 HEN DFNA
336 HEN DFNC

Name	(PLEASE PRINT)	
Address	Apt.#	
City	State/Prov.	Zip/Postal Code

* Terms and prices subject to change without notice. Sales tax applicable in N.Y.
** Canadian residents will be charged applicable provincial taxes and GST.
  All orders subject to approval. Offer limited to one per household and not valid to
  current Harlequin Superromance® subscribers.
  ® is a registered trademark of Harlequin Enterprises Limited.

SUP01   ©1998 Harlequin Enterprises Limited